Decision of a Heartbeat

by

Danielle Deneault

1663 LIBERTY DRIVE, SUITE 200
BLOOMINGTON, INDIANA 47403
(800) 839-8640
WWW.AUTHORHOUSE.COM

This book is a work of fiction. People, places, events, and situations are the product of the author's imagination. Any resemblance to actual persons, living or dead, or historical events, is purely coincidental.

© 2006 Danielle Deneault. All Rights Reserved.

No part of this book may be reproduced, stored in a retrieval system, or transmitted by any means without the written permission of the author.

First published by AuthorHouse 01/11/06

ISBN: 1-4208-8538-3 (sc)
ISBN: 1-4208-8545-6 (dj)

Printed in the United States of America
Bloomington, Indiana

This book is printed on acid-free paper.

This is for Raymond

I would like to thank everyone who believed in me and made this book possible. Thank you!

~Danielle

Prologue

1993

James Martin stood up from the oak chair and walked over to the long mirror across the room. He was dressed in his tuxedo ready to marry his fiance Victoria Brenden.

I'm ready! Stop thinking about Lavender! James told himself aloud. He couldn't help it. Lavender Springer was always on his mind. Her beautiful green eyes haunted his dreams on countless nights. She was perfect and had always been perfect. James shook his head and paced around the room. *No! No! No! Stop it James! You're getting married to Victoria in fifteen minutes; Lav is part of your past!* James told himself. He had never told his childhood friend that he was madly in love with her ever since they met fourteen years ago. James kept pacing until a knock at the door interrupted his thoughts.

"Come in!"

The doorknob turned and Victoria Brenden slowly walked into the room dressed in a long white wedding dress. Her plain, long, blond hair was pulled up in a bun with a few curls hanging down and string of pearls hung loosely around her neck.

"I know it is bad luck to have you see me before the wedding but I need to tell you something." Victoria said. She walked over to the chair that he had previously been sitting on. She smiled at him and folded her arms over her lap. "First, I had to tell a few 'select' people to stay outside the church just in case *she* decided to come."

James' mouth flew open but she began before any words could come out. "James, I just can't have her here! I just want you all to myself, and . . ." Victoria stood up and walked over to him and wrapping her arms around his neck, she let her smile get wider. "We're having a baby."

Chapter 1

Summer 1980

James watched as the girl walked up his driveway with her mother. He didn't know who she was but at the first glance he knew he had found his first crush. He was sitting outside his house, a two-story colonial in Oaklawn, a small community outside of Cranston, Rhode Island. His mother was also sitting outside; crocheting a blanket for his sister Grace, who was upstairs napping.

As soon as his mother had saw them, she waved and invited them in for lemonade. "A really stupid thing to say Mom," James thought. He brushed his semi short, light brown hair away from his face revealing his pair of stunning blue eyes. Only then did he realize that the smoldering heat was making his blue t-shirt stick to his back.

"You must be the Springers, welcome to the neighborhood! I'm Christine Martin and this is my son Jamie," James blushed; *She used my stupid nickname*, he said to himself. When he stopped blushing, he looked up at the girl. She was about his age, with long dark brown hair and sparkling green eyes. It reminded James of the crisp green grass that lined most of the front and back yards.

"Yes we are. I'm Mary and this is my daughter Lavender."

"Here come inside with me and I'll get the lemonade,"she began, showing Mrs. Springer into the house. "Mrs. Springer and I are going into the house, why don't you and Lavender talk, okay Jamie?" Mrs. Martin told them. James watched his Mom and Mrs. Springer walk into the house and disappear into the kitchen that was visible from the door. James looked down at his sneakers but he could still see her sit down crisscross next to him.

"I'm Lavender," She declared and stuck out her hand. James looked up and shook it.

"I'm Jamie. I mean, I'm James!" She laughed and he blushed again.

"So, you like The Stars*?" she asked and pointed to his t-shirt that had the group, The Stars* on it.

James' face lit up. The Stars* was like the greatest band ever! Out of the four members in the band, Max Page was the best one in James' opinion.

"They're the coolest!" exclaimed James.

"Max Page is the best!"

"He's my favorite!"

"Mine, too. What's your favorite song?"

"It would have to be "The Duchess's Calling". I also like "With Words" ." James explained.

"Cool! Do you want to go to the pool? I saw it when we were coming home," Lavender suggested. She stood up and made her way into the house to seek her mother's approval before James could say no. He sighed and went inside as she ran past yelling that they could go. He stalked up the stairs confused as to what he should do. How was he supposed to get himself out of this mess?

"You like her," declared a voice from the top of the stairs. James looked up and saw his older brother Erich standing at the top, his blonde hair pushed back on his head. James rolled his eyes and continued up the stairs.

"I just met her, she's just a friend."

Erich moved so James could get up the stairs. "Yeah that's what Adam said to the snake about Eve."

James and Lavender walked down the street that led to the Oaklawn pool. They hadn't talked since they'd departed the house. James hadn't changed and by telling his Mom that he had put on his swim trunks and then put his shorts over them, he avoided having to really put them on. She had done the same thing probably, seeing that she had the same thing on.

"So...what school do you go to?" she asked when they turned left on Colonial Ave. James noticed that she twisted her hair when not talking. School. Why school? Why did she have to bring up school?

"I go to St. Mary's. Catholic School.."

"I'll be going there next year."

"Have you seen the uniforms yet?" He asked.

"Yeah, the girls' aren't too bad, but I feel bad for you boys. Those gym uniforms you have to wear are horrible." Lavender laughed. James had to smile; at least he didn't have to wear them for another three months. The itchy blue shorts and gray long sleeve shirt would drive anyone mad if they had to wear it twice a week. "Well I am glad that I'll at least know someone at the school."

"I can introduce you to my friends; then maybe we can hang out together at school."

"Do you think that they are at the pool?" She asked. James' high sprit sank once again. "Do you?"

"Um...No and how about we not go to the pool."

"Why?"

"Because."

"Because why?"

"I just don't feel like swimming."

"Oh. Well do you mind if I just take a quick swim? I've been waiting to go to the pool for ages."

"Um...um..."

"James, are you okay?"

"Lavender-" he began

"Lav, you can call me Lav it's shorter."

"Ok, well I want to be truthful with you...um... see I...um... can't swim,"

"That's it?"

"You're not going to laugh?"

"No, why would I laugh? I only learned to swim three years ago," she explained. James let out a sigh of relief.

"Oh, so we're not going to the pool?" James asked her.

"Nope, come on we're going somewhere else," she said taking his hand and running. James tried to get his feet to catch up with her but he was always slow when it came to running. She let go of his hand after only a few moments and began to run faster and faster. When they came to the woods, they moved in and out of the small bushes and shrubs. James hoped that small ticks wouldn't jump on him.

"Come on, we're almost there!" she called to him. James continued to follow her and when she finally came to a halt it was in front of a huge pond. A small brook ran into the pond and green grass surrounded the area that was home to many rabbits. This was a place he knew very well, though never dared set a foot into. Blackmore Pond.

"I found it while I was exploring the other day, isn't it pretty?" she asked. James stepped forward and looked around to make sure no one was around.

"It's called Blackmore pond."

"Really? That's cool. So come on let's swim." James stared at her as she went to the water's edge, shedding her clothes and then placing them on the rock nearby. She wore a lavender colored one piece that matched her name.

"But I thought we weren't swimming!"

"I'm going to teach you how to swim. Now come on."

"But I didn't bring my bathing suit."

"You don't have it on underneath?"

"No! I thought I was going to be able to talk you out of swimming!"

"Well then swim in your jeans."

"But you've only been swimming three years; what if I drown? This lake is deep!"

She walked up to him and looked in front of him. He noticed that they were the same height. "James, trust me." She held out her hand.

James looked from her face to her hand. Firmly he grasped it and walked over with her. He pulled off his shirt embarrassed. She smiled at him and he watched her get in the water. She stopped after a few feet. *Must be cold*, he thought.

"Is it cold?"

"No, surprisingly it's warm," she answered.

James cautiously walked over putting his right foot in. He thought she was lying but found out she wasn't. Inch by inch he found himself slip in to the water. She grabbed his hand and led him deeper in the water.

"Ok, now relax and breathe, ok. So watch me first," she explained. She quickly showed him how to dog paddle. He nodded and did the same. He did it! He really did it! She laughed and showed him how to float and then how to go under, which he mastered. She got out and so did he, the bond between them had started.

"So when is your birthday anyway?" he asked her while they sat in the grass drying off.

"July 9, 1970."

"Really? That's my birthday, too!"

"No way! That's way cool."

"I've never met anyone with the same birthday as-" James was cut off when mounds of water hit him and Lavender. Wild screams came from all around them, and boys surrounded them. One of the boys was Nick Brenden.

"Hey James!" Nick yelled after climbing onto the nearby rock knocking down Lavender and James' clothes.

"Nick? What are you doing home?"

"My Ma got back early so she picked me up." Nick explained. He wiped his dripping, long blonde hair out of his face. The other boys came closer, water pistols still at the ready. They were ready to take any order from Nick, clearly one of the leaders of the group. The other leader was James, the shy quiet kid who stayed behind and let Nick give orders to the boys.

"Hey Logan, Anderson, and both of you too, Gabriel. You can lower your weapons but keep a few on the girl," Nick called to them, but he kept his gaze on Lavender.

James stood up and walked over to Nick. "No, lower the water pistols." James told them. They didn't and he knew they wouldn't. "Come on Nick she's my friend."

Nick gave James a face and then went back to Lavender. He hopped off the rock and walked over to her. He was taller than her by a inch.

"Name?"

"What are you running an army?" She asked him.

"Name, please."

" Lavender Springer."

Nick looked around at the boys who had their water guns at the ready. He waved his hand and they lowered them.

"Well, Miss Springer, My name is Nick Brenden and these are my troops. Raymond Logan, Ryan Anderson and Steven and Will Gabriel. So if you will be on your way, me and my friend Mr. Martin have important business to attend to."

"Well Mr. Brenden," she began, "I am right now talking to Mr. Martin and you and your 'troops' interrupted us. And no, I will not be on my way, also you have knocked my shirt off the rock that it was on and I would greatly appreciate it if you pick it up." Lavender said smugly.

Nick didn't know whether to be offended or to laugh but the expression he had on his face was priceless. James tried to hide his laughing, no one had ever stood up to Nick before. James picked up their things and walked over to them.

"I think that we should be going," James said stepping between them and handing Lavender her things.

"What, James, are you scared that I'll go psycho on her?" Nick asked.

"Yes. Now come let's go Lav." Lavender didn't follow James when he began to walk away.

"James I don't walk away from things," she said to him. He turned around and watched her try to stare Nick down, just as he was doing to her.

"Nick, come on."

Nick rolled his eyes and stepped back. "What would it prove if I beat a girl?" he asked the other guys. Nick turned around heading back to his rock but Lavender got there first. She pushed him by his side into the pond making him splash all the boys around them. They squealed and ran around trying to dry themselves. James and Lavender laughed all the way out of the woods.

"I can't believe that you pushed Nick into the pond!" James howled with laughter.

"I can't believe that you hang out with those guys! You let that jerk push you around." Lavender said after she stopped laughing.

"Nick isn't always like that. He is just on his high horse because he just got out of summer camp and is a free kid."

They continued laughing all the way back to the house, each in their own way re-picturing what happened. When they arrived back on the street, they made their way into James' house. Mrs. Springer was still talking to James' mother when they walked in.

"Hi Kids, did you have a good time?" Mrs. Springer asked them. Lavender was totally different from her mother; Lavender's hair was dark brown while Mrs. Springer's was dark red, in long curls.

"Yeah," They answered at the same time.

"Well Lav, we better get going, we're meeting your father for dinner tonight." Mrs. Springer explained. Lavender nodded and said goodbye to James and Mrs. Martin. Mrs. Springer and James' mother talked at the door for another moment before they left.

"Aren't they nice people Jamie?" his mother asked. James nodded and went upstairs to take a shower. A half hour later he could smell the fresh aroma of red Italian sauce that was just hitting the table.

Erich and James' father were already seated at the table. James' father was a tall man with dark brown hair and blue eyes that James had inherited from him. He worked as an attorney with a big law firm in Rhode Island. His father described the family as rich, but his mother described them as comfortable. Whichever it was, they had a lot of money to spend.

Grace had dark brown hair and light brown eyes like their Mom. Erich was the only one who stuck out, with blonde hair and steel-like grey eyes.

"So how was your day, James?" his father asked. Before James could even open his mouth Erich opened his.

"Jamie's got a girlfriend."

"Do not!"

His father looked at both of them. "Richard–"

"ERICH! My name is Erich, everyone has the name Richard Edward!"

"Okay, okay Erich then, don't worry you'll get a girlfriend," his father said, and then went back to his meal. James smiled and poked at his food, finally Erich was getting his share of embarrassment. James and Erich were never close. They were only three years apart but James held on to how Erich use to beat him up when he was younger.

James felt a hard kick in his leg from Erich, so James kicked back, and accidently pushed him off the chair. *Take that!* James thought with triumph.

Chapter 2

Summer of 1984

Three years had passed by and James and Lavender had become the best of friends. The summer of 1984 would be the same as always, hang out together every day, go to the beach, Lavender and Nick would fight; part of the same summer routine. However, something had changed. He couldn't put his finger on it, but James knew something was going to mark this period of time.

Their birthdays were now celebrated together, Lavender's hair was shorter, and he had a growth spurt sending him to be 5'9, still that wasn't it. So what was it? Why were things suddenly spinning out of control?

⁕

As fast as he could, James darted up the stairs to his bedroom carrying two sodas. His clumsiness made him almost trip a few times, and having two gigantic feet didn't help either. Lavender sat on the floor looking through a magazine.

"Why do you read that?" he asked, sitting down and looking at the magazine, "Cosmopolitan". He passed her a soda and took a sip of his.

"Because, it prepares me with valuable information for life," she retorted, flipping through the pages. Putting it down, she looked over to see a piece of scattered news paper outside James' door. Standing up, Lavender walked over and picked it up.

"James look! The Stars* are coming to the Convention Center!" she cried waving the paper at him.

James went over to her and looked at the newspaper.

The Stars* !
Coming to a Convention Center near you!

Boston, Mass. 8/1/84
New York, NY 8/5/84
Providence, R.I. 8/10/84
Hartford, Conn. 8/12/84

"They're coming this weekend!" Lavender exclaimed. "We should ask if we can go."

"Uh, Lav read the fine print," James told her. He pointed to small writing under all the tour dates. She pulled the magazine from the floor and propped it up in front of her face.

"Doors open at ten." she said flatly. James frowned and looked at her disappointed face. She sighed and sat down closer to him.

"I wish we were older. Then we wouldn't have a curfew." She sighed. James started to blush uncontrollably. He could smell her passion fruit perfume. He gulped, and then sat up.

"Do you want to go down to the roller rink?" Riverdale Roller Rink was packed with kids from the neighborhood and school all summer. Hopefully it wouldn't be like that today.

"Ok, I just have to leave a note for my Mom. Here, come over to my house and then we'll go," Lavender suggested.

"Yeah," James began. " Hey Erich, tell Mom that I went to skating!" Erich didn't answer him back and James didn't really care. He and Lavender walked down the stairs and across the street. Surprisingly, Rhode Island had been having great weather instead of the usual overcast days.

"Come on in, I'll only be a minute," Lav said stepping in the house. He followed her in and looked around. James had been in her house before but something was strange about it.

"Did you change the furniture?" he asked looking around some more.

"No, why?"

"Um, no reason. Are you ready?"

"Yeah. Hey, James, can you go up to my room and get my gym bag? My socks are in there. I have to do something really quick, it will only take a few more minutes."

James thought his heart was going to jump out of his chest, she had asked him to go up to her room. He wasted no time running up the stairs. Sure he had been in her room before, but once again, strangely something wasn't the same. The white walls had a pink border around the room.

Through her bedroom's huge window, was a view of James' room across the street.

He saw the bag and grabbed it, but looked up to see Erich staring back at him from his window. James shook his head and made his way back downstairs.

"Ready?"

"Yeah. Oh, thank you for getting my bag," she said, walking out the front door.

◈

Lavender pulled on her skates and stood up. James had already glided over to the rink but waited for her. A mess of kids from school and the neighborhood were talking loudly, skating and eating hot dogs from the concession stand.

"James!" a very familiar, annoying voice called from across the room. Nick Brenden and his friends skated over to James. "Where the hell have you been?"

James shrugged and looked through the crowds for Lavender. "She isn't with you, is she?" Nick whined. James frowned and looked at his friend.

"Look, she is my best friend."

"Yeah and I remember when we used to be best friends," Nick mumbled. James pushed past him trying to find Lavender.

"James!" Nick called to him. Nick managed to grab James' t-shirt. James turned around and walked back to him. "Look," he said pointing across the room.

James looked over to see Faye Waters, her long red hair draped over her shoulders. She was in the same school as them and lived in the same neighborhood. Her Dad worked as a police chief and her mother as a hair dresser. She had five year old twin brothers and to top it off, the family thought it was 1960. Hippie style was not in.

"Yeah so?" James asked.

"So? Well, um, seeing that Lavender knows her..."

"Wait! You just made a big deal about Lavender and now you want me to ask her to introduce you to Faye? Nick get a brain," James told him and began to walk away.

"Please James! Please I'm begging you!"

Sighing, James faced Nick and reluctantly nodded his head. Nick smiled and watched James walk over to Lavender.

"Hey! There you are." Lavender greeted him.

"Lav, can I ask a favor?" James asked her. She stood up on the skates and nodded. "Ok, well I was wondering if you would, um, introduce Nick to Faye Waters."

"Ok."

"Really?"

"Yeah. I'll be right back," Lavender said skating over to where Faye was standing. James did the same in going over to Nick.

"She said she would." James told him. Nick gave a smile.

"James I owe you for this."

"Actually-" James began but was cut off by Lavender who was standing behind him, Faye next to her.

" James, Nick, this is Faye. Faye, this is James Martin and his friend Nick Brenden." Lavender explained. James waved at her and walked away from Nick. Lavender followed him after saying goodbye to Faye.

"James, I suddenly don't feel very well, do you mind if I go home?" she asked him catching up to him. James looked back at Nick and nodded.

"Yeah, I really don't feel like skating." They took off their skates and handed them back in. As they left the building, Rockwell's "Somebody's Watching Me" song came on.

"I like this song," she commented.

"Really?" he asked.

"Yeah."

"Do you want to stay and listen to it?"

"No, come on, let's go."

⁂

The next day was Friday, the night of the concert. Neither said how badly they wanted to go see their favorite band. James was sitting in his room, reading a mystery book that he was almost done with.

"Knock, Knock!" a voice said from the doorway. James looked up and saw Erich leaning on the doorway.

"Yeah?" James asked annoyed at his brother.

"Oh come on Jamie, I know you want to go to that concert, but don't take your anger out on me," Erich said. James rolled his eyes and watched Erich walk over to the bed. "Now being a good person I decided to give these to you." Erich pulled out two long pieces of paper from his front pocket.

"What is this?" James asked, taking the papers.

"Concert tickets. For tonight."

"Really? Wow, thanks that's really generous of you."

"Yeah I know," Erich mumbled and walked out of the room. James jumped up and ran downstairs and across the street. Ringing the Springer's doorbell at least five times at once, Mrs. Springer answered the door.

"Hello Mrs. Springer, is Lavender home?"

"Yes, hold on James, she's got a friend over, I'll get her."

"No, that's okay." James said backing away from the door. He watched Mrs. Springer close the door and lock it. He quickly ran in the middle of the street, and stood so he could see Lavender's window.

"Lav!" he called to her, trying to keep his voice down. After a few minutes she appeared at the window and smiled at him. He held up the tickets and waved them frantically. She gasped when she realized what he was trying to tell her. She left the window and ran out the front door.

"James, where did you get those tickets?" she squealed.

"Erich gave them to me."

"Oh my gosh, we're going to the- wait, how are we going to get out?"

James thought about it for a moment. "I'll tell my parents that I'm staying over Nicks house and you tell your mom that your staying over Faye's."

"Ok..... I'll meet you at the bus stop at 9:00."

"Deal. See you tonight." James said turning back to the house.

"Wait! What should I wear?"

James smiled to himself and then looked back at her, "Surprise me."

James was antsy all through dinner; moving around in his seat was sure to draw attention so he stopped and poked at his food. James never saw his father and mother staring at him.

"James, honey is everything alright?" Mrs. Martin asked him, after giving Grace more juice. He looked up startled and tried to remain calm.

"Yeah."

"Christine, I think that it's time that I gave him the ' Talk '. I mean at twelve he's old enough really," his father said to his mother. James' eyes opened wide, He already knew about sex and he wasn't comfortable talking openly about it. With Nick being the most active, James more than often, had to hear of his sexual escapades.

"No!" James said immediately, " I don't need it."

"James, I was twelve when I learned-"

"Dad, I'm fourteen," James said still poking at his food. *This is just another reason why we were never close*, He thought to himself. He was always working, James couldn't even remember a time when they went out or did anything together. Erich didn't seem to care but it always had affected James.

"I know, I said that James, anyway-" Mr. Martin began, but James interrupted.

"Um, Mom can I go spend the night over at Nick's house?" he asked standing up and taking his plate to the kitchen. He saw his mother look over at his father and with out words ask if he thought it was ok.

She shook her head in agreement and began to clean the table. "I'll just call Elaine and ask her if it would be ok if you stayed over tomorrow too. Your father is working and I have an early appointment at the doctor for Gracie."

James began to panic. He wasn't really going to Nick's, how was he supposed to get out of this? Suddenly he had an idea. James ran into the living room and quickly dialed Nick's phone number. One ring...two rings.... three rings.... "Hello?" Nick's voice said over the phone.

"Nick, It's James. Listen I need your help. Remember yesterday when you said that you owed me?"

"Yeah?"

"Well I need the favor now. I need you to tell my Mom that you can let me stay over tomorrow while she takes my sister to the doctor. Oh and tell her that I'm sleeping over tonight."

"Wait, where are you going? I want to go."

"Shh! I'm going to see The Stars*-"

"Lucky."

"Nick, please just cover for me!" James pleaded. He heard Nick sigh and then quietly he said yes. "Thank you! Okay hold on... Mom! Nick is on the phone!" James heard his mother pick up the phone in the kitchen and he hung up the one in the living room. The phone call only lasted a minute and then she hung up.

"James!" Mrs. Martin called from the kitchen, "Everything is all set. Are you going to leave now?"

He looked to a clock. 8:45 it read. "Um... Yeah I'm just going to change!" He called back to her. James sprinted up the stairs and desperately searched for something to wear. Pulling out a pair of worn jeans and His new black Stars* t-shirt. He slipped them on and looked around for where he placed the tickets. Upon finding them he slipped them in his pocket and ran out the door and didn't stop until he reached the bus stop.

⁕

The sun was already set as Lavender and Faye went through Lavender's bag of outfits looking for something for her to wear. Both girls were in their pajamas; Faye in a long night shirt, and Lavender in shorts and a tank top.

"God Lav, you have nothing for me to work with!" Faye exclaimed pushing her long red hair out of her way. Lavender went through the bag and pulled out the "alternative outfit" of her green mini skirt and purple top. She really didn't want to wear it but that was all she had that appealed to her as "a date outfit" but it wasn't a date! Was it?

"Faye, help me!"

Sighing, Faye walked over to her best friend. How I wished I could be her. Perfection is the only way to describe Lavender, Faye thought. "Lav look, I think you should wear this," she began walking over to the open closet. She pulled out a pair of Lavender's wide leg jeans, which she had borrowed and never returned.

"Oh so now you decide to give them back!" Lavender laughed. Faye held them up to her and smiled.

"Go change into this and put on your Stars jacket and wear your white sneakers. Hurry its almost 8:45!"

Lavender laughed at her friend, then disappeared into the bathroom, it had taken her a near ten minutes to get the dark eye liner just the way Max Page wore it. Stepping out of the bathroom a moment later dressed, she thought she was ready to go. "So....tell me.....how bad do I really look?"

"You don't look that bad..."

"Faye!"

"Sorry, I'm kidding, no you don't look bad. Now go before my Mom realizes that I'll be the only one sleeping here tonight." Lavender walked over to her friend and gave her a hug.

"Thanks a lot Faye, I owe you!"

"Get me Tommy Klein's autograph."

"I'll try."

" Bye."

"Bye."

꧁꧂

She was already there waiting."You um.. Look...nice." James told her. It wasn't the exact word he wanted to say but it was the only thing he could think of that stayed away from totally hot, and even though I'm thinking this is a date I'm going to tell you that it isn't.

"You too... I'm a little under-dressed aren't I?"

"No." James said quickly. He looked at her again, she wore her hair down long. "So how did you get out of the house?"

"I went over to Faye's and changed there."

"Oh... So you're staying at Faye's?"

"Yeah, aren't you staying with Nick?"

"No." He smiled at her and looked down the street. He could hear the bus coming slowly down the narrow street and making its stop at the bus stop, They boarded the bus depositing 50 cents into the change holder. They took a seat at the front and didn't talk until they reached the Providence Convention Center.

Lines of adults and college kids lined the entrance; ticket takers were clamoring to get the tickets ripped and the people into the convention center. Beside each ticket taker stood huge men dressed in all black. James and Lavender got at the end of the line. It moved quickly but not quickly enough to them. Finally they were next in line.

James handed the ticket taker the papers but the guard stepped in front of them. He had a name tag on that read: Billy.

"Excuse me, hold up for a second!"

"What for?"

The man folded his hands over his chest. "Look, kids your age have been trying to get in here all night, and I'm not sure where you've been getting these but...," Billy said "These tickets are fake."

"What!" James and Lavender both exclaimed.

Chapter 3

"I'm going to have to call your parents," Billy said. He grabbed James and Lavender's shoulders and led them past the ticket booths. Floods of adults poured in the area, carrying drinks, and stuff that they had bought.

"The tickets can't be fake, my brother gave them to me!" James insisted. Billy led them to the security room where a few other kids were there, some crying.

Billy sat them down and kneeled in front of James, "Look the ticket numbers don't match up with the real ones. Sorry kids. So what are your phone numbers?" James gave him the numbers and sank down in his seat. He looked over at Lavender and tried to read her expression. At that moment The Stars* could be heard singing "The Duchess's Calling ".

"I'm sorry," James told her while trying to hear the song through the screaming. She looked over at him and gave a half smile.

"This is your song."

"Yeah I know."

"Do you want to dance?"

"Here?" he asked.

"Yeah."

"It's a slow song."

"So? I think we've know each other long enough to dance together," she answered. James looked around at the other kids who were sitting crying their eyes out.

"What about them?" James asked her. She looked over at them.

"W-" she was cut off by a loud noise from outside the door. Billy, the only security officer there, stood up and opened the door. A group of men and women were having a brawl outside the door! Billy tried to pull them apart from one another but was caught in the uproar. More and more people gathered to watch. James and Lavender wasted no time in getting out of there, pushing their way through the people.

"We made it." James said after getting out of the crowds. Lavender was out of breath by the time they escaped.

"Which way?" she asked. He looked around and couldn't decide.

"I don't know. To the stage I guess. Look over there!" James exclaimed pointing over to a door that read **Stage**. "This way." They ran to the door and slipped inside. The room was dark and only one light was coming from the end of the way.

"You don't think that it's the bright light do you?" James asked her. She shrugged but he couldn't see. They walked into the light and the farther they got the louder the lyrics of "Open Rage " sounded. Suddenly a curtain was pulled back from the front of them revealing The Stars* singing and playing their instruments on stage.

"James...I think I'm gonna pass out." Lavender breathed to him. The song ended and the band came near them. Max Page was a lot better looking in person. Each of the members, Max- Alex Globeman, Derek Michaels and Tommy Klein had on black t-shirts with tight black pants.

"Hey! Cool shirt." Max Page said as he passed James. Lavender and James both stood in shock at what had just happened.

"James, Max Page just talked to you! You're set for life." Lavender exclaimed. James peered on the stage and saw all the equipment. Max's guitar, Alex's bass, Derek's guitar and Tommy's drum set.

"Hey, can we play anything for you? What's your favorite song?" Max asked them when he returned. Lavender blushed and looked to James.

"Um...can you play "Vigilante" ?" James asked knowing it was her favorite song. He saw her face light up with excitement as Max nodded and walked on stage. Max ran back and walked up to James. "Hey is this your first date?" He whispered.

James didn't know how to respond to this. He saw Max wink at him and walk back to the stage. " Vigilante " started and once again Max came back, he pulled Lavender by the wrist onto the stage. James watched Lavender's shocked face as she walked on stage with him. Max motioned for James to come on stage also. Running, James ended up on stage also.

The song started and they both stood motionless on stage until people in the audience started jumping up and down to the song. Without thinking he grabbed her hand and spun her around. She laughed at him and they danced. Their song ended and after two more songs and an encore The Stars* walked off the stage.

Alex Globeman, one of the founders of the band, was the last to walk off the stage. His short dark blond hair was dripping with sweat just like the others who had walked past.

"You're cute kid," looking to Lavender.

"Um...Thanks."

"You two want to come back into the dressing room with us?" Alex asked them. James and Lavender looked at each other and both shook their heads in excitement. Following Alex they walked down a long passage and into a room where all the band members were. Tommy and Max were talking quietly, Derek was downing beer and some of the back up musicians sat around on the other chairs in the dressing room. Awkwardly they stood while Alex took a seat on one of the couches that was in the room. Thin white walls held two mirrors and a closet filled with wardrobe.

"So did you enjoy the show?" Tommy asked them. Tommy always appeared to be the only one who really socialized with fans.

"Yeah, we did. You guys are really great!" Lavender raved. Still standing, James moved closer to her.

They watched Tommy lean over and take the joint off the table. James and Lavender saw him light it then pass it to the rest of the guys. After they all were finished Max held it out to them. Lavender gulped and they both looked over at each other again.

"We're only kids."

"So? We've been smoking this shit since we were your age," he told them. "Come on it's not going to kill you."

James looked at all of them and shook his head. "You guys write about saying no to drugs, what about songs like "Yard " and "Hole in the Box"? You're an influence to kids our age and yet you're smoking weed in front of us!.... Come on Lav, let's get out of here," Lavender followed him out the dressing room door and both stood speechless at what they saw in front of them.

"Mom?!"

❧

"James Andrew Martin, how could you have lied to us? And to see a concert!" his mother screeched at him. Mrs. Springer and his parents were all in the Martin's living room. James and Lavender were seated next to each other on the couch while their parents stood. Lavender had been looking at her feet the whole time, red filled her face. James was faced to see the angry faces of his and Lavender's parents.

"Mom" he pleaded, " I told you Erich gave me the tickets! We didn't know they were fake! Why won't you believe me?"

His mother sighed, "James, Erich told us the story. You had gotten the tickets and showed him, when he found out that it was and "older concert" he told us before security called."

"And Lavender, look at you! You look like...like...like... something I will say when we get home!" Mrs. Springer cried at the sight of her daughter. Her father was shaking his head, as was James'.

"Mom-" Lavender began. She looked up at her mom her big green eyes filled with tears that she was trying to hide. *I really wish I could cry now*, James thought. Suddenly, he wanted to reach out and grab her and hold her until she stopped crying. "He gave James the tickets-"

Cutting her short, Mrs. Martin spoke once again, " I think that is enough for tonight. James, you're grounded for two months."

"What!"

"We'll talk about your punishment when we get home Lavender." Lav stood up and walked with her parents out the front door. James didn't know who to be angry at, Erich, his parents or himself. In fact he didn't know what emotion to express. Not making eye contact with his parents, he stormed up the stairs and slammed the door. He pulled his shirt over his head and flopped on the bed; burying his head.

He looked over at the clock on his night stand. It read 12:22. Only two hours ago he had been at the concert on stage with The Stars*, with Lavender. With Lavender... He looked across the street. She was walking into the house. That was it. It had not been obvious to him before, she used to be his best friend, sure he had a slight crush on her years ago, but now it was different.

"I think...I *really* like her," he said aloud.

※

Lavender walked across the street with her mother silent next to her. It had seemed so great up until they had brought out the pot and when James' mother caught them. Lavender looked up at her mother who was walking up the front steps of the porch.

"Mom?"

"What?" Lavender swallowed hard and then walked up the porch.

"Nothing," she watched her mother put the key into the lock of the door, then open it. The light inside was bright, blinding Lavender as she stepped in. Her father was standing near the stairs, his bottle of vodka clutched in his left right hand.

"Where have you been?" he slurred.

"No where," Lavender looked at her mother who had disappeared into the living room.

"You sneak out with that son of a bitch across the street?"

"No," Lavender started to walk to the stairs, she was ready to escape all of this, she was so tired of his abuse towards her.

"Get back here I'm not done talking to you!" he grabbed her arm and pulled her back down to him.

"Well I'm done! Leave me alone!" He grabbed her again and yanked her back to him. Lavender looked into his cold green eyes. His skin was pale and his face was rough with stubble.

"Don't you dare talk to me you little whore!" he yelled lifting his hand to her face and striking her. It knocked her down, her knees banging on the wood floor. "I know you've been fucking him! Next thing you know you'll be pregnant and end up just like your mother!"

Lavender looked up at him, her brown hair splayed across her face. She wasn't going to take it this time. For the past seven years she had been putting up with his physical and emotional abuse, all because he wanted to be a drunk. She felt hot tears welding up in the corners of her eyes. Lavender stood upright, stabbing pain was hitting her legs. Staring at her father all she felt was hate.

He reached out to grab her again but Lavender seized his hands and twisted them in a unnatural position. He we was so stunned he didn't move. "Don't you ever touch me again! I'll break everyone of your bones if you even try to touch me!" Lavender twisted them more and something popped in his finger. " Got it you crazy bastard? You fucking do anything to me or my mother again and I'll kill you!" With a quick movement, Lavender jabbed her aching knee into his groin sending him tumbling over.

She looked for her mother but didn't see her. It didn't matter anymore, all she wanted was to go upstairs and be safe in her bedroom. Lavender dashed up the stairs and threw herself against the closed bedroom door. After locking it she ran to her bed and cried. A while later, a knock came to her door.

Standing up, Lavender walked over and opened it. Her Mother stood silent. Lavender fell into her open arms and sobbed into her chest.

"He's leaving, sweetheart, he's not going to hurt you anymore."

James awoke the next morning, his head hurt and his back was freezing, seeing he had slept with no shirt on. Instead of waking up to the usual sunny days that Rhode Island was having, dark grey clouds kept the sun locked away.

He groaned as he got up and walked over to his closet. After pulling on a grey t-shirt, he made his bed. "That's just how I feel...grey" he thought.

Shades were opened and with making his way downstairs, he could smell the left over breakfast. Earlier that morning in a half awake daze, he had heard his father leave for a trip to Boston. Halfway down the stairs he turned around again and went back up.

"I'm not even in to mood to see that jerk," referring to Erich. "He belongs in an asylum." James muttered angrily. He took a long shower and then dressed. Two months was the rest of the summer. It would be gone; soon school would start and it would go back to the same thing. Was it really worth it last night? Of course it was, he wouldn't have traded anything for last night. Well maybe some things. Already dusk was upon him. What had he done all day?

James took out the scrapbook that was under his bed. Sitting on the blue and green comforter, he turned the pages. The first few were taken back when he was younger, him and Erich playing in the yard, well James playing Erich was staring at James like he had thirteen heads. He and Nick sitting eating Dels Lemonade, a popular treat that was only open in the summer. He had finally arrived at the recent pictures; the first one was them.

She had been in her bathing suit . Her hair was down and curled up at the ends. He had been wearing a blue button up shirt with denim shorts. A large pink piece of bubble gum was at her lips in a huge bubble. She had it pressed against his cheek. He was smiling.

James didn't even know that someone was watching him from the doorway. "Knock Knock!" he looked up and the smile that was on his face faded to a frown. Erich's blond hair was slicked back, his sneakers were making marks in the carpet. Stepping in the room he left the door partly open.

"What do you want?"

"Now Jamie, is that anyway to talk to your older brother?"

James sighed and went back to the book. But Erich grabbed it away from him. "Give it back!"

"Why? It hasn't even been a whole day and you're longing for her." Erich sneered. James reached over and tried to grab the book from him but he pulled it back. "Tisk, tisk, James!"

"Those tickets were fake!"

"Yeah I know. I come off as the good kid and you as the bad." He stood further from James and began flipping the pages. "James I would say that you are obsessed with Ms. Springer."

James held his tongue tight in his mouth not saying a word. He hoped that he would leave soon. Erich looked from the album to James. "I'd like to get near her." James stormed up to him and grabbed the book.

"Leave her alone," he said firmly.

"I wouldn't even try Jamie. I'll just leave you to be horny for her." James threw the album on the bed and pushed his way past Erich, making his way to the cellar. James had gotten in the door when he heard his mother calling him.

"James! James!" He peeked his head in the door and saw her standing next to Grace, his little sister. "Me and Gracie are going to Stop and Shop, we'll only be a little while. Erich is upstairs." He nodded and walked slowly down the cellar stairs. The dark cellar had always scared him when he was younger; it had at least thirteen rooms and each had a small window. One of the rooms, James had made his own.

It was one of the large rooms. It was also the only room where you could exit out to the backyard, though you had to climb up or down the rocks. The heavily insulated rooms keep most of the cold out and the sound. He had only been in the room a minute when a loud, sharp knock came at the door. He ran to the door and found Lavender, tears splattered across her face.

She threw herself into his chest and began to sob loudly. Stunned for only a moment, James wrapped his arms around her back and tried to calm her down. "Shh...Shh...Shh... What's the matter?" she looked up at him and then sobbed more.

"I- couldn't- take- him- anymore!" she said, between sobs. "I told him to leave me alone and he did! He did! He's leaving right now!" James pressed her head down on him and held her.

"They're getting a divorce and I couldn't be happier!"

"That's best right?" sniffling, she looked back up at him and smiled.

"You're such a good friend James,"she looked down and struggled to get something in her pocket, but in the process lost her balance and fell, bringing James down with her. They laughed and rolled on the soft navy carpet below them. James found himself on top of her. She gently placed her hand on the back of his neck and pulled his face down to hers.

They were only inches apart when his Mother called him from up the stairs. He jumped up and looked down at her. "I'll be right back," he told her and then raced up the stairs. Breathless, he opened the door and saw his mother taking brown grocery bags in from the garage.

"James, I was calling you, what were you doing down there?" His breathing became normal again and as fast as he could he helped her with the groceries; then darted down the stairs. When his eyes saw what was happening, he felt as if he had died. Her body was under his, being held down. He was trying to take her shirt off while trying to hold down her struggle, she kicked and hit but it didn't help. Erich had Lavender pinned down.

Without thinking he ran and jumped on top of Erich and hit him as hard as he could. Erich swung back sending James to the wall. His back felt broken and his neck twisted. Somehow he got up and ran over to him again, punching and kicking at him, Erich stood up and backed away. Lavender had crawled up against the wall, tears poured onto her face. James stood in front of her blocking her when he could.

"You little shit! " Erich screamed at James. Lunging forward to James, he grabbed his neck and held him against the wall. Squirming and trying to get loose before he ran out of breath. Somehow he managed and shoved him to the ground.

"You sicko! You're seventeen, we're only fourteen! How dare you come near her!" yelled James, who was unaware of how the words didn't make sense. Erich rose and stumbled over himself.

"I'll get you! I'll even kill you if I have to! Take it seriously!" James and Lavender watched him run out the basement door. James sprinted to lock it and then put a chair under the knob. Running back over to her, he wrapped his arms over her trembling body. Her sobs were worse than before.

"Are you okay?" he asked her pulling away from her. She nodded while keeping her head down making as little contact as possible. " Come on, we have to tell my Mom."

"NO!" she exclaimed and grabbed his hand. "We can't! He said he would hurt you if I said anything. We can't tell her! Please don't tell her! Just stay here, I'm fine! You're fine and please, just stay here!"

※

At 9:58 James and Lavender walked out of the basement and climbed down the rocks and found themselves on the street. A dim streetlight was the only sign of life. He sighed as he walked her over to her house. They stood in the middle of the street, both looking down at their feet.

"I'm sorry. If I hadn't let my hormones out, this would have never happened," James told her. She looked up at him and caught his eye.

"No, James it's my fault. I should have never came over in the first place," she said turning to her house. He watched her walk up the porch and then pause. She walked slowly over to him and stood in front of him. "Wait."

She stepped in closer to him and leaned in. He did the same and when their lips met, they felt that the world had overturned. After a minute she pulled away and smiled at him. "I wanted to do that earlier," she ran back to the porch, opened the door and disappeared behind it.

Chapter 4

James limped up the stairs making his way to his mother's bedroom. "Thank God, that I survived last night." James said to himself. Bruises covered his body and face, deep blue and purple marks were set into his legs....

❦

Mom will be in bed by now, she always goes to sleep early when Dad is away on business, James thought. Just having his first kiss was enough reason to celebrate to him. On top cloud nine, nothing could go wrong. Slipping quietly in the door; he locked it behind him.

"Psss.....psss..." James squinted in the darkness.

"Erich?"

"Jamie come on I gotta show you something downstairs." Erich's voice was not even above a whisper. He could see Erich's outline standing near the door of the basement. James walked over and looked at Erich. A scary grin was upon his face.

"What?"

"Come on it's downstairs."

"Can't it wait?"

"Come on Jamie." Erich slipped through the door and it seemed to James that he floated downstairs. Cautiously James followed. It was darker than up stairs but an eerie glow peaked out from the very bottom. When James reached the last stair, Erich grabbed James' body and shoved him to the ground. Placing his hand over James mouth, he dragged him into the eerie glow of bright florescent light like a rag doll.

James twisted, turned, kicked and punched but couldn't escape. James gasped at each stabbing pain that ran up his chest from the nasty meeting with the concrete floor. Nothing looked familiar. Finally Erich stopped and stood up upright.

After getting use to the light James looked around; no sound could express his fear. The room was filled with chains and other torture equipment. He felt himself being lifted and before he knew it he was up in one of the chains.

"Where did you get all this?" James asked, tears were forming in his eyes. Erich smirked at him and walked over to him.

"Oh Come on, that's really not important. What is important is that I get you back for your little escapade today," Erich shut and bolted the door behind him. "Don't start something you can't finish Jamie."

***

He had been awake all night. Erich had left after the first seven hours. Before he left he unlocked the chains and let him fall to the ground. The pain was unbearable but he had to get help. His mother would be up in her room, while his father would be getting home from his business trip to Boston. Church would begin at nine sharp, though he doubted that he was going to be able to make it. Still the sun hadn't broke through and it made the house dark and dreary.

Mrs. Martin was in her room and was the first to see her son. Hearing him approach she put away her romance novel. She ran over to James and steadied him against the wall.

"Oh my God."

***

Lavender opened her eyes and looked around her bedroom. She had slept sounder than she had in a long time. Her hair was neatly sprawled across her pillow and the purple covers were drawn to the top of her thighs. Her pink sweatshirt she had fell asleep in came to her knees. It was about eight o'clock, her mother must be in her room and her father... where was he? She could care less. Hopefully he was far away. They had watched him pack his stuff into his car.

She had been awoken for a minute when she heard a mild siren coming from outside but she had fallen back to sleep. *"I must be dreaming,"* she decided. Still laying in bed, Lavender smiled to herself and touched her lips with her left fingers. For her first kiss it wasn't that bad. In fact it had been great.

She had to see him again, she had to be with him. Today, she was going to see him in church!

She forgot all about church!

Quickly she jumped out of bed and ran to the bathroom and washed up. Picking out a pink skirt that fell to her knees, a yellow top, and a pair of white dress heels that she rarely wore.

She glanced at the vanity which held the make-up she wore last night. She shook her head. After the incident that night, her mother had let it go that she had been at the concert. She walked to her mother's room and shockingly she found the door open and not a single trace of her. "Mom!" Lavender walked down the stairs and into the kitchen. Her mother wasn't there either, where was she then? "Mom?" Lavender called again. That was when she saw a note propped up on the table by the vase her Grandma Molly had given Lavender's mother and father on their wedding. She had always admired it, a clear glass vase with flower design. For being so plain it was so beautiful.

Lavender picked up the note and began to read: *Dear Lav, There has been an accident with James. I went over with his Mother, to Providence Hospital. -Love Mom.*

What happened? What was going on? Suddenly it hit her, the sirens weren't a dream, they came early this morning! What was wrong with James? The loud doorbell rang and it made her jump. She tip toed to the front entry and looked out the peephole. Lavender let out a breath when she saw that it was Nick. Quickly she opened the door and saw his somber face.

"Nick, what's going?"

"You don't know?"

"No, I don't know!" she said getting angry, "What happened to James? Is he okay?"

"Your Ma called my Ma, I'm supposed to take you back to my house and then we will take us to hospital."

"Why!" she asked taking the collar of his green shirt into her hands. "Why is James in the hospital?!"

Nick gulped and then answered. "Erich tried to kill him." Her hands let go of his shirt and she felt herself spinning but she wasn't moving. "He beat him up pretty bad, I saw him a little while ago and he says he is fine, their watching him for any bleeding. They just don't know."

❦

"Fourteen year old male, physically abused by his older brother,"someone said. James had his eyes open then but he only heard every other word. His mother's hand clung to his and in back of her he saw his Mrs. Springer on his mother's side holding his sister back. He heard the voice of his father rushing up to his mother. Mrs. Martin's frantic crying did not help the situation. Mr. Martin got her to let go as they pushed James further into the hospital. A moment later he passed out.

⁂

He awoke a bit later, his eyes bloodshot and his body aching. A few visitors had come by, Nick, who was desperately trying to hold in sickness and his mother who burst out in tears every six seconds and his father who avoided eye contact. From what he understood, his parents had gone down to the police station to answer some questions about *him*.

Drifting off to sleep again, he heard the door open. The newly familiar voice of his Doctor filled his ears. "Mr. Martin? How are you feeling?" He opened his eyes and tried to smile but nothing could make him smile. "You're pretty strong. That beating nearly killed you. Your parents will be back soon but until then you have a visitor." James tried to sit up and managed to move one inch. The doctor excused himself and left the door open. She walked in slowly, bracing herself. She wasn't looking at him; her gaze was to the floor. When she got near him she tried to look at the paintings that were hanging on the pastel blue walls.

Awkward moments of silence followed. Finally James spoke, "Lav, look at me." Her eyes were still looking at the paintings trying to block out his image.

"I can't."

"Why? Look its not that bad-" at that moment she turned as he showed her his arm filled with bruises, cuts, and welts. She winced and then turned away again. "Lavender please, please, I'm sorry! Just look at me!" Holding back her tears she slowly turned her head to him.

He smiled at her. For the first time all day he smiled. She could make him do that. Without thinking he grabbed her hand, but she pulled away. "James, I'm so sorry."

"I'm okay, don't worry about me."

"I'm so sorry, if I hadn't told you not to tell your mom, this is my fault."

"Lavender, it's not your fault. Please don't blame yourself," James pleaded. "I told you, I'm alright."

She wiped her tears and looked back to him. "It is my fault! I should be punished not you!"

"I would rather it be me, you're too beautiful."

"What?" James looked at her, she had heard him. "You called me beautiful."

"It isn't a lie Lav. You're gorgeous."

She didn't know how to respond. She mouth went dry and she could feel the blood rushing to her cheeks.

"I can't look at you like this James. I should go," she said turning to leave but he grabbed her sleeve and pulled her back over to him. Bringing her down their lips met in perfect harmony. His tongue slipped into her mouth, touching hers. After a second, she pressed her mouth into his. They parted and she ran out of the room leaving James with out company.

The door closed and she pressed her back against it. Something made he turn her head to see Nick staring through the window that let you see into James room. He stared at her and walked over to her. "So, you two are together now? When's the wedding?"

She stood there. He had seen them kissing. He had seen them french kissing each other in a hospital, her, with tears on her face, him, with bruises and scars. "You're such an asshole," she told him moving past him.

⁂

"Mom, I'm fine!" James told his mother later that night. His father had come to look at him but barely said two words. He was now on the hospital phone located at the nurses station. Visible through the glass, James watched his father hang up the phone and walk back into the room.

"They found Erich just a few miles from here. He's being brought into the police station."

"Dad, Erich is really sick, he had his own chamber in the basement, I never knew it was there!" James said trying to sit up. Mr. Martin stopped him though.

"James, I know. Everything is going to be ok. We didn't know about the room either. There are so many damn rooms in that basement it's hard to keep track. Look, an officer is here to talk to you. We are going to leave and let you talk to him ok?" James nodded and watched them both leave. A fairly tall man dressed in a navy police uniform. His light red hair was slowly receding to the back of his head. A few small wrinkles could be seen if he were to go under a microscope. James guessed he was maybe in his late forties.

"Mr. Martin, my name is Captain Kirkman. I'll only be here a little while." He explained. He took out a small notebook and flipped to a clean page. His eyes looked over James and he swore to himself. What did this kid do to deserve this? "Um...Okay, so Your brother beat you am I not correct?"

"Yes he did."

"Did anyone witness this?"

"No."

"Okay, do you know if he has hurt anyone else?"

"Well... earlier yesterday my friend Lavender and I were in my basement and I ran upstairs to do something and when I came back down he had her pinned down," James explained.

"And are you and your friend together?"

"What do you mean?"

"Is she your girlfriend?"

⊱ ─── ⊰

Two Sundays later, James was able to leave the house. Church was the first place he was allowed to go. Entering St. Mary's church was hard with all the people staring at him, small children pointing at his bruised face and hands. They all knew what had happened to him. Holding in his anger he took a seat with his parents and sister.

Minutes later, Father Daniels appeared at the alter. At thirty-nine, Daniels stood at five nine and a half with a full head of jet black hair. His white robes fit snugly on him and his voice was rather soothing.

"Dear Friends, Children of God, let us get started by saying that our hearts go out to the young man who was badly injured only three weeks ago. Today he is here, and let us pray to God that, God may soothe his pain. Please join me in prayer."

Winter 1984

James sat with his parents in the cold courtroom. The grey marble floors made the room colder. The grey walls didn't help. Erich sat at one table, hands folded neatly on the table. His hair was slicked back and his black suit didn't make him seem as nice as his lawyer had told him to dress.

"The defense calls Lavender Springer." Michael Kacnolls said to the courtroom. An older man of fifty-six, Kacnolls had been in law since he could walk. His father, grandfather, great grandfather, and great, great, grandfather had all been lawyers. The Kacnolls family was one of the best law firms in all of Rhode Island.

Michael Kacnolls's round middle gave away that one too many donuts had been eaten, but his sharp, black eyes would frighten anyone. James looked to the back of the courtroom and watched Lavender walk up the path to the witness stand. When she got there she stood and put her hand on the bible that was on the stand.

"Do you swear to tell the truth and nothing but the truth, so help you God?"

"I do," she answered quietly and then took a seat.
"State your name please."
"Lavender Springer."
"Your full name please." Kacnolls asked her again clearly annoyed but for some reason unknown.
"Lavender Diane Springer."
"Thank you. Now Ms. Springer, In your own words tell the court what happened." James watched her body tense as she sat more upright in the chair.
"I had gone over to James' house and I was crying-"
"Why were you crying?"
"My parents told me... that they were getting a divorce."
"I see, please continue."
"So I went to James' house and James told me everything was alright. Mrs. Martin called him upstairs a little while later and I stayed downstairs. Mr. Martin came in after James left and he... tried to... rape me." The words were sour in her mouth. *Mr. Martin. His name should be Mr. Asshole*, she thought bitterly. Gasps came from the jury, one lady even covered her mouth fearing she might be sick. Kacnolls had no feeling for this case, he didn't feel sorry for the boy but after hearing the girl, something inside him want to hurt the man he was defending.

Kacnolls' own daughter, Melanie, was the same age as them when she was kidnaped outside their home in Coventry. She had been later found in the wooded area a week later. The kidnapper was found but he was never sentenced to death. Melanie would be in college now.

"Ms. Springer, did Mr. Martin succeed, I mean, actually rape you?"
"If you don't mind I really wouldn't like to re-live that." Lavender answered. Kacnolls turned to the Judge.
"Your Honor it is essential to the case that Ms. Springer tell us what happened."
The Judge rubbed his temples and then looked to her. "Ms. Springer, please tell us." She nodded and looked in the courtroom to James.
"He pinned me down and tried to remove my clothes. If James hadn't come down, I would have been raped."
"Thank you Ms. Springer that will be all." Lavender walked down from the witness stand and made her way into the back of the court. Kacnolls took a seat next to Erich and tried not to look at him.

A short recess followed and when they came back, the jury fell quiet and James heart began to race. What would happen if Erich didn't get put in jail? What about his parents, his friends, was he going to hurt more of them?

The man on the last seat of the jury stood across from the judge. James sucked in breath.

"What has the jury decided?"

"We find Richard Martin....."

James was going to be sick at any moment....

Chapter 5

"We find the defendant Richard Martin.... guilty." James let himself breathe again and tried to hide the smile that was playing at the corner of his mouth. Looking over at his parents, he saw his mother holding tears and his father holding her hand tightly.

"Richard Martin, I sentence you to eighteen and a half years in prison. Ten years attempted murder, eight for attempted rape. Case dismissed." the Judge said. He banged the gravel, stood up and walked out of the court.

He looked to the back, but she had already left. His parents had got up and started to leave too. Standing up, he fixed his shirt and looked over to where Kacnolls and Erich was standing. Erich was staring back at him.

"Jamie....Have a great eighteen years."

The fierce winter wind blew snow into his face as he sat on the stairs of the courthouse. He had told his parents that he would get the bus home. Surprisingly they let him do what he wanted for once. James pulled out his gloves and put them on. School had started in August and everyone looked at him different.

I'm not different! He thought, *Stop looking at me as though I murdered someone!* She hadn't talked to him in over five months. Not in the neighborhood, not at school, not even when they all had to work in a group.

I blew it, I blew it by kissing her. He said to himself. Suddenly through the icy wind he saw a figure coming close to him. Dressed in her heavy burgundy winter coat she took a seat next to him. The long brown hair she had been growing over the summer was tied back into a french twist and the heals of the black boots she had on were digging into the snow.

"Hi."

"Hi."

"So...how are you?" Lavender asked him.

"I'm okay and you?"

"Fine...James can I tell you something?"

He looked over at her face and tried to read her expression. "Anything."

"I had a dream last night-"

"I good one I hope."

"A great one."

"That's good."

"And I saw you." Taken aback he continued to look at her.

"Oh."

"Yeah."

"So what was I doing?" She lifted her big green eyes to him and smiled.

"This..." she said taking her right hand on the left side of his face and bringing her lips to his.

❊

As I sit here in Mr. Berreti's ninth grade English class, I'm watching her. Watching her with awe at the sight of how much she has changed over the summer. When the mothers of Oaklawn got together they comment on how she is becoming more beautiful everyday.

Sometimes I catch what they are saying when I am walking through the neighborhood on a cool summer night when no one is watching the street for nosey kids like me. Seems as though walking the neighborhood at eight- nine o'clock when the sun has gone down has now become a new thing of mine.

I pass the old ladies who are sitting on their porches trying to listen to the crickets chirp without their hearing aids on. I laugh to myself when you can hear them saying "What? What did you say Claire?" when they think that their daughter is listening. Other times I will see them shake their heads at me when I pass by.

I know why they are shaking their heads too. They know that I've broken every one of their granddaughter's hearts by taking their virginity and then forgetting they are even alive. At fifteen I do get around. I guess you could say that I'm the way I am because I grew up without a father and I am "resentful" or so that's what the quack doctor told my ma when she took me.

I wouldn't have had to go if to see a counselor if he hadn't been caught with Emily Flynn in the bathroom. Ok so that was a mistake, but I'm not perfect. The counselor told my ma that my step-father Mr. High and Mighty Real estate agent should spend more time with me. My Ma didn't say anything though, as long as he keeps taking in the bucks from his "job" she could care less.

My eye's are now drifting over her again and studying her every move, I watch as she slowly starts to write her name on the white lined paper in front of her. During the time between Christmas and Spring I had discovered that I was smitten with her. From then on I guess you could call me a stalker.

I then saw what he saw, that she was gorgeous, and smart and everything that every one of those stupid Catholic school girls weren't. I haven't felt this way about a girl in a long time, once I did but it was nothing. Feeling this way about her it wouldn't be meaningless fucking, it would be something special.

Would it really? Am I really sure of that? I don't know but for now all I know is that I must have her.... but there was a problem. My gaze went over to the left side of the room. I fixed on him and sneered. What the hell had he done to deserve her?

First of all did he really have her? Over the summer he has asked her out to the movies. They saw "Back to the Future" and then went out for ice cream at Newport Creamery. After that they walked around the quiet neighborhood. I guess this is where the stalker part come in. I walked about ten feet behind them until they came to a stop in front of her house. They held hands all through the walk and they talked of everything: the movie, the new marriage of her mom and step-father- lawyer Jeremy Ryan, her new step-sister Elizabeth.

The way he looked at her made me sick, I don't know if he knows that he looks like a complete moron or if he is doing it on purpose! I was surprised that they didn't hear me behind them, even at the point when I stepped on a pinecone. When they got back to the house, he kissed her and she kissed him back.

Again I became sick knowing that she was kissing him, putting her tongue in his mouth. Gag me! Ever since I started to like her I've turned against him, we used to be cool but now I kind of hate his guts.

I mean what did he do to deserve her? So what if he was almost killed? Then I would have an open chance with her. I was so tired of him, tired of being treated as though he was God and listening to people feel bad for him just because he went through all that. Boo hoo hoo!

He isn't that innocent! She's probably lost her virginity already and here they go to church every Sunday like good little Catholics. Always polite, always doing what they are told to do, when really he must be screwing her any chance he can. Only I'm the one who sees through them and everyone thinks that they are so cute together!

The bell snapped me back to reality. For a second I sat there and watched her get up and then watched him go over to her. She laughed and followed him out of the class room reaching for his hand.

One day I'll have you.

"Nick?" Mr. Berreti's voice called to me. "School's over."

James walked down the hall and turned right going to his locker. High school wasn't that bad, in fact he kind of liked it. He liked all of his teachers- except for Coach Malone, the gym teacher. Oh yeah and Kirk, his son who was a complete jerk. He tried to think of his numbers of the lock, 5- 13-36? Or 5-13-26? It was the last digit he couldn't remember.

"5-13-36" he said aloud, as he opened the locker. As soon as it was wide open it slammed shut again making James jump back. Kirk stood on his left with his hand on the locker. He was 5'10 making him taller than James by two inches. Kirk had a army haircut and lots of freckles on his face.

"Look Martin, I don't like you."

"Good, I don't like you either," James said to him as he reached to open his locker again, but Kirk's hand was still in the way.

"Don't you want to know why I don't like you?"

"I don't care. Can you please move?"

"I don't like you cause all the girls like you. I don't like it!"

James turned and faced him. "Well I'm sorry. For the rest of the year I'll wear my ugly mask so then we can match."

"You think that you're so much better than me, well you're not! Just cause you survived that beating doesn't mean that you are special!"

James narrowed his eyes and tightened his right fist into a ball. He knew he couldn't hit him, he had to remain cool. James looked around out of the corner of his eyes and saw a crowd starting to form.

"Look Kirk," James said cooly "maybe people would like you if you weren't such a pain in the ass. If you spent as much time bulling people around, as you did on your school work they wouldn't have had to fail you last year. So go and be a pain in the ass to someone else cause I'm not going to take it, now fuck off!"

Kirk backed away as the red started to form on his cheeks. He looked around, and then ran, pushing his way out of the circle. James shook his head and went back to his locker, ignoring the other people around him.

"5....13.....36..." he said under his breath as he turned to lock for the second time. Suddenly he felt a tap on his shoulder as he was getting out his books. Turning around he saw Lav standing there with her backpack on and two books in her arms.

"Are you ok?"

"Yeah. I'm fine."

"I've never heard you talk like that," she said quietly. She started to walk down the hall with her back to him. Puzzled, James scooped up his books and ran after her. The green jacket on his arm was dangling in the air as he went.

"Lav! Wait up!.....I don't understand what you mean," he told her when he caught up. The door was a few feet away as she paused and looked at him.

"Just what I said James, I've never heard you talk like that to anyone."

"So I was just supposed to stand there and let him say stupid things to me?"

"No James, but you didn't have to say that he failed."

"Why not? It's true!" Lavender sighed and walked out the school doors. It was pouring and she didn't have an umbrella. He walked after her through the doors, as he was trying to get his jacket from his arm.

"What did I do wrong?" She whipped around and faced him again. Her wet hair clinging to her face and shoulders. His own hair was rapidly becoming flat and water was dripping into his eyes.

"James Martin, how would you like it if someone said something about what happened to you last summer?!" she yelled to him.

"He did say about last summer!" He yelled back.

"And you felt really shitty didn't you?!" James lowered his head.

"Yeah."

"So how do you think he felt?"

"I get your point." jogging over to her he put the jacket over her head to cover her. She sighed again and took the jacket from him, then grabbed his books along with hers and wrapped them in the coat.

"If you get these wet the school will charge you." James tried to hide his smile as he took his jacket from her. "Come on, I have to be home to see Lizzie off the bus." James walked with her slow steps. Her pink polo shirt was clinging to her body soon and her jeans were soaked through. His were the same.

They neared the house in no time. He looked down at his watch which read 2:00. His mother wasn't home from her new job at Bee's Hair Salon and his father wouldn't be home until late tonight. So he too needed to see someone off the bus....Grace.

As he got older it seemed as though Grace got more annoying. She was always going through his things; his closet, his dresser, his bathroom. She had her own bathroom, why did she want to go through his? Sometimes he would find her hidden in his closet when he walked in. She would be real quiet and then jump out at him. The first few times he jumped but after that he got use to it. Now he was waiting for his father to put a lock on the door. Which would never happen, he planned to go and get one and put it on himself this weekend.

"You want to come in my house and wait? Or do you have stuff to do over at yours ?" Lav asked when they came to her porch.

"If it's okay with you then I'll come over."

"Yeah it's okay. My Mom started helping over at Bee's Hair Salon as a receptionist so we'll be alone. Jeremy has the same hours as your dad, so we won't see him till late." Jeremy Ryan, her step-father was also an attorney, that's how her Mom and him met, through his Dad.

"My dad is messed up, says his case is hard. Then again he is always messed up."

"I think that is the one Jeremy is working on too."

"Can I use your bathroom?" James asked when they got inside. It was nice and warm inside and the fresh scent of cinnamon filled their noses.

"Yeah you know where it is." She answered as she walked into the kitchen.

A note was left on the table for me when I walked into the kitchen. I picked it up and started to read it.

Dear Lav,
Bee has Mrs. Martin and I working until closing time at nine. Jeremy won't be home until late tonight so I need you to make dinner. I left chicken in the freezer and some side dishes in the fridge, I'll call later to see what's going on.

Love Mom.

Great just enough to add to my day, I thought as I whirled around the island in the kitchen. Occasionally I'll cook for Jeremy before I head up to bed, when he is going to get home really late. Jeremy always made fun of my cooking but he was just joking. I have really liked Jeremy ever since I had met him and there hasn't been a single day where I haven't been grateful to James' father for introducing him to her mother. Though I always feel bad for James his father doesn't know what he is missing.

⋆

Jeremy tapped his pen on his wood desk. The rain splattered on his office windows. He really hated the rain sometimes but today he found it comforting. He looked over at the family portrait that had been taken before the kids' school had started.

Mary had Lizzie on her lap, with him standing next to her. Lavender sat next to her Mother, smiling the very beautiful smile she had. Lizzie's thin, long blond hair was pulled back into a braid and she was dressed in her blue party dress. He remembered that day clearly because Lizzie had wanted to wear her pink dress instead of the blue one. He would have let her except the pink one was dirty.

He looked at Mary's pretty face and wondered why on earth could he had not met her sooner. Rob Martin, his best friend all through law school had introduced him to her at the New Years Eve party they had at their home every year. He instantly fell head over heels.

Jeremy had been on his own for about three years before that. He dated women but never took the time to get to know them. Ever since Carol he had been reluctant to settle down again. Carol Degario, a beautiful blond, had wandered into his life at a bar on the night of his graduation from Harvard.

She took his heart right out of his chest and placed it in her purse. Carol was a Harvard teacher's daughter. She had been studying law under the watchful eye of her dear Daddy but then dropped out to pursue an acting career. He found her interesting in every way. They decided to move out to California to get her career in drive.

Jeremy received a job at a law firm and Carol went on auditions during the day. When her father found out he flipped and promised to send Jeremy into the deepest depths of hell if he ever married her. Carol didn't care and she persuaded him into marriage.

They were married in Vegas at the Little Chapel Of Flowers. Soon when they got back to California, Carol learned that she won a part in a low production independent film. Before the movie started, Carol insisted that she should have a baby.

Thinking of this Jeremy frowned, he knew what happened next, he played it over in his mind many times. "I remember saying no, now is not the time," he said aloud. She did it anyway, with the young director Peter Mere. She told him that she had been unfaithful and that she was pregnant and that she needed him. So he stayed.

They moved back to Rhode Island before she gave birth and he started work with a firm that his father's friend owned. Come to find out years later, she had only given him half the truth about the birth too.

She had twins a boy and a girl, but she had given the boy up for adoption. The boy she had named Joel and the girl Julie. Peter demanded rights to see his daughter but Carol had told him no, He could never come near her, she claimed that she had a restraining order. One day Carol ran into the store and she left Julie in the car with the doors unlocked. Peter had been following her and he had kidnaped Julie. Julie later died with Peter who had smashed his car on the freeway.

Carol turned to drugs then, Jeremy remembered, cocaine, acid, and everything else she got her thin fingers on. How she got pregnant with Lizzie is still a mystery. Jeremy was thrilled when *his* daughter entered the world. She looked like a mini Carol and he cherished every movement, every smile. Carol kept on the drugs and Jeremy paid for rehab twice but nothing helped her. He left Carol and was never going back.

On the morning of Lizzie's first birthday, Jeremy got a call from Carol's roommate saying Carol was missing. They later found her in a ditch outside of Cranston.

"I thought I couldn't go through it again. With marriage," Jeremy thought. He stood up and crossed the room. He promised himself a long time ago that would never happen to Lizzie. Now he had Lavender who was closer to the age of drugs, he wasn't going to let her slip into them either.

With the thought of his step-daughter, he smiled. It seems as though the little boy he knew from the very second he was born was madly falling for the girl next door, well across the street. *The first night of their date was very funny as I recall*- Jeremy thought silently. *Chaos, really.*

Lavender had gone through one-hundred different outfits before picking one. On that night she had her personal assistant, Faye Waters helping her pick out which outfit to wear.

He didn't realize that his new secretary, Joanne, was walking in his office. "Sorry to bother you sir but I just have a message to give you."

"Fire away Joanne."

"Your Daughter called, the eldest I believe. She said for me to tell you that James can't get a hold of his dad. Can you tell him that his Mom is working late tonight?"

"Will do, thanks Joanne."

"If I may say sir, she is very charming."

"Thanks Joanne."

⁂

"Hey um, can I ask you something?" James asked Lavender as they were walking back from the bus stop. Grace and Lizzie were running up ahead splashing around in the rain.

"Shoot."

"Well...um... do you think that you would like to go out again? I mean if you don't want to you can just say no. Last time we just went out as friends and the kiss was really unexpected and all-" He was cut short when she put her index finger to his lips.

"I thought the kiss was planned," Lavender said softly. She stood on her toes and placed her hands on his shoulders to lift herself to him. Leaning in his cold lips pressed against hers. His eyes closed lightly and he felt as though it was one of his dreams.

"James and Lavender sitting in a tree, k-i-s-s-i-n-g! First comes love, then comes marriage, then comes the baby in the baby carriage!" two very off key girly voices sang. They broke apart and looked next to them to see Grace and Lizzie, standing there, singing their hearts out.

James lunged jokingly at his sister. She squealed and ran far away from him. He ran up behind her and lifted her up and put her on his shoulders. She was laughing and yelling when James ran back over to Lavender.

"So? About that date....."

"Want to come over for dinner?"

Chapter 6

May 1988

I remember it, Jason Allen thought as he walked through the dimly lit corridor and into the bright study. The fire was roaring, when he realized he wasn't in the room alone. "I've been waiting for you Jason," *the sweet seductive voice of Bridget Allen rang through his ears. It couldn't be, Bridget had died in the car crash that had also killed his mother. Bridget his darling wife, alive? No! A ghost!*

James paused and re-read the words on the paper, did it make sense? He was working on a short story for his college resume, desperately hoping to get into Brown or UCLA. He wanted to write, he had always enjoyed reading and writing, it but now he was sure that he wanted to make it his career.

He and his father were barely speaking, every other day his father would bring up law school, but it wasn't for him. He didn't want to be a lawyer! *God can't they just leave me alone?* James thought. High school was almost over and then college, getting a job and then getting married and then... he stopped himself at marriage.

I'm taking it way too far, he told himself and then went back to the story. The cold spring day brought showers and the deep dark clouds brought depression. He had been inside all day sitting in the quiet living room. Grace was at the mall with his Mom, Lavender and her Mom and Sister. His father was at work, *practicing law*.

Today was Saturday, but it felt like Monday. He suddenly was tired of working on the story so he pushed it to the side. Slowly he stood up and made his way upstairs. Walking by the mirror on the stairs he did a double take.

I look different, he studied ,turning his head a little more. His nose was straight, his blue eyes still as brilliant as the day he was born-or so he heard from his mother every so often. He thought his full lips looked girls' but it was one of the things that Lavender said made her go crazy. He smiled at himself in the mirror revealing that all his teeth were straight from wearing braces for the past two years.

"Everyone changed, not only me," James said aloud. His father's hair was slowly turning grey. His mom's was also, but she covered it up with brown hair dye. Grace was getting older and some-what less annoying. She and Lizzie, were with each other all the time, so he didn't have to worry about getting angry with her for doing stupid things to him.

He passed her room few times. When they were together the door would remain closed and Grace would bring over Lavender's "Cosmopolitans" and they would read all the articles. Boys were a favorite topic of their's, this week it was between Jake Higgins and Ryan Quin.

James ran up the rest of the way and walked into this bedroom. His red Fender was sitting on the bed. He started playing the guitar after he got it for his fifteenth birthday. His teacher, Bif, a soft spoken guy who had played with a few really big names in music, was really cool. James lifted the guitar and put it on.

He really liked it, recently he had started singing. He thought he sounded like a frog but Bif said he sounded good. Recently, he had tried his hand at song writing and found that all the songs he wrote were about Lavender. He gave her every song to read and she found she liked each one better than the last.

Hearing the phone ring from downstairs James put down his guitar and made his way down. On the fourth ring he decided to run.

"Hello?"

"Hi, is James home?" a high pitched squeaky voice asked.

"Speaking."

"James, this is Erica Wright."

"Hi Faye."

He heard Faye sigh on the other end and then go back to her regular voice. "Damn James how do you do that? You do it to everyone." She complained.

"It's a gift I guess or it could be that I've been getting phone messages from Erica Wright who incredible sounds just like you!"

"Anyway, who are you taking to the prom?"

"Why?"

"I'm just wondering! Geez!"

"Did Lav ask you to call me?"

"No. I was just wondering if you would be taking her."

"Why did she say something?"

"She casually mentioned that you hadn't asked her and the prom is in three weeks."

"Well I have three weeks and I just might be asking Erica Wright, the biggest snob in school," James joked.

"James you're a jerk you know that!" Faye yelled into the phone and then slammed it down on the cradle. James laughed and replaced the phone on his end. *Of course I'm going to ask her*, He thought, *I'll ask her tonight.*

❧

"Have you decided what you wanted yet?" Lavender asked Grace and Lizzie. They were standing in line at the food court at the Providence Mall. She hoped she would be able to get a look at the prom dresses in Macy*s or Fileens. If only she hadn't volunteered to take the girls to get something to eat.

"We don't know!" Lizzie whined.

"Look, we've been standing here for about ten minutes, it isn't that hard. Please pick something!" Lavender nearly screamed. Grace and Lizzie stood speechless in front of her. Realizing that she had raised her voice to them, she turned in the other direction. "Sorry I just want to go look at dresses."

"Prom dresses?" Grace asked.

"Yeah."

"I read that brunettes with green eyes look good in purple, orange, and red. Those are their key colors." Grace began, " All the colors really look good, I mean you don't have to pick those."

Lavender looked at James' sister in surprise, *Lizzie must be stealing my magazines again*, she thought. Letting out a sigh she turned and faced them. "Do you guys want to help me pick out my dress?"

"Yeah!" they both yelled at the same time.

"Shh! Not so loud, now come on let's go to Fileens." Lav had only taken a few steps when she bumped into someone. "Oh my God, I'm so sorry!" Lavender looked up straight into the eyes of Nick Brenden.

"Nick?"

"Hi Lavender, how are you?"

"Um, fine how are you?"

"Fine. Who do you have with you?" Nick asked peering at the girls next to her. "Oh, it's Grace and your sister, Lauren right?." Lavender looked him over, she hadn't seen him in a while but she had heard the talk. How many hearts he had broken, and how many girls he had been with. His KISS tee shirt barely held his worked out biceps and he, like James, was taller. His baby face remained the same and that was said to be what pulled girls in.

"Her name is Lizzie."

"So uh, what are you doing tonight?"

"Nothing really."

"Oh."

"Yeah."

"Well do you want to go out?"

❦

"Hey Mom, where are you and Dad going out tonight?" James asked his mother when she got in from the mall. He was leaning on the kitchen counter eating an apple. He towered over her by a foot now but he still resembled her greatly.

"Oh I don't know. I'm sure that *you* will be in our conversations. I haven't had time to talk to him about you lately."

"You guys talk about me? Good things are being said I hope."

"Ever since the day you were born we've talked about you, we've talked about what school you'd be going to, what kind of girls you would date," she began. She walked and stared into his eyes. "No matter how old, or how *tall* you get, we will continue to forever talk about you. In a good way."

"Wait, you said school, you mean college?"

"Yes, that's something you and your father can't seem to agree on these days." James looked at the apple still in his left hand. Suddenly he didn't feel like eating it. The subject of college always made him sick to his stomach, especially when he wasn't finished with his paper.

"Mom what am I supposed to do? I don't want to go to law school but, I don't want Dad to hate me."

"Your father will never hate you James. He just wants you to follow in his footsteps. Whatever you do, your father will always love you."

"Are you sure about that?"

"James, I have been with your father since 1965. Trust me I know him better than your Grandmother. God rest her soul." James nodded. *Would he really except that I don't want to be like him? Not only in work but in other things*, James thought. He was never around, never spent time with him. He was always too busy with work.

Few times he had problems with Lavender and every time he wanted his Dad's input he wasn't around. At least he had his best friend Nick. He and Nick went back to pre-school, James remembered. Nick had been standing guarding the slide and James wanted to go down, surprisingly he let him go. From then on they were friends.

"Today Lavender was looking for prom dresses with the girls. Do you already have your outfit James?" his mother asked.

"I didn't ask her yet."

Walking over and taking the bag of corn from the fridge, she picked it up and took it to the sink. "Oh, I thought you had."

"I don't know how to ask her." he mumbled.

"Come on James, be creative. You get your romantic side from me," his mother laughed. "Just ask her."

James stood there for a minute thinking of ways to ask her and suddenly the idea popped into his head. "Mom can I break curfew a bit and take Lav out?"

"How much is a bit?"

"Maybe one o'clock."

"I don't know James, I really don't trust you with that car." His car, a gift he had gotten for his sixteenth birthday was a 1973 candy-apple red Ford Mustang Convertible. He loved the car but his mother thought it to be a monster.

"Please Mom, let me just stay out longer."

"Fine. You'll have to get Mrs. Ryan to agree. Lavender has a curfew of midnight too."

"Thanks Mom!" James exclaimed. He ran over and kissed her cheek. Grabbing his jean jacket from the coat hanger, he quickly put it on and ran across the street.

⚜

12:54 Saturday Night

James quietly opened the door with his key and slipped inside. He had six minutes before the curfew extension came to an end. It had been a nice evening, he had taken Lavender to Rocky Point, a hang out for teens on Saturday and Friday nights.

He turned the double bolt lock on the door and then looked around. He knew he was paranoid but could anyone blame him? Three years ago still seemed like today and he wasn't going to take any chances. Looking around he saw nothing moving in the dark house.

Earlier this year he had started working out to be able to protect himself. Why he had started only this year was something even he could not figure out. Around January his parents had gotten a letter from the prison, saying *he* was doing very well. They hadn't wanted James to know but he heard them talking. He couldn't have picked a better time to wake up that night.

That seemed to be happening more and more to him. Sometimes he would wake up and hear them talking in hushed voices.

Most recently that his Grandmother, his father's mother, was dying. They didn't want to tell him and Grace that is was lung cancer that was going to take her. A loud creek came from the stairs making him get on his guard, just as soon as he had let it down. His father's tall figure appeared at the bottom a second later.

James sighed in relief and then slowly removed the cold jacket. "You're past curfew." his father's stern voice said. James hung up his jacket and then looked at him.

"Mom said I could stay out until one."

"It's one now and you've just come in."

"I was in here six minutes ago!"

"Shut up or you'll wake your mother and sister." James narrowed his eyes at him. "So that will be two weeks grounding for your tardiness."

"I wasn't late!" his Father walked over to him and stood right in his face. He was still taller than James, but James was quickly catching up. His father's large right hand reached up and slapped him across the face.

"Don't you dare talk back to me!" James' cheek burned with pain, pain he hadn't felt in a long time. James wanted to push him and so he did. His father fell on the hard wood floor. He heard his mother's footsteps coming down the stairs.

"James! What happened?" she asked frantically as she helped his father up.

"You son of a bitch! You better get up to your room or get in that fucking car and drive until you are forgotten! You've been pissing me off for too long!" screamed his father

"Why is that? Cause I don't want to go to college to become a crook lawyer like you? Because I don't want to end up like you, a big asshole who ignores his kids and wife?" His father fell speechless. "You know I'm right, you know it so just goddamn admit it!" James yelled.

"James head up to bed right now," his mother said firmly.

"No let him talk I want to know what he really thinks about me. His father who has taken care of him all of his life and given him everything he's wanted. His father who has let him go without a job for the past few years. When I was his age I worked for my first car and my collage money. What has he done?"

"Materialistic things, where were you when I needed advice and where were you when I had questions?!"

"What was it that you needed advice on? Some new sex positions perhaps ?"

"Rob-"his mother pleaded.

James felt light headed, his heart was nearly coming out of his chest. What right did he have to assume that he was having sex with Lavender? It just went to show how great of a father he was. He knew **exactly** what his kid does in his spare time.

"Shut the fuck up! Just shut up! One, If I'm not having sex with Lavender! Two, My sexual relations are no business of yours and three, If I went and jumped off the fucking Newport Bridge you would give damn! I wish I was the one who was sent to jail then I wouldn't have to deal with you, you -"

"You know James the more you talk the more you're making me mad. You know I can throw you out at anytime!"

"You won't though. You just want to make us look like we're the perfect family, nothing goes wrong in front of your stupid friends that you invite from the office. I wonder if you treat them the same as you do me? Of course you don't cause they are special! You pay more attention to work than anything else. Have you ever once when I was younger taken me to the movies, taken me camping or even asking to sit and watch tv with you? You know, I'm pretty good on my guitar, have you once asked me to show you what I know, I mean you are paying for the lessons right?!"

"I haven't asked because you don't care what I think! You let everyone else see all your retarded stories that you make up in you head!"

"That's cause you don't even have a slight interest in me! Mom and Lavender actually care!"

"Oh but that's where you are wrong, James see I read one. If I remember the words correctly, I don't think that you would show your mother that one, I think it goes: He put his tongue in her mouth gently as he massaged her-"

"Shut up, that's private! You have no right to go in my things!"

"I'm done with you. You'll be sorry when I'm gone James count on that!" his father yelled as he stomped up the stairs.

"Go ahead and run from this, just like you do everything else!" James yelled back.

Chapter 7

Prom Day

"Shit!" James swore loudly as he stumbled out of his bed. He had forgotten to set his alarm clock last night and now he was going to be late for school. The room was freezing, giving him goose bumps on his bare chest. Luckily his mother had put out clothes for him last night. At times he wished she would stop treating him like a baby then times like this, he was thankful that she still did stuff like that for Him.

James ran into the bathroom and took the fastest shower he had ever taken. In less than five minutes he was dressed and was running out the door. His mother was shouting after him but he didn't have time to talk. Jumping into the driver's seat of his car he put the key in the ignition fast.

"Come on, come on!" he said under his breath. "Come on please start!" He had been having problems with the car recently and today of all days it decided not to start. A few second later the car started up. He backed out of the driveway and headed off to school.

Cranston East High School was only a few minutes away from the house. If he hurried up he could get there at the perfect time. With a small jolt, the car suddenly stopped moving down the road. "Oh shit." James said softly. This was not the time for the car to die! Not now!

He put the key in the ignition and turned it. "I don't have time for this!" He yelled. Suddenly it started again. He was at school in seconds. Sloppily parking the car he hopped out with his bag and ran into the school. Mr. Anthony, his home room teacher's class room was on the first floor, thankfully.

James' tennis shoes squeaked as he ran over the slippery floors in the halls, making it the only sound that could be heard. *Almost there*, he thought to himself.

Bringgggggggggggggggg! The loud bell sounded as his feet touched the entrance to the class room. Everyone's eyes were on him, staring at him. Mr. Anthony sat up from his desk and walked over to him. His receding hair line was once again covered by the few pieces of thin hair he still had. Mr. Anthony pushed his falling glasses from the bottom of his nose to the top.

"Nice of you to join us Mr. Martin. I hope you have a good excuse for being late and why you make so much noise when going down the hall."

"I was having car trouble and.." James began but Mr. Anthony interrupted him. James looked around at the eyes, Lavender sat in the second row Nick behind her. His seat, the only empty one, was near the front.

"Oh yes, that car quite a hot little number...well Mr. Martin, I'm sorry to say that I'm going to have to give you an hours of detention." James' mouth flew open to protest. He caught Lavender's pained expression. *How idiotic could he be? He had forgotten all about the prom tonight!* Lavender thought.

"But Sir, I was only a few minutes late and tonight is the prom. I've never been late for this class can't you excuse it? Please?" James asked as nice as he could. Mr. Anthony looked at him in disgust.

"If I let you off Mr. Martin then should I just excuse the whole class for today because it is the prom? I don't think so. Please take your seat." James swallowed hard as he walked to his seat and sunk down low into it.

"You old bastard, I hope you rot in hell," James thought to himself. He looked over at Lavender and could tell he was being ignored. He still hadn't picked up his tux. By the time he gets out of detention and into Providence it will be close to five. Then, shower and shave and be at the dance for six. He wouldn't have to eat when he got home, after the dance they could always go and get something.

That is if she still wanted to go to the dance. He had everything figured out, now it would be ok... he hoped.

The traffic coming back from Providence was torture. Cars were bumper to bumper, horns honked and curses flew. It was close to five o'clock when he got home. He was making better time than he thought. *Watch now the damn suit will be the wrong size with my luck.* James thought as he stepped out of the shower. He wondered how Lavender was doing....

<hr>

"Mom its too tight!" Lavender cried out. The strapless pink ball gown with silver sequins had fit her perfectly in the store two weeks ago and she hadn't gained weight since then. With her hair perfectly curled, half tied up into a bun and her manicured nails in place, she looked like she was ready for the Oscars instead of the Cranston East prom.

"Lavender did you have your bra on when you tried it on?" Her mother asked as she unzipped the back of the dress.

"No."

"Well that's probably why, you're wearing a strapless bra now and when you tried it on you didn't have one on. So just take it off and then I'll zip it back up."

"I'm not going braless!" Lavender looked over on her bed to see Lizzie laughing at her. "What's so funny?"

"Nothing." Lavender gave a half smile. Walking into the bathroom, she took off the bra and then walked back over to her mother and let her zip up the back. "Thanks." Her mother turned her around and smiled at her.

"I remember my prom. I went with Nicholas George. We had such a good time." Sighing, she brushed a stray curl off Lavender's shoulder. "It seems as though just yesterday you were a baby and now you're all grown up."

"Please don't start crying or you'll make me cry and then my make-up will smear," Lavender joked.

"Okay sweetheart. I'm going downstairs, your prince charming should be arriving soon."

"Hopefully," she muttered under her breath. Of all days that James has to be late, it had to be today. She knew he hadn't gone to pick up his suit yet so that took some time to get into Providence and out during rush hour traffic. "One day Lizzie, I'll be helping you get ready for your prom. That's only seven years away." Lavender told her.

"So who are you going to the prom with?" Lizzie asked taking a pillow and squeezing it tight.

"James, you know that."

"What about that other kid? Nick." Nick. Oh God, she tried to block that out. He had asked her out more than twenty times already and every time she declined. If James ever knew....

The ringing phone in her room scattered her thoughts, as she ran for it. *It must be Faye,* she thought.

"Hello?"

"Hi Lav."

"Nick?"

"I expect you were waiting for my call." He said flirtatiously. She sucked in breath and tried to grasp the phone with her slippery palm. She always got like this when he talked to her, she got flustered and instead of saying what she should say, words didn't appear.

"No I wasn't."

"Oh, well am I disturbing you?"

"Yes you are actually. I would rather not go to my prom nervous."

"Are you going with *him*?"

"Yes I am."

"Come on, just go to the dance with me," he said quietly.

"Do you know that if James ever found out that you his best friend was asking his girlfriend to go out with him that he would kick you ass? You're scum you know that? I never liked you from the day I met you!" She yelled into the phone and then slammed the receiver down and walked to the window.

"I have a very bad feeling about tonight Lizzie and I shouldn't." She watched the long black limo pull up in front of his house and then heard the door opening behind her.

"It's almost time Lav, everything is going to be great!" Her mother said walking up and planting a kiss on her forehead. She turned to leave but paused before she reached the door. "And Lav?"

"Yeah?"

"You have to tell him."

"I know. I know." She answered quietly.

⁂

"I think you put too much on James," Grace said to James as he applied his cologne. The tux was fine and the shoes were fine, the hair was good, but Grace was still there offering tips on how much cologne he should wear. He heard the limo pull up outside and then checked himself in the mirror again.

"Ok this is it, prom night. All the girls have been waiting a long time for their prom and tonight is the night. At least for Lav. I have to make it special." James reached for his wallet and keys and made his way out the door. Grace stood in his bedroom still, rubbing her feet into the carpet.

"James?" she called to him. He came walking back, holding the bedroom door half way open.

"Yeah?"

"Don't let Lavender get around Nick tonight."

"Why?"

Grace walked over to the window and peered into the night. "Nick has been asking Lavender out. He asked her out when we went to the mall and Lizzie says that he keeps calling her." Grace turned around to see his reaction but there was none.

"Grace, that's the most moronic thing I have ever heard. Did you make that up so that I wouldn't go to the dance or something?"

"James, it's the truth! I wouldn't lie!"

"Look Grace, I don't have time for this. You're lying," James told her. He walked out of the room and down the stairs. His mother walked out with him over to Lavender's house where she was already downstairs waiting.

"Wow......you look gorgeous," James told her. She grinned wide then walked over to him and took his hand.

"Thank you."

"Are you ready?"

"Yeah." Both their mothers had tears in their eyes as they watched their children enter the limo and drive away. Grace stood from the window and shook her head. *He should have listened,* she thought.

⁂

The high school gym was decorated with colored paper and balloons were scattered all around. "Open Your Heart" blared through the D.J.'s stereo and a few of their friends were on the dance floor already. James could see Will Gabriel with his date, Lav's best friend Faye Waters. He could also see Ray Logan and Patricia Lerman standing alongside the tables.

"So?" James asked her. She looked up at him and smiled.

"Even though the decorations are a bit corny, I'm glad that I have someone as handsome as you to look at." They danced to the songs that they had listened to over and over again in their bedrooms and in their cars. The albums so worn out that they had to go out and buy another copy.

"I'm gonna go get punch, do you want some?

"Sure." He left her a moment later and walked over to the long tables were the punch was. When he was getting his glass, Steve and Ray walked up to him and literally slapped him on the back.

"James come on, I thought that you would be smarter than that, the *real* punch is over there," Steve told him pointing out the table across the gym. When Steve said *real punch* he meant the alcohol.

"No thanks," James told him and went back to getting the punch.

"I'm surprised that you even showed up tonight James," Ray said to him when James was done getting the drinks.

"Why is that?"

"Well with the talk around the school of your love triangle. I would have thought that Lavender would have come with Nick to the dance."

"What? What love triangle?"

"You mean you don't know?" Steve asked him.

"No, I don't know what are you talking about."

"Dude it's been all around school!" Ray exclaimed.

"James, Nick has been asking Lavender out and word is that she's been saying yes." James stared at his friends in disbelief. No, Nick wouldn't do that. Lavender wouldn't say yes. He looked over at Lavender and saw Nick trying to get close to her.

"Hold this for me," James told Steve and Ray passing them the punch cups. James walked fast over there and pushed his way in front of Lavender.

"What's going on here?" James asked him.

"Nothing James. Nothing is going on."

"Really Nick? Cause I keep hearing is that you've been asking Lav out!" James' voice was raised making a crowd start to gather.

"It's not what you think James! I only asked her out to dinner!" James looked away, his eyes locked on a sign in the gym. He shook his head and stared Nick right in the eyes.

"You son of a bitch...you know, I should have listened to my sister," James said calmly. Without hesitation, James threw his fist into Nick's face making him fall to the ground. With the second from Nick, La Bamba had started playing. Both were now rolling around on the gym floor, blood from James' nose that he was sure was broken was flying everywhere.

"James! Stop it! James!" he could hear Lavender's voice through out the chants of the word "fight". At last two teachers pulled them apart. James was struggling to get out of their grip and get back over to Nick.

"Let me go! Son of a bitch, let me go!" James yelled as the teachers who were holding him back grabbed his waist and pulled him out of the crowd that had formed. He saw tears in Lavender's eyes as he was being pulled aside. He knew he couldn't fight the teachers any longer so he just let them take him to the boys locker room.

He recognized them as his gym teacher, Mr. Malone and his math teacher Mr. Kenner.

"Martin, what the hell were you thinking?!" James wasn't paying attention to them. He was more worried about the blood around his face that was still coming from his nose. The only words he heard were "clean up and get out." He had to find Lavender, he needed to know what she had done.

He cleaned up and then walked out the parking lot where not a soul was in sight, except her. He walked over to her; her face showed disgust.

"James, you are a loser do you know that?"

"I'm a loser? If I were you I wouldn't be going out with my boyfriend's best friend!"

"Look I don't know what the hell you think you know but if you and I are really that great of friends, then you would know that I would never do that to you!" He paused and looked at her tear soaked face.

"You didn't go out with him?" he asked.

"No! James you mean everything to me! I thought tonight was going to be a nice night and then I was going to tell you..."

"Tell me what?"

She stepped closer to him. Her mascara was running down her cheeks. "James, Jeremy got a job in New York. I'm moving."

"No."

"I'm sorry. I should have told you sooner. I found out the night you asked me to the dance and I was supposed to tell you then. So yes, I am the loser!" Lavender screamed. James felt his world crumbling to pieces. He hadn't expected any of this, not that his best friend would betray him or that the only girl he had ever been with would be leaving. He didn't expect that he and his father would have that blow out.

"You're not a loser. I'm sorry. I'm sorry I ruined the dance and we got kicked out. I'm sorry that anything ever happened! God, you can't even imagine how much I hate my life right now!" James yelled through the parking lot. She walked up to him and wrapped her arms around his waist and pulled him close to her.

"Will you dance with me?"

"Lav..."

"Please?" James closed his eyes then jogged over to their limo. The driver seemed to be passed out in the backseat so the doors were unlocked. He turned it and let the radio play. A song was just ending when Bryan Adam's "Summer of 69" came on. He turned it up loud and went back over to her.

"Can I have this dance?" he asked. The tears disappeared as they started dancing. He forgot everything when he spun her around. College, his father, his car, Nick, and even that she was going away.

Chapter 8

James stood grim faced next to Lavender in T.F. Green Airport. He didn't know how long he had been standing there with her, tightly squeezing her hand. Lizzie, Jeremy, and Mary looked over at them every once and in a while. He knew the time was nearing where she would have to leave.

"Come on Honey," Jeremy said to his wife and daughter "Let's take a walk and grab something before we leave." James caught a glimpse of Jeremy's sorry face. Lavender seemed dazed, her face pale and lifeless. Even the bright magenta top she was wearing reflected no color to her face.

He, on the other hand, looked like he was going to a funeral. Black tee shirt, jeans and dark converse sneakers.

"Did you get your admission to Brown yet?" she asked breaking the silence.

"No, not yet."

"Are you nervous that you won't get in?"

Yes. He didn't want to tell her that though. He didn't want her last thoughts to be that he was a nervous wreck with only the imaginable things happening; his father, that weasel Nick, her, and above all going to college.

"No, I'm not nervous."

"My Mom already has me in NYU. I got the letter Saturday."

"That's great!?"

"No." She looked up at him, eyes becoming wet with tears. Placing her arms around his waist she pulled him close to her and tried to hold in her sobs. "I can't do this, I can't leave! Everyone is here, everything I know is here. I just can't leave it all behind! James you can't imagine how much I hate my mom right now! It was her idea for Jeremy to take the job. He was going to turn it down! She's fucked everything up."

Without warning, she grabbed his wrists and pulled him with her to the bathrooms three feet away. He stumbled a few times as he was being pulled by her into the ladies restroom. Moving to the biggest stall, she locked it and pushed him against the tile wall. Her mouth pushed hard against his as she let her hands trail from his chest to his hips. Pulling back she looked down and unbuttoned her jeans and let the zipper undo.

His eyes went wide at her in shock, only in his fantasies did she do something like this. From the very beginning she had made it very clear that she was well worth the wait, and he had agreed.

"What are you doing?!" he cried aloud. Urges that he held for a long time told him to keep his mouth closed but his heart said no. She pushed on to his lips again and let her fingers run through his hair. She brought her mouth to his ear and whispered softly.

"If I can't stay then I want to know that I was your first. I wanna screw you." her cool breath made a chill go down his spine. He closed his eyes, mesmerizing her. A moment later he saw her reaching for the button of his jeans.

"Wait! Wait! No, We can't do this!" James said firmly, pushing her away. She looked as if someone had slapped her hard across the face. "Lav, I can't-won't- make love to you in a public bathroom!"

Stepping away from him and turning the other way he heard her zip up her pants. James walked over to her and knelt before her. "Lav, it's not that I wouldn't dream of doing this with you.....It's just.... I don't want you and I to remember that we went at it for the first time in a bathroom where people can just walk in." He pulled her chin up so that she was looking straight.

"I know that you don't want to go. I know that you don't want to start over in a new city again. I know that you are really hating your Mom right now but listen to me, I promise you that I will talk to you and come and see you whenever I can and when we do have sex, it would be so much better than it would be here."

The door of the bathroom creaked open and a pair of heels could be heard outside the door. Immediately he jumped on the toilet so that who ever it was could not see his feet.

"Lav? Lav? Are you in here?" The voice of her mother came from the other side of the thin door. Lavender wiped the tears from her eyes and called back.

"I'll be out in a few minutes!"

"Okay. Hurry up, the flight is leaving in a few minutes. Where is James?"

"Oh....um.... he already said goodbye. He went home."

"Alright sweetie. I'll be with Jeremy and Lizzie." Her mother's footsteps disappeared out the bathroom door leaving them in complete silence. He stood up again and walked over to her.

"I have to go," Lavender said quietly wiping the tears from her eyes and walking out of the bathroom. Before she left she ran back into the stall and kissed him, her arms around his neck.

"I love you," were her last words to him before she ran out of the bathroom leaving him pushed against the wall fighting the urge to bring her back to him and place the engagement ring he bought on her delicate finger.

Fall 1987

Standing outside Slater hall- Brown University for the first time, was something James would never forget. All things around him seemed magical, even the freshly mowed green grass. The red mustang held the first load of his dorm room belongings that he had brought with him from home.

This is my current place of residence now, for the next four years, James thought to himself as he lugged box number one labeled clothes up to his room. Setting it down on the bed he looked around at the room. Light beige walls, hardwood floor, the long windows looking out to the grass and trees.

The room held two people, he wondered who he would be sharing with. Suddenly loud footsteps made its way into the room. James' mouth opened at the sight of the boy standing a few feet away.

"Dammit, what are you doing in my room?!" Nick yelled loudly at James.

"Your room? This is my room! Get out!"

"No this is my room! See it's right here on my paper!" Nick retorted holding up his paper and pointing at the words.

"I'm not sharing a room with a bastard like you!"

"And I'm not sharing a room with you...you...you..."

"See you can't even think of a word to call me! How the hell did you even get in here? You failed everything in school!"

"If you must know you asshole, my step father paid for me."

"Well ring-a-ding-ding! Little Nicky gets saved by his big rich father!"

"Hey that's step-father! Heard about the blow out with your father! I heard it from Maggie Roman," Nick said moving into the room.

"You're a sick pervert, how did you find that out? Screw her and then ask?"

"Righty-o! You call me a pervert? What about you? Sneaking off to be alone in movie theaters and where ever else!" James shook his head at Nick and picked his box up off the bed. "Yeah that's right, be the baby that you are James, run home to Lavender!"

Keep walking, James told himself, *just keep walking.* He stopped at the end of the hall, dropped his things and went back.

"You were supposed to be my friend! How could you ask her out?! We were supposed to be best friends! How could you do that to me?!"

Nick walked over to the window and looked out for a moment. James' face had turned red with the anger bottled up inside of him.

"I don't know," Nick responded turning to him. "I don't know James. One minute I hate her for taking my best friend away and then I like her for I don't know what reason. All I do know is that all summer it was on my mind and I felt like shit. I know it was wrong. I'm sorry James. I really am sorry."

James watched Nick completely face him. For the first time he didn't feel like ripping his face off and throwing it into the Providence River. He let out a breath and walked over to him.

"James, I don't know what to say to you. I'm sorry, I truly am. I wish that I could take back what I did but I can't. Just please don't hit me again," Nick nearly begged. James laughed and held out his hand to shake.

"I'm not going to hit you. *Friends* don't hit each other. Sorry."

"My face was black and blue for nearly a week."

"That should teach you not to screw with other guys girlfriends." Nick got quiet suddenly then backing away he walked over and flopped on James' bed.

"Sorry about your nose. Was it really broken?"

"No it wasn't broken after all. So where is your stuff?" James asked him returning from the hall where he had left his things.

"I have my mom's car **packed** with suff. In July I got into an accident going to the beach. Guess who hit me?"

"Who?"

"Remember Brad Lusren? He used to live down Pontiac Ave, always used to hang out with..um... you know who." Nick said quietly when he realized how James was connected to Brad. James had stopped in his tracks, it was the first time anyone had really mentioned his brother in a long time.

Brad and Erich were complete opposites. Brad, the nice boy who mothers' often compared their own sons to, had been the same age as Erich when the accident took place. Lursen had always been a bit of a geek when it came to being social and story was that Erich-yet another outcast- took him under his wing.

"It's okay say it Nick, it's not like it never happened. It's over and done now," James said firmly. He thought he had let it go a long time ago but James could never let it go. No matter how deep he tried buried it.

"Anyway, my step dad got him to pay up for the damage. I guess I should get to unloading the car. I only have it for a day so I crammed my things in."

When they were finished bringing in their belongings James and Nick set up the phones and television.

"Dude, didn't we talk about being roommates when we were about nine or something?" Nick called to him.

"Something like that." James finished hooking up his phone, then moved on to unpacking his clothes. He stopped in the middle and looked at the clock : 7:30. He should call his mother and let her know that he was okay. When He had left the house earlier she was crying but really trying to hide it. Two rings...three rings....

"Hello?" a girly voice said into the phone.

"Grace?"

"Oh, sorry Grace it's just your brother!" he heard the voice say. "This is Jane. Grace's friend. Hey, by the way, cool bedroom-" but Jane was cut off by Grace who snatched the phone out of her hand.

"Hello?"

"Hey Grace, is Mom home?" Grace fell silent and her voice fell to a near whisper.

"I think they are busy, they're yelling about you."

"Who's yelling?" James asked his sister. He wished that Grace wouldn't have to hear every word they said.

"Daddy. He says that you're trouble and that you have always been trouble. He told Mommy that if you ever came to the house again you would be in deep shit. I don't want you to leave forever. You're not going to leave forever are you James? Please tell me you're not." Grace sniffled into the phone.

"No Grace, I'm not leaving. I told you don't swear you sound like a tracker trailer mouth. Can you go and get Mom for me please?"

"Hold on." After five minutes he heard his mother's voice on the other end. He could hear the back round noises: crickets, rustling of branches from a breeze. She was outside.

"James I'm so glad that you called. Are you settled in okay?"

"Yeah, everything when good. Nick and I are sharing a room."

"His mother didn't tell me that he got into Brown. Good for him."

"Yeah. So um... how are things? A lot can happen in seven hours." James asked her. He saw Nick jumping on the bed.

"Cut it out or it will fall through the floor!" James yelled.

"Thanks Mom! I didn't know that you would follow me to college too!" Nick yelled back.

"You boys seem like you're having a good time." His mother said. Her voice sounded shaken and upset. It seemed like it was forever since he saw her, when he had only kissed her goodbye this morning.

"Mom is everything ok? Grace said that you were yelling."

"Oh James don't worry about it. You have much more important things to worry about right now. Have you talked to Lavender lately?"

"I called her last week when I got the letter. I told her that I would call her when I got settled....Mom what is going on? You know with Dad and everything?" She let out a sigh and started to speak low into the phone.

"Your father is just a little....upset right now. He would have really liked you to follow in his footsteps. You're his only son."

"I know, but Mom I'm not lawyer material. I don't want to become him. I really can't stand what he is about."

"Now James your father is a good man. I will always support your decisions because you are my son and I will love you until way past the day I die. But you must understand that he is my husband and your father and I will stand by him also. What I am trying to say is that I am not taking sides here. I just want you to know that I want you to talk to your father. You need to respect him."

"Yeah okay," James answered gravely.

"I'm going to get Grace's girlfriend home then get her into bed. I'll talk to you on Sunday when we go out for breakfast. You're still coming aren't you?"

James thought about it for a minute. "Yeah I'll be there."

"Good. Bye Sweetheart, I love you."

"Love you too." James replaced the phone and sat for a moment. He had talked to Lavender all summer, never mentioning the ring he had bought her a week before she was going leave. He had taken all the money he had saved from birthdays, lawn mowing in the summer and everything else. It was the perfect diamond in the perfect gold band. He had bought it on impulse, having a crazy notion that maybe they could have gotten married and then she wouldn't have to leave. Picking up the phone again he dialed a New York number.

"Hello?" The voice of Mary Ryan came through the phone.

"Hi Mrs. Ryan, it's James. Is Lavender around?"

"James listen, I've let you call Lavender all summer. I've even let her talk to you for more than half the night but I must enforce that I do not want you to call and talk to her any longer. She needs to concentrate on her school work and nothing else. Let her move on and don't make it harder than it already is for her."

"Wait! Mrs. Ryan-"

"Goodbye James." she said simply hanging up the phone. He still clutched the phone in his hand hearing the dial tone.

"Goodbye."

Chapter 9

Fall brought many new things for James. New friends, classes, and experiencing the world of job hunting. He hoped he could get something close to campus, but that was no luck of his. As he drove down Waterman Ave. he noticed a sign in the window of a diner that read **Hiring**.

The sign above it read **East Side Diner** and it looked like a blast from he past. Silver outside with medium sized windows James felt as though he was living in 1950 instead of 1987.

Opening the door to the restaurant he noted that the white walls and black and white tile made it seem somewhat even more out of the fifties than he expected.. Not a soul was in the place except for a tall, lean older woman who wore too much make-up and put too much hair spray in her big teased hair. James read her name tag from a far : **Sharon**.

"Hi, the sign outside said hiring. I'm wondering if I can put in for the job." James told her stepping into the diner. The woman walked out from behind the counter. Four inch heels, a short mini skirt and a shirt that held only ten percent of her cleavage walked over and looked him over from top to bottom.

"Ya be seeing Lee," she said to James smiling. "Lee! Someone's here about the job!" A few minutes later a short man with a thick middle appear out of a door near the entrance to the bathrooms. His receding black hair was nearly gray and his suit looked as old as the diner.

"Hello, I'm here about the job."

Leroy looked James over too and then waved his hand at him. Turning back to his office he mumbled follow me. James did as he was told and followed the man through the entrance that he had seen him use. Passing the bathrooms and walking down the small corridor, James and the man came to a door leading to a basement.

The wood stairs creaked beneath James' feet at every step he took. A door led off a the bottom of the room, in which they passed and made their way to a small lighted area.

The office was panted a grey and the concrete floors casted a gloomy look to the basement. Lee took a seat in the large leather chair in front of a desk filled with papers.

"So....you want the job."

"Yes sir."

"What's ya name kid?" Leroy asked pulling open his desk draw and taking out a cigar.

"James Martin. I'm a student over at Brown." James looked at the chair in front of the desk. He slowly took a seat.

"Uh huh. Did I say you could sit there?"

James stood up immediately and pushed the chair back in.

"Naw, Naw I'm just yank`in ya leg. Sit! Sit!" James nodded and sat down in the chair again.

"I was looking all over for someone who was hiring and when I saw your sign outside I ran right in to see if I could apply."

"How old are you kid?" Lee asked him taking another puff of his cigar.

"Eighteen."

"Eighteen...interesting.....well kid, I'm in need for the help. Ok you got the job. I'll give ya four-fifty an hour plus tips. Fridays, Saturdays, and Sundays are when we are busy most so come in then. Sharon will get you a uniform." Lee told him. He went back to smoking his cigar a moment later.

"Thank you sir."

"Kid, be here at five on Friday."

"Got it."

"And kid-"

"Yeah."

"You're alright."

"Thanks." James stood up from the chair he was sitting on and walked into the diner. Sharon was standing at the counter once again, this time filing her nails. "Excuse me? He told me to have you get me a uniform." Sharon looked up and flashed a smile.

"Sure hon. Now what size?"

"A large, in the pants and shirt." Sharon looked him over again.

"I bet you are."

"What?"

"Not a thing hon." she said walking away from him down into the basement he had just left. She returned a moment later and handed him the uniform. She walked behind him and caught James off guard by nipping her fingers at his rear.

Friday

Well I guess this is what it is like going to work. James thought as he slipped his uniform over his clean, chiseled body. When he had told his mother about his job finding, she congratulated him but made a fuss about where he was working.

"That Leroy is trouble James!"

"I need the job Mom," James had protested and he did need the job. He should have gotten one a long time ago. His father's words repeated in his head *"His father who has let him go without a job for the past few years. When I was his age I worked for my first car and my college money. What has he done?"*

The short sleeve shirt and black pants fit him perfectly. His watch read 4:30. He planned to get there early just in case he needed to know anything. Nick wasn't in the room when he returned. James figured that he was put with the new girl he had been seeing, Paula.

James parked and walked into the restaurant. A few older men sat at the counter. One sipping a coke, another tea and the last a steaming coffee. They stared at James when he walked in until he made his way over to the counter.

"Hey Shar, is this who Lee got to be the new waiter?" The one drinking the coke called out. Sharon's face appeared in the order window.

"Yup that's him. Hey babe what's going on?"

"Um...nothing much. I came in a bit early to see if there is anything I have to know," James responded. The men's gazes stayed on him as if he were about to pull a gun.

"Well you can meet Dino, the chef. Come on back and I'll introduce you to the other girls," Sharon told him. Making his way out of the room and into the kitchen, James saw there was four other girls in the kitchen with a short white man in a chef's hat.

"Girls... and Dino, this is James. He's our newest waiter. James this is Betty, Sue, Darlene, and Amanda. And of course our chef Dino."

"Hi," James said quickly. He looked over at the girls. Betty and Sue looked to be in their late fifties. Each had pale white hair and wrinkled skin on their hands. Darlene looked as old as Sharon-maybe younger. But Amanda is who caught his eye. *Big time flirt.* James thought looking at her. Long strawberry blond hair, tight mini skirt and tight top, she looked as if she belonged out on the street trailing for men.

"Hi James," Amanda waved as she licked her lips. James nodded at her and stood for a moment looking around the kitchen. Plain and ordinary as they come.

"Well it's almost time for you to start your first day here at the diner," Sharon began tossing him an apron. "Good luck."

◦◦◦

Eleven o'clock could not come fast enough for James. He had never worked as hard as he did tonight. Tired and worn out, James trudged to the dorm room. His feet felt like they had chains that were dragging behind him. He supposed it wasn't all bad, he had made 50 dollars in tips.

He opened the door and discreetly made his way in. Nick had the T.V. on channel three, James was too tired to see what show it was. He turned around when he saw his friend come walking in and then quickly hit the pillow.

"I am so fuckin beat," James moaned as he covered his head with the pillow. "All night it did not stop. Not once. I just want to got to sleep!"

"Dude come on. It can't be that bad."

James sat up and looked at Nick with the last bit of strength he had. "Have you ever worked in a restaurant where people send back food because they find that it is 'Not golden enough' or cleaned a table that five kids made a mess of? Or perhaps you've had the waitress who is a total sex maniac up your ass, asking you over and over again if you would like to join her in the back room."

"I'm guessing you didn't go to the back room." after a few moments of not an answer back Nick looked over at his friend. Passed out on the pillow James' breathing was steady. Saturday morning another day of work.

◦◦◦

The hot blankets on top of Rob Martin caused him to awake at three in the morning. His wife slept soundless next to him. He heard a light wind outside as he stood up from the bed and walked out the bedroom door. This wasn't the first time that he had walked the quiet halls of his home with no one to see him.

He had been waking up every other night, too many thoughts running through his head. James was a main problem. At times he regretted saying those things to him, other times he hated that James fought him on the subject of careers. Sometimes he knew James was right, right about what he had said to him that night he came home. Was work really holding him away?

Rob hadn't meant to do all those things. Christine knew that and he thought James knew too. Grace didn't seem to really care. She was just interested in what went on in her little world. James was another story all together. He should have seen it coming after everything with Erich. He should have done something more.

What could he do? What more could be done? He was in jail. He wasn't coming out. By that time....hell he couldn't predict what was going to happen next week! Rob walked down the steps and into the hall where they had fought at the beginning of summer.

Now he was in collage. Alone, gone, out of the house he had been born into. A smile played at his lips thinking of it. How overjoyed he had been to hear that it had been a boy. Christine had wanted a girl at the time but as soon as she saw James' face she forgot all about the girl names that ran though her head during her pregnancy.

Walking into the living room, Rob stopped at the mantle over the fireplace. Where the family portrait hung. It had been taken when James was sixteen and Grace was six. It was like looking at a mirror of himself when he looked at his son. Same brown hair and same deep pools of blue eyes.

He had gotten his father's eyes who was a tall, stocky man with too many bills he couldn't handle. Rob reminisced on a time when at only thirteen He had been working with his Godfather Freddie at his fruit stand on Park Avenue in Cranston. The money hadn't been a lot and the people who visited the stand often made him add up the prices for the fruit more than once fearing that he was ripping them off.

At fifteen he had gone to work at his uncle's flower shop on Pocassit Avenue in Silverlake. The money was more and the hours were longer. Uncle Joe was always busy with orders and often had Rob deliver them if the regular delivery boy wasn't there. That is where Rob met his first girlfriend, Carol Degario. Carol was year younger than him with a gorgeous body and flowing blond hair. Carol lived with her aunt Angelina in Silverlake. Her mother had died when he was very young in a car crash that took the life of her brother Richie.

They dated on and off for about two years, enjoying each other's company. Late in the fall of 1962 when he was seventeen, his father died of lung cancer from a cigarette habit. He left his mother in a mess with no money to pay the large remaining bills.

One night while they walked the beach Carol mentioned that her father might be able to get him into college.

He started pre-law only a short time later and in no time he was in Harvard studying and balancing his school life as well as a job for his mother. Later Carol said she wanted to see other people. The loss took nearly all of his school time to get over but when he finally bounced back he forgot her. Who knew that his best friend and dorm room mate, Jeremy Ryan would marry her later in years.

Fresh out of college he found himself in a law firm and hit it big when he won the case of a convicted murderer.. He moved back to Rhode Island and the rest as they say is history.

Rob moved silently through the kitchen, opening the fridge. A minute later he closed it and went back to the living room. Dropping into the large sofa he eyed the phone. It was really early. Too early to call him. The debate to talk to James nagged at him until the early morning when the sunrise started peaking though the windows.

Christine had told him about James' job at the East Side Diner. He wondered how he liked it, what he thought. He was really curious but just too stubborn to admit that James was right about some things.

"He's right that I'm an asshole," He muttered under his breath. His hand reached for the receiver again but he stopped himself. Did he even want to talk to him over the phone? Would it be better if he went to see him? He couldn't figure out what to do. The phone suddenly rang making him jump.

It was six in the morning who would be calling at this time?

"Hello?"

"Rob? Is that you? I didn't think anyone would answer," Jeremy Ryan's voice asked.

"Hey Jer, what's going on? How is everyone?"

"Great, great. Mary and Liz had a great time picking out furniture for her bedroom. That's the latest news. How is everyone there?"

"We're fine. You're settled alright?" Rob asked rubbing his temple. He could feel the a headache was coming on.

"Yeah, I didn't realize how much I miss it there though. Even out in California I missed it. So uh....how are things going with you and James?"

"I haven't talked to him. Nice isn't it? All I know is what his mother tells me."

"He got into Brown right?"

"Yeah. On one point I'm proud but on another I'm pissed that he isn't going to law school."

"Gotta let him made his own choices Rob. Think about it, did you get to make your own choices?"

"I have thought about it Jer," Rob said holding back his anger. "Since three o'clock this morning I've been thinking about it. I know that I had to go to law school and I know that really it was kind of my Mom's decision. If I hadn't she was going to lose the house and well...you know the rest."

"Anyway, What else is He up to?"

"He got himself a job. Over at East Side Diner. Why don't you know this? I thought they were talking constantly."

"They haven't talked. The only reason I sort of knew about Brown was because I answered the phone. He was really happy."

"I know."

"How is Lavender? What's school tossing her?"

"Med school is in effect, which is good. At least now if I need to have an operation I can get one at a fair price," Jeremy laughed. Rob saw Christine come down the stairs her robe hugging her body.

"Jeremy I have to go get ready for work. I'll call you this week."

"Okay, see ya. Take care."

"You too." Rob said then hung up the phone. He walked over to his wife and pulled her close to his chest.

"I love you. You know that right?" he asked her.

"Oh of course...So what is it that you want to know?" she asked pulling away from him and looking into his eyes.

"I was just wondering how um.... James is."

"Just talk to him and stop being an ass. You should be asking *him* how he is not me."

"I swear that I will not ask you anymore just tell me what he said when you went to see him yesterday." he pleaded.

"He said the usual. The job is fine, school is fine. He is seeing his friends. But he's still the same as he has always been."

"Which is?"

"See you miss the important stuff because you want to mess around. James has a broken heart. And he'll have one for a long time I'm sure. He's just that way, he always falls too hard." she said kissing him and then going to make breakfast.

Maybe James and I are more alike than he thinks.

Chapter 10

Spring of 1990

James reread the note that his journalism teacher, Mrs. Rayburn left on his desk earlier that morning. She wanted to see him after class about his latest paper. The rest of the class piled out on that April morning. Mrs. Rayburn sat at her old desk looking over papers.

Rayburn was one of the most strict teachers and not a favorite among test time. He wondered what she wanted with him. During his years, she often took him as an open target to pick on in class. If he had to do it over again he would have never picked the front seat.

Her white hair was pulled back into a knot at the base of her neck and her blue sweater hung on her rail thin body. James gulped and walked over to her desk. In the four years that James had been at Brown he had become the talk of all the girls around campus. Their gossiping was usually about how nice he was or that he was drop dead gorgeous or the fact that he hadn't dated any of them. They had come to the conclusion that someone had broken his heart. Or that was what his friend Nick Brenden told everyone of those girl who were interested in James.

"You wanted to see me Mrs. Rayburn?" James asked her. Looking up from her papers she smiled at him.

"Yes Mr. Martin I did." She rummaged through he papers looking for a certain one. At last she found it and handed it to him. It was his paper on the history of Brown. An 'A' was on the top of the paper. "This Mr. Martin is beautiful work."

"Thank you. I worked really hard on it." He had too

"I can tell. This is what I wanted to talk to you about. Where do you plan to be after your graduate in a month?"

"To tell you the truth Mrs. Rayburn, I don't know."

"Here is an idea," she began standing up and moving away from her desk. "I have an old friend who is one of the top editors of The Providence Journal. I seriously think that you could have a future there. That is if you want it. Your writing is superb."

"Wow, thank you I'm flattered. To answer your question, yes I'm interested definitely."

"Well then I'll call him and set up the meeting."

"Thank you, thank you so much!" James exclaimed reaching for her outstretched hand. They shook hands and moments later he set off down the hall at a brisk pace. A job at the journal! Wow, that was something he never saw coming. Wait until he told his Mom and .... well his Mom could tell his Dad.

He hadn't spoken to his father ever since the fight. He had tried though. One night his mother brought him into the diner and they sat down to eat. He didn't say one word to James.

Thinking about what Rayburn had said James almost went into shock. Graduation! Graduation was only a little while away. He wasn't ready! He wasn't ready to move out of the dorm! Where would he go?

He didn't have anymore classes today so he decided to go looking for an apartment. James walked back to Slater Hall and into his room. It was quiet for a change. *"Maybe a bit too quiet,"* James thought as he let his hand open the door.

The bathroom door was closed when he walked in, Nick must be back. Dropping his backpack on the floor beside his bed he went to the phone and dialed the operator asking for relators.

"Good afternoon Turner Realty. How can I help you?" a woman's voice said over the phone.

"Hi I'm looking for an apartment to rent," James told the woman. Suddenly he heard a loud bang come from the bathroom.

"Okay what are you looking for?"

"Um... something small. Maybe one bedroom, one bath."

"Are you in a certain price range?"

James thought about it for a second, "about 150 to 250."

"Okay Sir hold on for just a second." After a moment the woman came back on the phone. "I think I might know a place for you. 21 Marshall Street. Apt.3. I can have one of my realtors over there anytime you would like to see it."

"How is today?"

"Today is just fine, Sir," she said. James took down the address, directions and other information. He grabbed his jacket and then headed out the door. After he left, Nick poked his head out of the bathroom to make sure no one was there. Behind him his date was putting her clothes back on.

◦◦◦

James pulled into the small courtyard of 21 Marshall Street. The outside was kind of nice. A short woman was already standing outside dressed in a black pant suit. She had flaming red hair that was pulled back into a bun. He stepped out of the car and walked up to her, hand outstretched.

"Hi, I'm James Martin."

"Samantha Bradshaw," she said simply shaking his hand. "Well let's get started shall we?" Samantha opened the door she was standing in front of and walked inside. The hall way was dark with only a window of light peaking through. He followed her up the two flights of stairs. At the top a door stood, a plain brown door with a handle.

She went up to it, took out the key and opened the door. James walked in after her. The kitchen was right there when you walked in and the door and the living room was visible from where he was standing.

"It's a two bedroom penthouse with one bathroom. Charming isn't it?" she asked him as she walked through the place. *"I guess,"* James thought. It was in his price range and it would only be until he could get a really nice place. The walls had dark plaid wallpaper that was hideous but he could always fix that. The floor wasn't bad either. James walked through the rest of the house . It was the perfect size for him.

"So Mr. Martin, how do you like it?" Samantha asked him walking out of the living room. Sighing, James looked around.

"I'll take it."

◦◦◦

"How much more stuff is there?" Nick panted as he dragged James' boxes up the stairs. James had set down his box of stuff already. The man from the phone company was hooking up the lines for him in the bedroom and kitchen while the cable man was working in the living room.

"Not much more," James told him taking a drink of his water. He set it down on the small kitchen table that he had recently bought along with pots, pans, dishes and all the other essentials. The place was actually starting to look good. He had stripped the plaid paper off the walls and repainted them a light beige.

His new bed was being delivered later today and the couch tomorrow. "Thanks again for helping me Nick. I really couldn't have done it without you." Nick shrugged and walked across the room staring into the spare bedroom.

"Say James, I was wondering…"

"Save it Nick. I already know what you've been thinking. Dude, I thought you were going to move back in with your parents."

"Come on man! I don't want to go back with my parents. Ma is going to treat me the same as when I lived there before. Like a baby."

"Nick you are a baby. Instead of chasing all those mini skirts you should have been getting a job and then you might have your own place."

"Then I would end up like you. When was the last time you have female contact?" James fell silent and went back down the stairs to get the remaining things. *Don't think about it! Don't think about it!* James firmly told himself. He heard Nick coming after him, panting all the way.

"James! James, wait up! Come on will you hear me out?" James whirled around and stared at him.

"Look. I'm happy the way I am. Okay? I don't need you to remind me about the last time I was out with a girl." James reached into the car and grabbed another box.

"I didn't mean to bring her up. I know what happened with her but James you can't have a broken heart forever." Taking the box labeled clothes James looked up at Nick.

"Try ripped out, stepped on, ran over and stabbed until all the blood ran out," seriously James responded. Going back up to the house he thought about what Nick had said. They hadn't talked since the summer before school. Her mother told him basically to fuck off. Hadn't she read the letters that he wrote her? He must have not been that important to her otherwise she would have taken the time to respond.

Perhaps Nick is right, James thought. *Maybe I should move on and see other girls.*

◈

The cup of Dunkin' Donuts hot coffee shook in his hand. It was almost twelve. His interview with Mrs. Rayburn's, Mr. O'Mally, friend had been at eleven. Did he get the job? Did he mess up in the interview?

He was positive that he had. He made so many flaws in his speech the man had looked at him funny. With a bushy moustache and a huge balding spot on his head he reminded James of his mom's brother, Uncle Terry.

They said that they would get back to him in a week or so. He really hoped he would get the job. He needed it. He didn't want to remain at East Side Diner for the rest of his life. The hot coffee burned his tongue when he drank it but he was too busy trying to get the butterflies out of his stomach.

Last night when he called his mother and she immediately invited herself over. He didn't care but that meant that she would change everything he had around the apartment. Things were actually going really well for him in the apartment. It was cozy and comfortable. He liked it, being out of the dorm and not having to share it with anyone. The only thing that he needed to do now was learn how to make something other than a sandwich.

Starting up the Mustang from his parking place in the Dunking Donuts, he drove further downtown to a little book shop called Buck-A-Book. He picked up a cookbook for himself. On his way home he passed his father's law firm. Shaking his head he went back to looking at the road.

The dark grey sky said rain was coming in. It said that it might be like this all next week. He hoped it wouldn't. Graduation was next week and supposedly it was outside. Lightning lit up the sky and thunder shook it. It was going to be a bad storm.

At home, James parked in the garage and ran upstairs. The rain had began to fall hard just as he pulled in the drive. Going over to the answering machine he clicked the button.

His mother was one of them. "James I have to run out for a little while today I hope you get this message before I need you. I was wondering if you can pick up your sister today and bring her home with you. I'll get her when I come over there tonight. Love you."

It was almost time for James to leave when the phone rang. He picked it up and heard loud voices and music and knew instantly it was Nick. Recently, Nick had secured a job at the radio station and so far everyone ranging from teenagers to adults loved Nick's late night show.

"Hello?"

"James?! James?! Can you hear me?" Nick's voice screamed over the phone. James pulled it back then got back on again.

"Yeah, I can hear you, where are you?"

"I'm at a party."

"What?"

"I'll explain when I see you. Listen remember my-" Nick got cut off before he could finish. The storm must have knocked out the phone line. James hung up and ran outside to the garage. He put the top of the car up and drove away.

~~~

Grace was quiet in the car as they rode back to the apartment. She said "hi", but nothing else. *The wipers on the car need to be changed*, James thought as they drove. *They're were starting to get old.*

"James?"

"Yeah?"

"Can I ask you something?" Grace asked. James glanced over at her. Tears were filling the sides of her eyes.

"Grace what's wrong?" she then began to cry.

"I was thinking about someone."

"Who?" suddenly it hit him after a moment. She was thinking of the best friend she had lost. "You're talking about Lizzie right?" Grace shook her head in agreement.

"I always feel sad when it gets around this time. This is when she moved away." James came to a red light. Looking over at her he felt bad.

"Grace, I know what your feeling. See it wasn't only you who lost someone, it was me too. Grace I know that you and Lizzie were close, but think about me and her sister." He couldn't bring himself to say her name. Just talking about it brought out memories that just a little while ago he had tried to lock away. "We did everything together Grace. We had our birthdays together and we more or less got in trouble together."

Grace looked up at her brother. She didn't know their history, she didn't know about the accident. "How long were you guys friends?" she asked wiping the tears from her eyes.

"I've known her since I was your age."

"Wow."

"Yeah. See we basically hung out everyday, so Mom and Mrs. Ryan," yet another name he didn't want to say, "They were friends. Lizzie's dad and her mom met through Dad."

"I know."

"Oh. I didn't think you knew."

James turned into the driveway, he almost hit the wall because he wasn't looking where he was going. Pulling into the garage Grace and James sat in the car for a moment.

"James?"

"Yeah, Grace?"

"I was thinking about Lavender the other day too."

"Oh."

"Did you love her?"

James sat speechless for a moment. He turned to his sister and smile grabbed the corners of his mouth. "Yes. I love her very much."

Chapter 11

The flash went off, blinding James. His mother's old camera had the most outrageous flash on it. After all the long years at school he had finally done it. He graduated from college, got his own apartment and recently found out that he was now the newest reporter for "The Providence Journal".

"Okay Mom, I think you have every step I've taken on that camera." James said sarcastically. His mother walked over to him. She was dressed in her favorite pink dress, and pearls. Grace had dressed up too. His father hadn't shown up.

"James you did it! I always knew that you would be great." She said pulling him tightly.

"Christine! Hi!" Elaine Crain, Nick's mother called her. Elaine, Nick's stepfather Gary, Nick and a young blond walked over to them. Nick was dressed the same as James was but his cap was off revealing the short blond hair he recently cut.

"Elaine! Gary! How are you?"

"Great, great! This is so exciting! My oldest is out of college and my youngest is back with me!" James peered at the girl next to Nick. They could pass for twins. Same color blond hair, same light brown eyes. James knew that Nick had a sister, but he had never met her.

"Oh how rude of me! Christine, James, this is my daughter Victoria. She just came up from Florida. Victoria lived with Tommy." Tom Brenden had what Nick called "abandoned" Nick when he was three and his sister was two. Tom was a truck driver and was always going back and forth down to Florida, so he just settled there.

James caught Victoria's staring eyes. He smiled at her and saw her blush. She was cute, quiet and reserved. "Mom I'm gonna go see a teacher

I'll be right back." James told his Mom quietly after he spotted Mrs. Rayburn in the crowd. He walked up to her and smiled.

"I got the job!"

"Oh I'm so happy for you! You'll be wonderful."

"Thank you so much for thinking about me when the opening came up."

"You're welcome. Now have a great summer and get to work on that job. I'll be seeing O'Mally every now and then. So don't think I won't know what you're doing."

"Thanks again." James called to her as he walked away. His mother stood with Grace still talking to Elaine. He wanted to get back to the apartment, he hadn't eaten all day.

⁂

Nick took light steps as he and his baby sister walked away. *She had grown up so much!* He thought. The last time he had seen her was when he was thirteen and he went to Florida to visit his dad.

Had she really changed. Her small fragile body now held a pair of huge breasts that Nick hadn't imagined she would have. He always had a soft spot for his sister and if he found out she was showing off anything he was going to flip.

"I'm glad you're back." Nick told her breaking the silence. She flipped her long hair over her shoulders and took his arm.

"I'm glad to be away from Daddy. His drinking problem is getting worse. When he married the woman from the AA meetings I knew that I would have to get out of there." Victoria looked up at her handsome brother. His profile was almost alike to hers, small nose, same small brown eyes, small lips. When most people saw them together they thought they were twins.

"Nick?"

"Yeah?"

"What's James like? He seems very nice."

"Do you like him or something?"

"No, I was just asking."

"He is too old for you anyway."

"What? And if I did like him he is only a year older than me." Victoria retorted.

"What about him Vicky? What do you want to know?"

"Is he single?"

"Yes."

"Gosh, how could he be? He's gorgeous!" she thought aloud. Nick eyed her and saw her smile. "He is!"

"No."

"Please Nick! Please I want to go out with him! Can't you ask if he likes me?"

"No Victoria! I won't do that ! I don't want my baby sister and my best friend dating." Nick stated firmly.

"I'm not a baby anymore!"

"Trust me you are."

"No I'm not!"

"You are a baby. Instead of chasing the boys you should be getting a job and get a place of your own," Nick said taking James' words, but switching them to his own advantage.

"Well then, I'll ask him out myself."

"Fine go ahead. He'll refuse you though."

"How do you know that?" she asked. How did he know that James was going to refuse her? No one had ever refused her. All the boys in Florida absolutely loved her. She hoped to death that Nick and her Mom wouldn't find out what she had been doing back home. Otherwise she would be dead.

"James is an old fashion person."

"What's that mean?"

"It means that he would ask you out if he wanted to."

"Oh."

"Come on it's getting cold," Nick said looking to the overcast sky, "It's probably going to rain."

Later on that night James laid soundless in his bed. The rain hit his windows making him stay up. It was a Friday night and he had no where to be. A long time ago he had promised himself that after college he would get out more. But now he had no place to go!

Victoria suddenly popped into his head. Why was he thinking of her? She was pretty, nice, she had a nice body...really nice. He pushed the covers off and walked into the kitchen. His hair was a mess from moving it around on the pillow.

Maybe he should ask her out. Would Nick care? Would she say yes? The only way to know was to ask.

A week and a half later, James drove his Mustang to Nick's old house in Cranston. He had asked Nick if it was alright if he asked Victoria out. At first he was reluctant, but then he agreed. She, on the other hand, *quickly* agreed.

James planned to take her to RISD, Rhode Island School Of Design to see the paintings and such. He put on his dress shirt and slacks that he had on underneath the robe he wore on graduation. About ten minutes later they walked out of her house, her arm hooked around his. She was wearing a pink top with a pretty white skirt.

"So I was thinking of taking you to RISD. Have you been there yet?" he asked her.

"No, I haven't. I left Rhode Island when I was very small and this is my first time back since I was in first grade."

"How did you like Florida?"

"I loved it. We lived in West Palm, my Father has a house near the beach. I've mostly lived near the beach all my life." Victoria told him. Thinking back to the beach made her think of Scott Benson, her first serious boyfriend. He was a surfer. She met him when she took a job at the Surf Shack Pizzeria. Scott had taken her breath away the day he walked in there and she hadn't been the same since.

"So what brings you back to Rhode Island?" James' eyes fluttered over her but then went back to the road.

"My mom and dad had an agreement where she was to get my brother and dad was to get me, when I turned eighteen in May, I decided that I wanted to be with my mom. My father had remarried and things weren't working out right." Images came back to her, horrible ones she wished she could forget. The drugs, the sex, the horrible tragedy that made her wake up and realize what she was doing to herself.

"I've lived in Rhode Island all my life. Sometimes when I think about it I ask myself why I never left. Nothing is holding me back."

"What about school?"

"School yes, but I could have gone to another college. Then again, things are just going right for me now."

"How so?"

"I'm becoming a reporter at the "Providence Journal" and I have my own apartment and not to mention that I have the pleasure of being accompanied by a beautiful young woman." James smiled at her.

She blushed and turned away. She was happy. Thinking back Victoria couldn't remember being this happy. Yes she could. It was right before Scott had committed suicide.

It's almost the two year anniversary on Friday, James thought. For the past two years he and Victoria had dated. He planned on proposing, then soon she would be moving in... James stopped himself. Laying in bed on that Saturday morning something struck him hard.

He still thought about her sometimes. But not as often as he had before. Her memory lingered like a cold that wouldn't, couldn't be fought. *Lavender is gone! She's never coming back James. Just forget her.* He could hear Nick's words but not believe them. He had to believe them. He was proposing to Victoria on Friday night.

He loved Victoria. He really did.

"I do love her," James said aloud getting up from the bed. He went to the kitchen and got himself a cup of coffee. Settling down into one of the kitchen chairs he felt at ease.

The doorbell rang loudly unexpectedly. Getting up to answer the door, James' neck hurt suddenly. His father stood at the door his hands deep in his pockets. The two men stared at each other for a moment before James moved aside so that he could enter.

"Nice place you have here," Rob commented. "How long have you been here?"

"Two years."

"Oh...did you fix it up? You know wall paper, paint, carpet?"

"Yeah, when I got here it was a plaid wall paper. I took it off and painted."

"Well you did a nice job." An awkward silence passed through them.

"Would you like some coffee?" James asked him. It was as if a homeless man had wandered in and claimed to be his father. This man James was looking at with the sprinkle of grey though his hair and the fine wrinkles around his eyes was not the father James remembered.

"Coffee, yeah. That would be great thanks." James watched him take a seat at the table. James thought of how he took his coffee, two sugars and one cream. When he was young, he would watch his mother make the coffee for him, then have James bring it up to him. His mother yelled when he dropped some coffee on the stairs. It seemed so long ago that he was a small six year old. James set it down in front of him and took the seat across from him.

"So... how is work?" James asked quietly.

"Oh, you know the same thing...What about you? How is your job over at the mail room?"

"I work in the newsroom," James answered, clutching his teeth.

"That's right. I always get those two messed up." His father took a sip of the coffee and looked at his son. "James, it's been too long."

"I know it has."

"Look, I've been the asshole that you said I've been whether it's been all the years you were a kid or the past five. I was wrong. Okay? I was wrong to do those things and say those things to you."

"Wait-"

"No, hear me out," he began. He set down his coffee and stared at James. "James when I was a kid, my father couldn't supply me with a Mustang or a nice house and he was never really there. I'm not saying that I had a bad childhood, I'm not saying that you're Grandfather was an ass. I'm not sure what I'm trying to say really. So I guess I'll just start this way; I'm scared of new things. I'm scared of the world that you have been brought into. I'm afraid that I'll lose you."

"Listen about the college thing, I just wanted you to when you are ready to start a family then everything will be taken care of. In terms of money, I mean. Your mother and I are not going to be around forever."

"I know." James said. He felt like a teenager again, sitting listening to lecturers, and things.

"I want to know before I die that everything will be alright for you. As for the many other things, I cannot even express the feeling of wanting to go back in time and fix them all. As I recall, you said that we had nothing in common, well I want to clear that up."

Rob Martin sat in the kitchen with James until four in the afternoon that day. Each telling stories about what they had been through. They talked of life, love, work, school, everything James had ever wanted to know he now understood.

When Rob left that day he knew things were going to be alright. James would be fine, he had a good job and he was getting engaged. Rob arrived home later that night after going for a drink at the bar. Christine was waiting up for him in bed. He looked and saw how lucky he was, beautiful wife, daughter, a son who he now was more connected to, this house that would one day be James' and his wife's.

He imagined grandchildren, running around the house. Once he told Christine what James was planning to do on Friday night there was no stopping the mental images.

"My God! I have to call Elaine! We have to go over wedding plans!" she had cried when he told her.

"No, you're not calling her. Remember you don't know about the engagement. James wants to tell everyone himself."

Chapter 12

Friday

James rushed out of Mr. O'Mally's office. He couldn't believe it! It was amazing! He hadn't expected it, especially with all the other things going on. He had been made top editor for the Providence Journal. James was taking O'Mally's place seeing that he was retiring.

Mr. O'Mally had said he had done fine work on the Kaufman murder trial. Perhaps that it was that he had managed to get a interview with the ever mysterious Lyle Kaufman. Whatever he did, he made it. He was on top.

He was planning on proposing that night when he took Victoria to dinner. Things were set, he had talked to her parents, talked to his parents and as of Monday he was the proud owner of his parents' home.

They bought a house in Newport a few months ago, so they gave James the house as a starter. He rushed by his desk so quickly that he forgot his jacket.

"Hey!" a voice called behind him. James turned around and saw Rasheen Corts heading to him. He and Sheen had worked on the Kaufman story in the beginning and they soon became friends. Sheen's dark skin was the trademark of a Middle Eastern descent.

Sheen had a wild spirt like Nick, but Sheen knew when to tame it.

"What's the rush?" he asked going up to him.

"I have to get to my pare- my house- O' Mally promoted me to editor!"

"Congratulations man!" Sheen said patting James on the back. "You know this calls for a celebration! We can go get drunk tonight." James and Sheen began to walk down the corridor.

"Sorry but I have other plans, besides I don't drink."

"What?! You've never had a drink before?"

"Well only at church, I've had the wine."

"Dude, one night I have to take you out. So what are you doing tonight?"

"I'm proposing to my girlfriend," James said proudly.

"No way dude! Right on!" Sheen exclaimed, throwing him a high five. "Let me guess, you're a virgin too?"

"Yeah."

Sheen's mouth dropped open. "You're shittin me! You're no virgin!"

James laughed and nodded his head. "This wedding is going to be quick. Trust me." He smiled and so did Sheen.

"Congrats dude, I'll see you on Monday! Later!"

"Later!" James called back.

⁂

Victoria sat in her bedroom looking at the blank stare she had on. The vanity was dusty, she should wipe it off but she didn't care. Tonight was yet another glorious night with her boyfriend.

"An anniversary," Victoria said aloud. Two years. Best two years of her life so far. Every time she was around James her heart did flip-flops, kart-wheels, and handstands. Everything about him was perfect.

The day had started out as a mess but it was going to end with a passionate kiss from his beautiful full lips. She wished it were more but James had said that he wanted to keep to the rules and wait until he married marriage.

I had told him it was only for women but he claimed it was just something he had to do, Victoria thought to herself. Her memory of Scott came back to her. He had been the one. She was sure that what she was doing had been right.

It was getting close to the time she should be using to get ready. After showering, putting on make up and doing her hair, she had to pick between which of the two outfits she had laid out. The new dress she had bought at Fileens, or the classic little black dress that showed the soft skin on the top of her legs.

Choosing the black dress that fit her perfectly, Victoria looked in the mirror. Hard to believe that she was Victoria Brenden. White trash from the smelly trailer park in Florida. Tears welled in her eyes, she wasn't supposed to be thinking of that! Besides it would ruin her mascara.

Everyday she prayed that her birthday would come sooner so that she could return and be with her Mom. Be with her dear brother who was her role model. Nick hadn't know what it had been like growing up in a trailer park where your father was a drunk. He had lived the high life.

Gary was a millionaire, he could get Nick anything he wants. Always living with nice things, her on the other hand had to work for things that she wanted. She had saved up for tickets to a concert when she was fifteen by working, slaving at the pizzeria. In the end she never got to go to the concert. *The money was spent for other things...*Victoria thought. *I bought these,* Victoria looked at her huge chest.

Stop now! Or you will start crying! Victoria gave herself a once over in the mirror. The long blond hair she once had now was cropped to her shoulders and the small brown eyes she possessed looked larger tonight thanks to eye liner. *He should be here anytime soon,* Victoria wondered what they would talk about, James was always a surprise.

The doorbell rang a second later, sending Victoria running to the window but it was only the pizza delivery. Letting out a sigh she walked back over to her vanity. Loosely picking up the still hot curling iron she took a worn out straight piece from the front and twirled it around the strand.

Her and James' picture was on the corner of the vanity. It had been snapped when they went to Rocky Point. That night she remembered was the night she learned from Nick that she was the first girl James had dated since he was seventeen. Nick didn't tell her why so she asked him.

He didn't responded at first, then later on the drive back he said that James was in a really rocky relationship and it had ended badly. *"Whoever the girl was, she must have been a real dip shit, James was gorgeous!"* Victoria considered herself lucky to have him. Girls stared at them when they were out. If she was one of them, she would too.

Sometimes when she thought of that night, she wondered what the girl had done to hurt him so. What did she look like? What happened between them? It was none of her concern, the girl was gone. James was smart enough to not go back with her if he ever saw her again.

Besides, they were happy. Victoria smiled to herself. She was positive that James was really "The One". The doorbell rang again and this time she knew it was him. Grabbing her black purse and light shawl she walked out of her bedroom, closing the door behind her.

⁂

"You look stunning," James told her again when they walked outside. She blushed at him and let her hand slip into his. He looked just as stunning as she did. Was that a new suit he was wearing?

He opened the passengers side door for her before getting into the drivers side. The reservation at Twin Oaks was at eight and it was seven thirty now. James looked over at her and saw the dress she was wearing was showing the top of her thigh. Controlling himself, he started the car and they took off.

The place was packed. Usual for a Friday night. The bar held the Friday night drinkers while the dinner room held either families, husbands and wives and the occasional dates. He took her arm as they walked through the crowded dining room. The waiter placed them at a small booth near the window. The candle on the table flickered, exposing light to her eyes in the darkened room.

"How did you ever manage to get reservations? This place is always packed," she said taking off the shawl and setting it on the side of her.

"Well its easy when you top editor of The Journal." James told her proudly. She gasped and covered her mouth.

"James! You got promoted?!"

"Today. O'Mally is retiring and he chose me to take his place and guess what?"

"What?"

"My parents bought a house down in Newport and they gave me the house they are living in now."

"Oh my gosh James that so amazing!" she raved. Their waiter came a moment late to take their order.

"What can I get for you this evening?" he asked.

His name tag red Phil. "I'll start off with a bowl of the clam chowder and the prime rib."

"I'll have the same," she told him. The waiter walked off and James looked at her.

"Are you going to be able to eat all that?"

"Trust me I'm starving. I skipped lunch today. Mr. Angelo kept me through lunch." Victoria had started a job at an advertising firm a little over a year ago. She had made friends quickly, one of them becoming her best friend, Jessica Horace.

They talked through the chowder and steak, each moment bringing him closer to asking her to become his wife. "The landlord wants me to rent the apartment to someone new now, the guy is in construction and he has a wife and an infant. Or so that is what she told me. I'm lucky because if my parents didn't give me the house then I wouldn't have a place to go."

"It'll be just in time too. They're moving out next month," James finished. He set down his fork and knife and looked like Victoria. Beautiful, vibrant. She was everything he needed right now, and everything that he would ever need.

"Victoria?" He slipped out of his seat and walked over to her. Standing next to her he took the ring out of his back pocket. "Will you marry me?" She jumped out of her seat and threw his arms around his neck.

"Yes! Oh yes I will!" she whispered into his ear. Slowly he got the ring out of the box. A gold band held two diamonds. He held her left hand and slipped it over her finger. He stood up and kissed her lightly.

"I'm going to call Mom and Gary!" Victoria exclaimed. She stood up and made her way to the phones. By the time she came back, James had paid the bill and was ready to go.

"Ready?"

"Yeah," She said picking up her shawl. They held hands walking out the restaurant. The sky was filled with stars as they walked out the door. James turned around at the sound of his name being called. It sounded very familiar...

"James! I thought that was you!" Faye Waters came rushing over to him.. The smile James had been wearing nearly turned to a frown. He hadn't seen her in years and she was *her* friend not his. *She did look good though*, James thought looking her over. The light blue dress she was wearing went along with her hair great, which was still a red but more of an auburn.

"Faye hi!" James tried to sound excited. Faye laughed and moved her hand to his arm.

"It's so great to see you, it's been forever! God of all the places to meet!" Victoria seemed confused, why hadn't James introduced her? Could this be the girl that left him? She had seen how his expression changed when she came up to him. "I just recently found out you were with the paper, that's awesome!"

"Yeah," James said. He felt awkward to her, as if he hadn't know her, hadn't know that they had talked about him when she was across the street. "How have you been?"

"Oh busy, I just finished real-estate school, so I'm kind of frazzled but other than that- When I saw you I just had to come and say hi. I'm so rude to not say hello to your friend! Hi I'm Faye!" Victoria nodded.

"Okay......well James I better be getting back in, it was really nice to see you."

"You too Faye." Faye turned away but looked back at him. Her expression different, not like herself.

"James? I um... bumped into someone recently."

"Nick right? He's been all around lately." James said half annoyed half not caring.

"No.....I got a call while I was downtown yesterday. Lavender came back to Rhode Island."

※

The world had seemed to stop, as well as James' heart. *No. It wasn't true. She couldn't be back!* James frantically turned the wheel of the car onto Victoria's street. The darkness was brightened by his headlights.

Victoria had been quiet all the way from the restaurant, she didn't know what to say. Never had he driven like this, never had be acted this way. Pulling to a stop in the front of her house he leaned back in the seat. Running his fingers through his hair he asked himself questions over and over again.

Why now? Why after all this time? Did she expect to find him? Or start over? He didn't know what to do, every second was worse than the last. Victoria sat in the car staring at her bag in her lap.

"James-"

"What?" he snapped. She pulled the hand she was going to put on his hand back. "Sorry."

"What is going on? Tell me!"

"Nothing is going on."

"So you took me on that roller coaster ride home for nothing? James tell me."

"There is nothing to tell!"

"Yes there is! Now you've been a jerk since we left the parking lot. This is supposed to be a great night!" James turned his head away. He couldn't tell her, she wouldn't understand. He had put his past away, locking it up so it would never escape.

"You wouldn't understand."

"Try me James? You know if you loved me so much this would be easy for you!"

He snorted and shook his head. "This is just something that I really don't want to bring up."

"Is she the one?" she began, "Is she the one who broke your heart?"

"Nick tell you that?"

"He might have, just answer it. Tell me why you haven't been with other women before me! Tell me what she did to you!"

"What would it do? Huh? What good would it do you knowing?!"

"Fine," she said opening the car door. "Don't tell me. Let me just have this loom over me forever!" she yelled.

"Don't yell," He said almost calm.

"Then tell me James! Tell me what is going on. I have a right to know. As your fiancee-" That was all James heard from her sentence. The word ran through his ears and the visions he once had over took him. He had planned to marry Lavender. He had planned to do all the things he had done with Victoria with Lavender.

"Shit," James mumbled.

"What?"

"Nothing."

She shook her head and walked over to him. Kissing his cheek she turned to go inside. "I'll call you later." Disappearing into the house he was left alone on the street. A footstep scared him, making him turn around and face his past.

"Hi James."

Chapter 13

Her beauty captivated him. She was everything he remembered. Her face was slightly different, but the eyes that haunted him remained the same. How did he know if this was real? She left him speechless, neither moved, nor spoke for minutes. James tore his eyes away from her face and looked at her body.

The low cut light blue sweater she was wearing hugged her and showed off her large, round breasts, the designer jeans were tight around her hips. Moving back up, he noticed her hair was longer almost to the middle on the top part of her arm.

"James?" she asked. That voice, so familiar but changed. A lot of things had changed since 1987. He swallowed hard and blinked his eyes.

"Wha-..you- I mean..." James couldn't find the words to fit what he wanted to say. What did he want to say anyway? She threw her arms around his neck and held on to him tight. Burring herself into his neck she began to mumble.

"I told myself I wouldn't do this. I hadn't planned on seeing you this early." He felt dizzy, confused, sick even. He pulled her away and grasped her arms.

"What are you doing here? How did you find me?"

"I'm staying with Faye she lives across the street. I was getting out of the car and I saw the mustang. At first I thought it was someone else but then I saw you."

"Lav, what the hell are you doing here?" Her expression seemed strange.

"I don't know."

"Why the hell don't you?!" he yelled. It was her turn to be the one confused.

"What? James....can we talk somewhere?" she asked quietly. Letting out a breath James released her and walked over to the car and started it.

"Get in," he said flatly. She walked over and sat in the seat that Victoria only a little while before sat. It smelled the same, it looked the same. It felt as though she had never left it. Turning around she looked at the backseat and thought about the nights they had kissed back there.

Before long they were at his apartment. He watched her take off her jacket and place it over one of the kitchen chairs. She looked around and then to him. His paleness made him seem almost albino, but it brought out his eyes.

"This is a nice apartment."

"Thanks."

"You're welcome." *She was nervous too*, he thought as he watched her. He shifted his weight from one foot to the other before taking off his own jacket. On one hand he wanted to grab her, his feelings for her were back, on the other he loved Victoria.

"So..."

James breathed deep and walked over to the table. She had taken a seat there already.

"So...James...how have you been?"

"Fine, and you?"

"Fine."

"Lav, what is it that you want me to say?" he asked jumping up from the chair. The temptation to yell and scream at her was pushing at his throat. How after everything she put him through, not calling, not writing back, she could sit there calmly.

She stood up and faced him too. "I don't know James! You want to know why I'm here? I'm here because I missed you. You know perfectly well that I hate what happened!"

"Look! Things aren't the same!"

"What are you saying?"

"What I'm saying is that I don't know what you want me to do! We can't just pick up where we left off!" She was quiet for too long. He had to say something but the words were not making its way out of his mouth.

"I knew I never should have come here. I should have listened to my Mother." Lavender mumbled. "I should have listened when she told me the real reason you stopped calling."

"I stopped calling?" James questioned her.

"Yes that's right you stopped calling! She told me that you must have found someone else and I'm starting to believe that it is true!"

"First of all your mother told me not to call you anymore! So I wrote you but I guess you were too busy to get any of the letters!"

"You're a liar! I've never received a letter from you! If I had I would have written back!"

"Your mom is a liar! Don't you see?"

"My mother would never lie to me! How dare you even say something like that!"

"I'm only saying the truth!"

"How do I know what the truth is from you? I feel like I don't even know you." Becoming quiet, she wiped a small tear from her eye. *Things were a mess. How could they even possibly get worse?* James thought. He walked over to Lavender and stood tall across from her.

"I'm sorry you feel that way. I'm sorry that *I* feel the same," Lavender looked up at him, almost in disgust.

"I'm still the same."

"Then how can you say that you don't know me when I'm the same person that I was back in 1987!"

"Cause you've changed!"

"Dammit Lav you're not making any sense!"

For a long period of time yet another silence passed between them. The room seemed to get cold, the air surrounding James gave him goose bumps.

"James....I want to start over. If we can. I've missed you," Lavender told him softly. James felt like a boulder was in his throat. What was he going to say?

"We can't." She was stunned at his words! He didn't want to, that was it. Pain was surging through her veins at he went on. "I'm engaged."

"What?! When... I mean, no I don't know what I mean!" The pain was now joined by sadness, almost betrayal.

"I became engaged tonight," he choked out the words slowly. "Her name is Victoria. She's Nick's sister." Lavender's heart had stopped at that moment. Her lungs stopped working. It felt as though someone was stabbing her with a knife every second, cutting out the memories that she held on to forever.

"You're.....engaged....to Nick's sister?" James shook his head in agreement Lavender stepped forward and slapped him hard across the face. "You bastard! You let me go on with everything and then you tell me you're engaged?" the tears were threatening to show.

"I'm sorry."

"Sure you are!" She grabbed the jacket and ran to the door. The quicker she got out of there the sooner that she could cry. She didn't ever want to see him again, what he did was unforgivable. *I told him I loved him!* Lavender thought arriving at the last landing of the stairs. *"That day at the airport I was ready to give it all up!"* Upon hearing his footsteps behind her she sped up.

"Lav! Please wait!" he called out. Shoving the door to get into the building open she ran outside. Sooner or later as she ran with her heels on she was going to break her neck. A moment later he was outside with her, only she was far ahead of him. Turning left off the driveway she began walking fast down Marshall St.

"Lav, please! Get in the car and I'll drive you home!" She turned around and looked at him. The moonlight illuminated his facial features, the strong jaw, the straight nose.

"Get in the car... The same car that once I sat in with you and talked about our dreams and what we wanted to do with our lives. You want me to get into the same car where she just sat before I saw you?!" She started to take off down the street again.

"Lav, listen to me!"

"It's Lavender, you lost your right to call me Lav. Only the people who really care about me can use it," she said turning around once more.

"I care about you!" he screamed. A few lights went on around the street.

"Fuck you!" she yelled back at him. When she got to the end of the street she was sure he had went back inside. He was gone, she never needed him, never wanted him! The dimly lit gas station was at the corner. A pay phone was under a blinking street light. Depositing the loose change she found in her pocket she called a cab. She had enough money to get home.

Lavender took a seat on the curb and waited for the cab. She was sure her sobbing was heard throughout the neighborhood.

Saturday

The telephone was ringing. Over and over again. James lifted his head of the pillow. The clock read 5:59. The three aspirins he had taken didn't help the pounding head ache he had. He felt around for the phone on the night stand, please hang up whoever it is. James pleaded.

He picked it up and put it to his ear. "Hello?" James asked groggily.

"James?" his mother's voice asked him. Something was wrong, she was crying. "James are you there?"

"Yeah Mom I'm here, what is it?" He sat up from the bed, rubbing his eyes. The brown t-shirt clung to his muscular body. Loud sobs like he had heard last night from Lavender beat out his ear drum.

"James...your father is dead."

⁂

Speeding down to the house he grew up in, James thought of what his mother said. Ditch....no seatbelt....faulty brakes...a roll over... It seemed like a blur but he was sure that he had thrown up somewhere between his bed and the driveway. He had thrown on a shirt and pants not even bothering to shower. His hair was a mess, his unshaved face a mess. Arriving in front of the house he turned off the car and slammed the door to the mustang.

Police cars were around and in the driveway. Neighbors were outside murmuring about what had happened. The front door was wide open when he went in. He heard his mother in the sitting room crying and trying to talk at the same time. James rushed over to her pushing past the two policemen who were talking to her.

"James! Oh my God!" she sobbed as she wrapped her arms around his torso.

"What happened?" he asked them. The older police man spoke up. He looked, vaguely familiar, Captain Kireman.

"Mr. Martin was driving and from what we believe the brakes were tampered with. He rolled over into a ditch." James' stomach rolled over and he felt he was going to throw up again. His father couldn't be dead. They had just started talking again, everything had been good! "We'll know more in a few hours."

"James, please don't let Grace come down here. She's still asleep in her bedroom." She let go of her son and nodded to him, as if she were saying she would be alright. Tip toeing up the stairs he quietly came to Grace's bedroom and opened the door. She was sitting near the window looking out down at the commotion below.

"Grace?" startled she turned around and looked at him. James shut the door behind him before going over to her.

"What's happening? Why are all the police here?" He pulled his sister close to him squeezing her tight to his chest, clinging to her like she was a stuffed animal. "James I can't breath." she said struggling out of his grip.

Neither can Dad. James thought. *Not anymore.*

⁂

The Mass ended earlier than planned. On the gloomy morning, Rob Martin's friends and family piled into St. Mary's church. James' Mother and Sister sat next to him on the right, Victoria at his left. The tiny black dress she was wearing was the same on she was wearing when he proposed to her one week ago.

James' trance like state was interrupted when Victoria nudged James to get up when everyone was leaving. His Mother and Sister remained seated. Father Daniels, older than James remembered him being from the last time he came to church two weeks ago, came over to them expressing his sympathies.

"James, I'm so sorry." he said shaking his hand. Victoria, his Mother and Grace had all went to the rest room leaving James alone in the church.

"Thank you Father." The sound of footsteps made him turn to see Lavender walking to him and Daniels. The tight black skirt fell to her knees and the long sleeve black top seemed unnecessary in the muggy weather.

"I thought that was you sitting in the back Ms. Springer!" Daniels called out. A smile washed over Lavender's face. She was ignoring him he could tell. "My look at you, look at both of you!" Daniels looked at both of them standing next to each other. "All grown up now. This place always seemed too big for you and now here you are. It's just so sad that we all must be together on sad occasions.

Victoria was back a moment later and when she walked back to James she pulled his arm tight around her. Lavender looked at her and thought she was acting very babyish. *She can have him. The bastard.* Lavender thought. She quickly apologized seeing she was in God's house.

"Now, who is this beautiful young woman?" Father Daniels asked James eyeing Victoria. She blushed and it made Lavender want to throw up. *She sure was young, what was she thirteen? Blond, what a shock James! With your new promotion did you buy her those implants? At least mine are a natural C.*

"Father this is my fiancee, Victoria Brenden."

"Fiancee? Well James is a very lucky man to have such a beautiful bride to be." Mrs. Martin walked back over to them. Her eyes went wide at the sight of Lavender.

"Oh my dear look at you, how gorgeous you are! You're certainly not the little girl I remember!"

"Thank you Mrs. Martin." James looked down at Lavender through the corner of his eye.

"Lavender why don't you come back to the house with us? Even though it's a sad time Rob would want us to be happy. I would love to hear how medical school is." *Medical School!* Victoria thought. *She must think that she is just top notch! Doctors wear loafers because they don't know how to tie their shoes*, Victoria laughed at her own joke.

The one thing about her father was that he was really funny, saying all stupid things out of no where. The loafers jokes was one of her favorites.

"I'm sorry Mrs. Martin I can't stay I have a train back to New York in a half hour. I would love to, but I can't. Maybe some other time. I'm deeply sorry for your loss." She said sweetly. James looked at her again, this time he turned his head. She looked up and smiled at him.

"I'm really sorry about your father James," Lavender, turning on her heel of her spikes, walked out of the church.

⁂

Lavender threw down her bag when she walked into her Mother and Step-Father's high rise apartment. James' words from the night that they had fought stuck with her. What if he really did write her? What if James was right, that her mother had been keeping secrets.

"Mom!" Lavender called out. Her mother stepped from the kitchen, her red hair tied up in a bun.

"Lav you're back so soon. How did everything go?"

"Did you keep the letters James wrote to me?"

"What?"

"Please don't lie to me. I've been through enough. Did you or did you not keep the letters he said he wrote?"

"Lav-"

"You did didn't you?"

"I only did it so that you wouldn't be hurt."

"Well you didn't think about years to come did you? How the fuck do you think I feel now?" Lavender grabbed her purse and stalked out the door, slamming it behind her.

Chapter 14

A week later James was parked back at his old house. Grace was upstairs in her room still in the grieving process. He was too but he couldn't lock himself up in his apartment. His mother on the other hand seemed to go back to the way things were as if his father had just gone on a business trip.

The police confirmed that the brakes were tampered with. They called it an open and shut case. His father had some enemies from work, cases that he won for the other side. James swore to himself that he would find out who did it. He swore to it.

His mom sat a cup of steaming, hot coffee in front of him before she took a seat at the wood table. James moved the spoon he had been given around in the cup watching it.

"Didn't I ever tell you not to play with your food when you were a little boy?" she asked laughing. He took the spoon out and sat it on a napkin. His mother sensed something was wrong with him and it wasn't just that his father had passed away. "How's Victoria?"

"She's fine."

"That's good. Have you two talked about the wedding at all? When I spoke to her mother she mentioned that you haven't decided on a date yet."

"Mom- I don't feel like talking about it." She nodded taking a sip of her coffee.

"I understand. James it's not your fault about your father-"

"This isn't about him!" James clutched the cup in his palms. "This doesn't even have to do with him."

"You're awfully upset James and if it isn't about your father then what the hell is it about?!" She demanded. Sighing James looked up at her.

"Mom tell me what your true feelings for Victoria are." She paused and looked confused.

"Dear, you love her-"

"That isn't what I asked," James interrupted.

"Would you let me finish maybe? Victoria is a very nice girl. She's sweet and kind, she's pretty. She loves you, you can see it in her eyes."

"And....what about Lavender?"

"Funny that you bring her up James."

"Please tell me. When you said You're not the little girl I remember, at the mass what did you mean?"

"Just what I said James."

"How would you know that she isn't the same?"

"I just know."

"Tell me how."

"Get rid of the tone and I'll tell you!" she said fiercely. James pushed the cup that he was drinking aside and settled back into the hard kitchen chair.

"Please tell me how."

"I don't know James she's just different. She is older and she has changed, just like you. I don't know what this is about but if you are trying to compare Victoria to Lavender or vice versa-"

"I'm not sure what I'm doing. I'm not sure if I'm even in the same universe! Lav is different, I know. I was in love with the old Lavender, not the new one."

"You're misinterpreting what I said James, she's still the same person,"

"I'm just so confused right now! I have so much stuff to worry about!"

" For one, are you talking about having to look after me and your sister? James you don't have to! We are financially and emotionally fine. You have your own life to live. You're young you can't do that to yourself."

"I'm gonna try to get the landlord to let me stay at the apartment. Or else I'm gonna have to look for a new place."

"You have a new place right here!"

"No I don't, you're not moving to Newport remember? You said that to me a few nights ago."

"James the house is bought down there. Besides it's where I have always wanted to go. This is your house now James."

"Mom you can't be serious. What about Grace? She has to go to school! And what about if you need me? Newport is kind of far away."

"Newport doesn't have schools? And James if I need you won't be that far away." She paused and looked James straight in the eyes. "Jamie don't worry about us. We'll be fine." James gave a half smile and grabbed the cold coffee, then stopped no one had called him Jamie since.....

Come on Jamie.

"I don't feel right about you moving."

"You want me to be happy don't you?"

"Yes."

"Well then let me move where I want to move. You know James I lived on my own for a few years before I met your father. I'm a big girl I can take care of myself." James got up to rinse the cup. He looked out the window onto the back porch and saw Grace sitting there. A notebook laid on her lap.

"How did she get out there? I thought she was in her room," James asked. She looked so sad. It was understandable. He hated to see her in pain as much as he hated to see it for his mother.

"Oh leave her. She's taking things very hard lately. She's disconnected from me won't tell me anything. All she keeps doing is writing in that notebook. Sometimes when I pass her room she's singing. I think she is writing songs. The other day she found your guitar up in the attic. I had forgotten all about it."

"Yeah me too. I stopped before I went into college. God that brings back memories. Do you know if Bif is still around?"

"Last I heard he was teaching still but he moved to Vegas."

"Why is everyone going to Vegas suddenly? Three people quit on me because they find the Vegas lights more amusing."

"I went there once," she told him as she started setting the table for dinner. "It was years ago though, its changed now I bet. Hey here is an idea, go there for your honeymoon!" His mother laughed.

"Mom there isn't even a date and you want to plan where I take her for our get away."

⚜

As he unpacked the furniture he brought from the apartment into the house he had lived in all his life, he couldn't help feeling the surge of happiness float through him. Movers were all around him, bringing in new furniture that he had bought with his big fat paycheck.

Everything was finally settling down.

"How many more boxes?" Victoria whined flopping into one of the couches in the living room.

"You sound like your brother."

"Why isn't he helping? He said he would. Besides we have to move all this crap to where I want it so that when I bring in my stuff I'll already be comfortable." James peered at her from around a corner.

"Excuse me? What do you mean, where I want it ? Remembering correctly I own the house. You're just going to be living in it," James said placing another box down. Victoria came over to him and wrapped her arms around his neck.

"But honey I just want to make it nice for us," a sad pout took over her face in seconds. "You wouldn't want my feelings hurt would you?" James felt like slapping her. He hated that baby shit. But it was going to be her house too....he nodded and watched her run off and start telling the movers where to put things.

James walked back out to the moving van. Something caught his eye across the street. A for sale sign. That hadn't been there when he was here the other night. From what he knew The Ryan's still owned the house. They had rented it and now probably decided to sell it to the people. James ignored the sign and continued to unload.

Later that night his mother called. She and Grace had been set up for a while in the beautiful almost mansion-like house on the beach.

"How is Grace doing today?" he asked her. With their father passing and Grace having to leave her friends it was tough. James could never leaving his friends and his school when he was her age. She was going to be in junior high soon.

"She is getting there. There are twin girls across the street. Christina and Caitlin. They seem to be hitting it off well. How are things over there? All unpacked?"

"Kind of. We just got done eating, so we're going to continue on working until everything is in its place.

"That's excellent. Who is over there helping you?"

"Victoria. Nick showed up a little while ago. He was supposed to be here when the movers were taking in the furniture but you know him." James laughed. His Mom sounded better today. He thought she was finally starting to get some feeling that his Dad wasn't coming home from his business trip.

"Well I better let you go. You guys want to get settled."

"I love you Mom."

"Love you Jamie."

"Mom..."

"Yeah?"

"Don't call me that."

"James-"

"Please, it brings back memories." She was quiet on the other line for a long moment.

"I'll come by tomorrow and help you get your stuff in order."

"Okay. Love you." James hung up the phone and walked into the living room where Nick and Victoria were sitting on the couch.

"Dude, remember when I slept over here and we watched that movie where the guy was chasing the girl with the cleaver? We stayed up all night to make sure he wasn't coming to get us."

"Yeah I remember. I still can't register in my brain that this is all mine now." Victoria smiled at him. Pulling her gaze away from him she went to the curtains that his mom had left up. She shut them and started unpack more boxes.

"Hey where are we putting this?" She asked picking up a box labeled magazines.

"I don't know just put it near the stairs."

"It's junk I'll just take it down to the basement."

"NO!" James yelled. She stopped and stared at him. He hadn't told her about what happened. Nor was he planning to anytime soon. He had avoided passing, going down, or being anywhere near that door. James knew that the police had confiscated everything in that room and that lights had been put up all around but no way would he ever go near it again.

"Why can't I go down to the basement?"

"Because the stairs are made of wood and they are old. It could collapse anytime."

"Fine..." she said slowly. James calmed down and went to get more boxes. Going upstairs he passed his room. The moonlight shone in making the beige carpet seem almost white. He walked in and looked around. *Some good times here*, James said to himself. The blinds on the windows were still even though the open window gave a breeze.

"Was this your room?" Victoria asked him coming around him. He smiled and nodded at her.

"This was it. For seventeen years of my life. Mom said that it was my nursery too. I don't think for one minute I ever left this room when I was younger. I used to sit in here and play with my cars and army guys. I would always make up stories while I would sit here. Either the world was going to be blown to shreds or some kind of storm was going to wipe out a city and only the army guys could save them. What did I know then?" James smiled. Victoria wrapped her arms around him and stared out the window.

Across the street the lights were off in the house. The bright green lawn was being watered with the sprinklers.

"Did someone live in that house?" she asked.

"Yes."

"I can imagine you and the boy across the street playing in the backyard and going to movies and things like that. I bet your parents were best friends and you did everything together. I also think that you would find it a relief to get away from Nick for a while. I can see you running in the street, playing tag or baseball or something."

"Or something."

"So am I right?"

"Everything except for playing baseball and tag." She hugged him and then reached up to give him a kiss.

"I'm beat I'll come by early tomorrow to finish okay?"

"Okay."

"Love you."

"Love you." She turned and walked back down the stairs and out the door. *You were right except for the fact that a boy didn't live across the street,* James thought.

※

Grace walked along the cold sand. *A storm must be coming in*, she thought to herself. Her mom was taking a nap in her oversized bedroom so she didn't know she snuck out. She wasn't allowed outside when her mother was asleep or out. *Ever since Mom had started going to that shrink and getting those pills she became tired in the middle of the day,* Grace thought.

James didn't know about Dr. Evan. Mom said it would worry him, and with the wedding to plan and everything he didn't need it. Grace let her path go into the water. The cold water stung at a cut on her foot. *But James should know, I should tell him but I never see him anymore. He's too busy with Victoria.*

Grace absolutely hated her. She had tried to be sweet to me and treat me like a baby. She's a phony. *I was excited when I saw Lavender in the church that day.* Grace said to herself. *I was sure that James was going to be with her. He did say that he loved her.* She had seen the look on Victoria's face when her mom had invited her over to the house, like something had crawled under her nose, rotting cheese or something.

Mom said she liked Victoria but she really doesn't. She just said she did to make James happy. Poor James, he's going to marry her! Eww that's gross! What if they had kids? Then what? He would forget me, and we wouldn't talk or see each other. Grace's head hurt from thinking about it.

I've lost my dad now I'm going to lose my brother. Life is so unfair! Heading back to the house she sighed. *What am I going to do? James can't marry her. I'm not being selfish here but I can see right through her.*

She had heard the saying that when you're in love, you can't really see what the person really is. Grace thought of Lavender and how pretty she looked. *Now if James married her then everything would be alright. I love Lavender she's always been a friend to me. And if they married then Lizzie and I would be family!* Grace was getting cheered up by these images. But deep inside she knew that Victoria was not going to turn into Lavender.

Chapter 15

June 1993

The guest list so far held 179 people, friends, family, coworkers, everyone was invited. The wedding was at St. Mary's and the reception at Quidnessett Country Club. August the twentieth was the date they had picked. Few things had to be worked out, the cake, the band and if Lavender was invited.

The fight they had on the night of June 2nd was concerning her. James walked around the table. The dining room light was shining in his eyes. Victoria had officially moved herself in three months ago, so he couldn't tell her to go home.

"You don't understand that we've been friends for years!"

"No James, you don't understand that this is my day and I don't want your ex there! Who ever heard of an ex girlfriend at a wedding?"

"Victoria, she's important, I can't not invite her!"

"I won't allow her to be there!"

"You're such a bitch!"

"You are a fool for even thinking of inviting her!" James marched upstairs and grabbed a bag out of the closet. She came rushing up behind him.

"Where are you going?" He was filling it with two days worth of clothing.

"New York."

"What? I won't allow you!" James pushed past her and went into the bathroom to grab his things in there.

"Then stop me!" She became flustered and stopped speaking.

"Fine, you know what? Jessica offered to go out tonight so that is what I'm going to do!" Victoria had been spending a lot of time with Jessica

Horace a girl from the office where she worked. It looked like Jessica was headed for maid of honor.

"Whatever you please!" James called after her almost laughing. He heard the door slam shut as he walked down stairs duffle bag on his back. He turned off all the lights and did the same as she only he walked into the garage.

What am I doing here? Victoria asked herself. Sitting next to a drunken Jessica, she felt out of place, sure she was old enough to drink but they would think she was stupid. She hadn't a clue what to order. Jessica leaned over to her, the slurred words making what she was saying unclear.

"What?" Victoria asked her. Jessica pointed a finger over to a guy across the room. He was really handsome.

"He's checking you out. Go talk to him."

"Excuse me? I'm engaged!"

"So? Look Vicky, not to be mean or anything but James is a pushover. You said yourself that James won't screw you and I've heard enough of you're complaining about how you need it so bad. What would James know if you went with some guy? Besides he is really hot." Jessica smiled and pushed her friend off the seat. Victoria let what she had said run through her mind. *James and I had a fight so why not be a little flirtatious?* Victoria asked herself. The man was as Jessica said "hot". The dirty blond hair and light grey eyes he had reminded her of Scott for some reason.

Slowly walking up she flashed a smile at him. "Hi."

"Hi, you want to dance?" he asked her. She head nodded yes as he pulled her to where people were dancing. After hours of dancing she was beat. "Do you want me to take you home? Your friend over there looks a little wasted." His voice was sweet and he seemed like a nice enough guy.

"Sure, let me get my coat." Turns out he drove a Jaguar. *An older one but still better than that ugly mustang James drove*, she said to herself. She told him how to get to the house and they were there in no time.

"Let me walk you in," he suggested. She nodded and led him into the house. When inside she saw him look around. It would have looked horrible is she had let James decorate it. "May I use your phone?"

"Oh sure." Victoria watched him disappear into the kitchen. How did he know where the phone was? He must be some kind of mind reader or something. She looked at the note James had messily scribbled. It said he would be back on Sunday night. What if he saw her? What would they do?

"Thank you for letting me use the phone," he said coming back in the room. Victoria turned around and faced him.

"No thank you. If it weren't for you I would have had to take a cab home." He came closer to her and leaned down to kiss her. She let her hands hold his neck as she gently kissed him back. The feeling was unbelievable. No kiss had ever felt like this. Soon he was upstairs with her.

She kissed him harder, letting her mouth learn every curve of his. Things were getting intense they both knew it. When she felt him moving up her shirt grasping at her bra, she pushed up from him.

"Wait I don't think I can do this." he pulled away and sat up.

"Oh come on, your boyfriend won't mind...."

New York City

The train James had been on came to a stop at one in the morning. After checking into the Regency he fell asleep on the king sized bed and didn't awake until nine o'clock the same morning. He had no clue where to start looking for her. He didn't know where she worked, didn't know where her house was.

James got the idea quickly. He reached for the white pages on the desk of the room. After what seemed forever he found her name in the tiny print. She lived in the city which was good. Quickly he showered and dressed, then made his way down to get a cab.

After waving his hand frantically for five minutes, a cab finally stopped for him. James climbed in and told him the address. The driver said nothing until they almost reached the building. He spoke with a middle eastern accent.

"Let me guess, you're getting married and your best friend is a woman but your new wife won't let her come to the wedding, so you're here to invite her anyway." James had to put his hand on his mouth to keep it from opening in shock.

"How did you know that?"

"Kid this is New York, I've seen and heard everything." The driver pulled over and let him out. James paid, then made his way over to the building. A short, balding man dressed in a security guard suit was standing at the door. *I guess they called rent-a-dope for this guy,* James thought.

"Hi, I'm here to see Lavender Springer."

"What's ya name?" The guard reminded him of Sharon back at the East Side Diner.

"James Martin." The guard made a few calls and then let him into the building instructing him to go to floor number 11 apartment 8. Good thing he wasn't claustrophobic otherwise he would have been terrified of the small elevator that was bringing him up to the floor.

He stood in front of apartment 8 for a long while before he built up the courage to knock. She answered the door minutes later. James expected that she knew he was there the whole time. He could see it on her face.

"Hi."

"Hello." The way she said it was cold, unforgiving, hateful. He looked at her. The tee shirt and jeans she wore were casual but she made them seem dressy. James stood awkwardly at the door, shifting his weight from one foot to the other.

"Can I come in?" She thought about it for a moment then moved aside to let him pass. The hall he was standing in was filled with canvases of paintings that looked like they belonged in a museum. He watched her walk into the open living room and take a seat on the tan leather couch.

The room was lined with windows looking out onto the city below. He followed her in and took his seat across from her. The kitchen was visible from the sofa as was the dining room with the hanging tiffany lamp.

"I needed to see you," James began, trying to not settle into the really comfortable couch. "The last time we saw each other wasn't a friendly visit. I'm sorry that we fought and I would like to make it up to you."

She nodded at him to go on. What he was saying wasn't what she really wanted to hear but it would have to do.

"Would you join me for dinner tonight?"

"James.... yes, I'll meet you for dinner."

"Really?"

"Yes." James stood up and looked at her. Still sitting she it appeared that she wasn't going to get up to see him out.

"And one more thing,"

"What's that?"

"I came to invite you for the wedding." Lavender jumped up at his words. Rage engulfed her. He was the asshole of the century!

"James you're a fucking moron! Why the hell would I show up at you wedding to that...that... plastic doll? You are perhaps the dumbest man on the face of this earth! Didn't I make myself clear last year? Well here I'll put it in writing," Lavender raced over to the kitchen where a yellow legal pad rested with a pen. She started to write the words she spoke.

"I will not go to the wedding of the asshole and his slutty, hooker, plastic doll!

Not even in the days of my death will I ever forgive him, because I, from now until eternity, hate him with a passion! The END!!!"

Lavender threw the paper at him and glared. James picked up the paper and looked over it.

Nodding he walked over to the front door and closed it behind him.

⁂

Kicking off her sneakers Lavender sat in the small office. The t-shirt she was wearing before was now in the dirty clothes and a big sweatshirt kept her warm. She needed to start studying for the test that was being held next week. All day she had been distracted and it was because of him. *Why did he have to show up now?* Lavender paused and thought about it he most likely said the same thing when she showed up.

Forget him! She told herself as she pulled a book from the bookcase next to the computer desk. *You got rid of him for good.* A long time ago she had convinced herself that what they had was in the past. And for a long time she didn't want to believe it.

"That's why I went," she said aloud, "to see if something was still there." There had been, as soon as she saw him she felt like a kid who still believed that Santa Claus came down the chimney on Christmas Eve. It was gone now. Bye-bye, sayonara, drown the drain. Was it though? That feeling came to her again today when she looked at him.

Going back to the book, she couldn't concentrate. It was already seven o'clock, what had she accomplished today? She hadn't studied, she just thought of him and what his face looked like when she yelled at him. Lavender walked into her kitchen, got a drink and then looked out of the tall windows.

Jeremy and her Mom had bought this for her on her twenty-first birthday. That had been two years ago. It seemed like only last week that the place had been bare of all the paintings and furniture. The doorbell rang suddenly. *Who could it be now, the repo man?*

Opening the door she looked at James leaning in the doorway, two brown paper bags sat at his feet. The rumpled hair was in its perfect place, she could tell he had been rubbing his head for a long time.

"What are you doing here?" Lav demanded placing her hands on her hips. He didn't move from the doorway, he just continued to stare at her. "I demand that you say something!" God what was his problem, he was looking at her like she had five heads!

"We had dinner plans." Her mouth dropped open. Unbelievable! He was so clueless! So stupid! So....

"Come in." *Why had she said that? You hate him remember Lav?* She watched him pick up the bags and carry them in. A red wine bottle was visible from the top of the second bag. He carried it into the kitchen and placed it on the counter.

"I brought take out. Italian. I hope you don't mind." Lavender shook her head and watched him unpack the items.

"Why did you do this?" James looked up at her.

"Before we ever went out, we were best friends. So think about that instead of thinking about when we dated." He continued to unpack the things, as she stood speechless. The sad thing was that he was right. Why hadn't she thought of that? James brought the food to her kitchen table.

"Do you have a bottle opener?" he asked holding up the wine. She nodded and got it out for him. Lavender grabbed the plates from the cabinet next to the stove and the silverware from the draw on her left.

They started eating soon after, she wondered if he felt awkward the way she did. Only hours before she had told him that he was the biggest asshole in the world and now he did this.

"What do you think?" James asked her disturbing her train of thought. She looked at his big blue eyes. It was something she always loved about him.

"Oh it's great." She watched him stand up and pour more wine into her wine glass. "James why would you do this?"

"I don't know."

"Yes you do tell me. I've been a bitch to you, why would you take this to me? I don't deserve it." James walked over to her and stood inches away. He took her hand and made her stand up. He pulled her chin up to his lips and kissed her. She let out a small moan as they parted.

"It could be because I've never wanted to be with you more than this afternoon...to kiss you and touch you like I've dreamed about since I met you. You drive me insane Lav," His mouth grazed her neck while his hands went to cup her breasts. Lavender closed her eyes and hung on to him. "I want to love you more than ever been loved before. I want to make you scream, I want your nails to leave marks on me," his cool breath whispered in her ear. Lavender pushed herself away from him and smiled

"Can you understand something in french if I say it?"

"Probably not."

"You're half french!"

" Okay, Okay, just try me."

"faites-l'amour moi."

"What?"

"Make love to me."

Chapter 16

What am I going to do?! Victoria asked herself as she paced around the bathroom. She had all the signs she was pregnant! Her one night stand that she had a nearly two months ago was the father of the child with in her.

She found out she was pregnant a week ago. She had planned to get James in bed, that way she could say it was his. Now as she got closer to the wedding date things weren't looking good. The small bathroom at the mall seemed to be closing in on her, the shopping bag filled with lingerie was sickening to look at.

Victoria hadn't told a soul except for Jessica about the pregnancy, she knew she could trust her best friend not to tell anyone about it. From one of the stalls behind her she heard the toilet flush. Turning around quickly she saw a middle aged woman exit from the stall. She had thought she was alone in the place!

Turning and ignoring her, Victoria looked at herself in the mirror. Four days before the wedding and she looked horrible. Tonight was her bachelorette party, something had to be done before tonight, otherwise someone would guess that something was wrong. She was going to make sure that James' pants came off. Tonight.

James sat next to Sheen at the bar. He had taken him out as a last night to be free, but he wasn't feeling very free. His mind had been elsewhere lately, the wedding was around the corner and he wasn't sure that he was ready to do it. He had been ready until that night in New York.

"Come on man order something," Sheen urged him. James looked at the many shot glasses that were around him and Sheen. There was no doubt that sheen was an alcoholic.

"I'm not really into this Sheen, can we go?"

"Dude, I'm far from done. Come on." Sheen called the bartender over to him and ordered James a shot. It came and James looked at the foul smelling liquid. Did he really want to do this or was it one of those peer pressure things he heard about when he was twelve.

"Here goes nothing." James said aloud. It tasted horrible, he decided as it went down his throat. But close to seven shots later James was feeling alright. It was then that Sheen suggested the tattoo.

Fortunate for them there was a tattoo parlor next to the bar. It had to be about eleven at night for there to be no one in the tattoo parlor. An overweight man with tattoos all over his arms was sitting in the chair reading a paper.

"You boys want to get inked?"

"He does." Sheen laughed. James looked at him confused.

"I thought you were getting one!"

"Naw, it's my treat to you." James stumbled over to the man and took his place in the chair.

"So what do you want and where do you want it?" The man asked. James' eyes closed for a second, a head ache was starting. Re-opening his eyes he smiled at the man.

"I want to small guitar, right here." James told him. Rolled down the top of his jeans and showed the man the left side of his hip.

"You sure?" Sheen asked him.

"Dude I was thinking about getting one when I was like sixteen but my mom wouldn't let me." Sheen laughed.

"You always listen to your mommy don't you?" James shrugged. When the man started the tattoo, James gripped the side of the chair.

"Damn."

"Oh don't be a wuss James." Sheen laughed again. He took a seat on the other side of James and watched him slowly get the outline of the electric guitar. "Okay, so it's only days before you're going to be a married man, anything you would like to share?" James' head started pounding, he didn't really feel like talking while the needle was slowly going in his skin.

"There is one thing..." James told Sheen about how he and Lavender met, about the concert, about the first kiss. He went on telling him about her and what happened at the dance and everything that recently went on with Victoria. By the time he was done, so was the guitar.

"So dude you ever.....you know screw around with her?" James smiled. Leave it to Sheen to ask such a question. Looking down he saw the tattoo. It was amazing! The rest was a blur to James until they hit the cool air outside. "You didn't answer my question, did you ever screw around?"

James let out a sigh and looked around. Suddenly he wasn't feeling very well. "You know for a first time drinker you sure hold your liquor well." At that moment James threw up on the side of the building. "Speak of the devil," Sheen said quietly.

August 24th 1993

"And do you, James Martin, take Victoria Brenden to be your lawfully wedded wife? To have and to hold from this day forward, until death do you part?"

"I don't." Gasps arose from the crowd behind him. Victoria's face was streaked with tears. "I'm sorry, I don't love you." James turned around and saw Lavender standing in back of the church. He ran over to her and lifted her up. He kissed her and then woke up.

Today was the day he got married, the day he would give up the memory of his first love. He was lying to himself, he was lying to Victoria, right now he was lying to everyone who was invited to the Church in just two hours. She had gone to sleep at her parents house so that she could get ready today at least that wasn't something he had to worry about.

He heard someone moving around in the other room. *Who the hell is it?* James soundlessly got up and grabbed the bat from the side of the bed. Holding the bat he felt like he was back in little league. Out in the hallway he could hear the strum of a guitar being played. The door to the room where he heard it was open.

Rushing in he was shocked to see Grace sitting on the floor playing the old squire.

"Grace!"

"Good morning, I didn't wake you up did I?" James rubbed his eyes and looked at his sister. She was dressed in the goofy, light pink flower girl dress Victoria had picked out. Her hair was pulled into a bun with small white flowers sticking out.

"What are you doing here?" James asked her. He took a seat next to her on the floor. She took the guitar off her lap and set it down on the side of her.

"Mom dropped me off this morning after I got ready. She went over to Victoria's house to help her get ready."

"Oh."

"Your friends should be here soon. They left a message on the machine that they would be over to see you. I heard them when I was coming in." Grace had a sad look to her, James decided as he studied her.

"Can you stand in that dress? It looks like its too heavy for you." She frowned and stood up. He hadn't noticed the matching, short pink gloves on her hands.

"Did you have any say in picking these dresses?" Grace demanded placing her hands on her hips.

"No, I only bought them. Wish I would have. It must suck having to wear them."

"Yeah and it must suck having to do what you have to do." James cocked his head to the right side.

"What do you mean?" Grace let out a sigh and walked over to the bed and flopped down.

"James...I don't know how to say this but I-" Grace was interrupted by yells and cheers coming from downstairs. Running feet came up, Nick and Sheen leading them.

"Dude! Come on time to get ready!" Nick yelled at him, James stood up and looked at his sister.

"We'll finish talking later okay?" James asked her. She nodded and watched him disappear with his friends into the other room. *Yeah we'll talk later*, she thought. Grace sulked downstairs and went into the kitchen. Opening the fridge she didn't see anything that appealed to her. Except for the two cartons of eggs.....

Grace snuck out of the bride's room and outside to the limo that Victoria and James were going to get into when they left. She didn't want to do this because James was also riding in here but it was something that just had to be done.

The basket she had been given to hold the flowers in early that morning had come in use for hiding the two cartons of eggs. All of them didn't fit so she had to stuff some into the one size too big bra she was wearing. No one was around, good she wouldn't be seen.

Grace threw the first egg and it landed on the fender some of the shell stuck but the rest fell to the ground. After throwing some onto the half open window of the limo and the tires and such, she took the other dozen in the limo itself. She put some on the seats on the floor, and even in the seat that held the small white pillow with **Bride** on it.

The driver had been asleep the whole time she was doing this but someone was watching her.

"What are you doing?" The woman's voice startled Grace as she was climbing out of the car. Slowly turning around she saw a old woman staring at her. *Only a passerby no need to worry,* Grace thought.

"None of your business," Grace told her snottily. The woman huffed and walked away from her. Quietly Grace closed the car door and ran back into the Church. The place was almost filled with all the guests. *I guess it's really taking place*, Grace thought, *He's really marrying that witch.*

How she hoped someone would stop them, when they were asked does anyone object she wished that she could be the one. When she told her mother that she said that it wasn't her place. She said James was in love with her no matter what anyone said. Grace sensed that was untrue.

When she watched her brother sleeping this morning he had been quietly been saying Lavender's name. That was who he should be with not Victoria! She really needed to see James but all his stupid friends were around him.

I really don't give a damn! Grace thought angrily as she ran over to where James was locked in the grooms room. Nick, Sheen, Will and Steven were laughing at something when she entered.

"Oh look what we have here!" Nick laughed at Grace. "Are you supposed to be the cake?" Everyone was laughing but James. He had a grim look on his face.

"I need to talk to my brother."

"He's busy right now leave a message at the beep." Nick said laughing. Grace was pissed off.

"Look you asswipes, I want to talk to my brother now!" Nick and the other guys became quiet and cleared out of the room. Grace stood across from James.

"James... I need to finish about earlier." *He is so sad, why?* Grace asked herself. Did he really want to do this? Marry her? Maybe he had seen what I've seen since day one. "Do you mind me asking if you love her?"

James gave a small laugh and stood up from the chair. "Grace all day I've been debating if I love Victoria." Grace held in her gasp. What he was saying, was it true? She looked at her older brother and smiled. He was so handsome, everyone went crazy over him. "Grace I haven't told anyone this but I went to New York and saw Lavender. And to tell you the truth.... I fell in love with her over again."

Grace wanted to dance, sing, everything she was hearing was great! "I don't know what I should do. I love Lavender, that is all I know. Something tells me that this wedding shouldn't go on and that I should be with Lavender. But Grace I just can't go out there and say that I love someone else. Not after all of this."

"But James you can't be unhappy. If Lavender makes you happy then you have to do what you have to do." James sighed.

"I can't do it. I have to get Lavender out of my head and out of my heart." Grace nodded and walked out of the room. Her brother's eyes followed her as she left. She sank down on the wall closet to the room. Why did it have to be this way?!

Father Daniels appeared next to her momentarily. "Miss Martin what are you doing sitting on the floor? The ceremony is going to take place in minutes." Grace looked up at the priest and shook her head.

"Not to be rude Father but I'm going to tell you now that God doesn't want this wedding to take place I can feel it. Something is going to happen." Daniels looked down at the girl questionably. Holding out his hand to help her up he spoke.

"You should go get ready. I think your mother was looking for you anyway. Grace stood up and heard lightning outside. *That means my eggs are going to get washed away... but not in the car*, she thought with a smile.

A moment later, no one saw Victoria disappear into the room James was in.

◦◦◦

James stood tall at the altar. A baby, this was all happening to fast! He had only had sex with her once and it was his luck, that was all it took. The faces in the crowd were filled with happiness as they watched Grace and the brides maids walk down the aisle. His gaze caught Grace's.

She hates me. He thought. James looked next to him and saw his friends standing in a line. Nick, Sheen, Steve, and Will. The music played and Victoria appeared at the beginning of the aisle. Gary Crain was holding her arm as he walked her down the isle. James fought the urge to run by putting on a smile.

In moments they were standing at the alter. The words Father Daniels said were a blur to James.

"If anyone should object to this marriage, please speak now or forever hold your peace." Grace's crossed fingers were behind her back. Come on, please someone say it!!!!

"Wait!" a voice called out from the back. Everyone turned to see Lavender standing in the back. Grace's eyes filled with hope.

"YES!!" Grace cried out. James looked at Lavender and smiled. She was dressed in an ice blue dress with matching heels, her hair was pulled back into a french twist. Her heavy breathing stopped just as he looked at her. He pulled himself away from Victoria and walked up to Lavender.

"Lav I lo-" James began to say but was interrupted.

"James what about the baby?!!!" Victoria screamed.

Chapter 17

James would never forget the look on Lavender's face when she heard what Victoria had said. Nor would he forget the gasps of the guests in the church. Lavender has stormed out of the church into the pouring rain. Victoria came over to him and shook her head.

"I've put up with you going ga-ga over her long enough! This is our wedding day!" Victoria grabbed his hand and lead him up the altar. Grace frowned and stood quiet on the steps. A short time later Victoria became Mrs. James Martin.

Grace watched Victoria's grossed out face as she slid in the limo. The eggs were sticking to her dress as she went in. Everyone around Grace ran over to help "The Princess" leaving Grace laughing to herself. James hadn't gotten in yet so he hadn't gotten any egg on him. Looking around he saw Grace laughing.

"James!" Victoria sobbed, "Someone egged our car! Who would be mean enough to do that?" With his gaze still on Grace he shrugged.

"I don't know Victoria."

Pausing as she went down the stairs, Grace listened for her mother. She hadn't been well since the wedding. She had been making calls to everyone there explaining some made up story why James had done what he did. The longest conversation so far had been with Mr. And Mrs. Crain who were downstairs right now.

"After all the money Gary and I spent James goes and does that! What was he thinking? Who was that girl and why was she there?" Mrs. Crain's loud mouth shouted. Grace was afraid to go down there fearing that she would have to sit in. The wind was making the trees move like crazy and the water fierce.

Her mother's calm voice was barely heard through Mrs. Crain's whining. *Like mother like daughter*, Grace said to herself. The shock of learning that Victoria and James were going to be parents still hadn't gone away. She hated the thought that another whining baby like Victoria would enter the world, plus she would be an Aunt!

The phone was ringing again, more people calling. How she wished this was over. Suddenly she heard James' name being used. It was James on the phone! The excitement rushed from her body. Now the next thing was going to be this baby. Everyone would start buying for him or her and then there would be babysitting.

The word Aunt rang in Grace's ears. What a terrible thing! I mean maybe if the kid had a different mother then it might be okay. She thought of the day at the Church. If she hadn't screamed about the kid then James would be with Lavender in the Carribean instead of Victoria.

Lavender was so pretty, how James went from Lavender to Victoria she had no idea.

"Grace! Come down here sweetheart," her mother called her from downstairs. Sitting up from the spot she had picked at the top of the stairs, Grace went down and was snubbed by the Crains as if she wasn't even there. Her mother handed her the phone and mouthed that James was on it.

"Hello?"

"Hi sweetie."

"Oh hi James. Having fun?"

"Tons of fun. One day I'll have to take you here the ocean is so different."

"Oh."

"We're bringing home lots of things for everyone. Wait until you see what I picked out for you."

"Oh, that's nice. I gotta go I'm kind of busy." Grace knew he was disappointed by the way he started to talk again. It hurt being on the phone with him, mostly knowing that in six months James would be a dad.

"Okay. Put Mom back on....and Grace?"

"Yeah?"

"I love you."

"Me too." Grace handed the phone back to her Mom and ran upstairs. She slammed the door for all to hear and ran to her bed. Reaching under her pillow she grabbed her old baby blanket that was now more of a string. Even though she was thirteen when things were really bad she took it out and sucked her thumb as if she were small again. Nothing would make this feeling go away.

Lavender laughed at her Grandma Molly's joke. Sitting in the living room with her elderly Grandmother, sister and Mom, Lavender almost felt back to normal. It had been two weeks since his wedding and with a little help from Faye back in Rhode Island, she had been better.

Molly Kingston, Mary Ryan's mother was pushing near eighty but she was just as healthy as thirteen year old Lizzie. Lavender looked at her and smiled. Molly had come down from her house in Maine for a once in a blue moon visit. It was good to see her again, the last time had been right before her sixteenth birthday.

"Mrs. Kingston, did you really have to walk all the way to the city and back when you got your first job?" Lizzie asked her. Lavender's gaze went over to Lizzie. *A teenager now. I remember that*, she thought with a grin.

"Dear it's Grandma, you best remember that. Yes, I had to walk to work every day from upstate New York. I babysat for Mr. and Mrs. Gold's twin boys. Gosh were they a handful!" Molly exclaimed taking a cookie from the plate her daughter had put out. Lizzie made a face and pushed her blond hair out of her eyes.

"I would never walk that far to watch some bratty kids!" she declared.

"Lizzie really doesn't like children, Mom," Mary told her. Molly smiled at Lizzie and Lavender.

"Here is some good advice to you girls, don't open your legs and you won't get pregnant. Besides both of you are too young!" She concluded. Lavender looked down at her lap and fixed the napkin.

"And what if I've already opened mine?" Lavender looked up and caught everyone's staring gaze. "I'm pregnant."

March 22nd 1994
Rhode Island

James collapsed in the chair outside of room 202 in Women and Infants Hospital. After four, long, grueling hours Victoria gave birth to a healthy baby boy. His mother had been there earlier along with his in laws to see the baby they had named Michael Adam. With Victoria sound asleep in the room, he decided to sit out here and relax.

The baby had been really late, he was supposed to be born the end of February but instead he was born late in March. Thinking about it James stopped, something didn't seem right....

James counted back nine, June....something didn't fit right. James yawned he was really too tired to care. He had rushed home when he got the call from Victoria and he hadn't been off his feet since. James had gone into work at five o'clock this morning because something was wrong with an article and the editor had to fix it.

He promised her that he would stay here tonight so that is what he had to do. With the last bit of strength James had, he walked over to the nursery where about a dozen babies were sleeping soundly. Michael was in the front of the row, moving around. He looked just like Victoria, his head full of blond hair.

Another man dressed in the same type of hospital garments walked up to the window and looked in. He looked over at James and pointed in the window.

"That's mine, right there. The girl. Her name is Samantha." James looked over at the baby he was pointing to.

"She's beautiful. This one is mine," James said pointing to Michael. The man smiled and looked at James more closely.

"I know you. You're James Martin, you work for the paper." James nodded and held out his hand.

"I don't believe I know you, what's your name?"

"Terry Shields, I was a lawyer on the Kaufman case. I remember you from your story on Kaufman. Great articles."

"Thank you."

"Say would you like to go down and get a cup of coffee with me? I sure need one."

"That would be great thanks." James replied. He followed Terry Shields down the elevator and into the dead quiet cafeteria. Getting their coffee they took a seat at one of the tables and started to talk.

"Is this your first?" James asked him.

"No, I have two older ones. The oldest girl is going into high school, and the middle girl is starting junior high. You?"

"Yeah. It's kind of weird though, when I was ten my sister was born and I spent a lot of time learning to feed her and change her. It kind of feels like I'm new at it though. Like I've never done it before."

Terry laughed watched James drink the coffee. "You'll be just fine. Remember kids don't come with owners manuals."

March 22nd 1994
New York City

Lavender sat up in the cold hospital room. The baby girl in her arms was sleeping soundly. She was the spitting image of her daddy and she wasn't even a few hours old. She had his dark hair, his blue eyes, his lips even.

Her Mother had gone home just a little while ago after they had fought. At seven months, her Mother had tried to push her into giving up the baby for adoption. Reluctantly she had almost said yes. But when she had held the baby in her arms she told her no.

"Stop holding on to him Lavender!"

"I'm not holding on to him!"

"By keeping this baby, that by the way you are not ready for, you **are** holding on to him!"

"I'll be able to handle school and still be with her!" She had felt like she was a five year old begging to get a puppy. Lavender looked down lovingly at the baby. *She has my nose,* Lavender laughed. It was hard to believe that the beautiful child was hers. It seemed as if it were a dream.

If only James could-

James. He came up when she looked down at her daughter. Lavender had told herself that she was going to that wedding only because of the fact that he had gotten her pregnant. *It was going fine until I found out she was pregnant too.* She might have been there earlier if she hadn't tried to fit into the blue dress that fit her only a month before. If only she had been there, he would be here with her looking at the newborn.

The memory of the night they had spent together replayed over and over in her mind. What a night it had been! The memory of waking up on the morning of the test and throwing up had also been an experience. At first it had came as a shock, but then again she expected it, she knew that the condom had broken.

The baby moved a little in her arms. She must have been the biggest baby born that night. She weight exactly eight pounds three ounces. Lavender looked down again and saw her open her eyes just a bit. She still hadn't decided on a name, two had stuck but they didn't seem to fit her. Suddenly it hit her!

Molly after her Grandmother who had recently passed away from an unexpected massive heart attack. Lavender thought more... James' Mother's name was Christine. So it was settled, Molly Christine Springer Martin had a name.

Victoria held Michael in her arms. Her Mother, Step-Father and Brother crowded her on her left side while, her Mother-in-law and Husband stayed to her right.

"Now can he see?" Elaine asked James. James exchanged glances with his mother and nodded.

"Yeah he can see."

"Are you sure because I'm pretty sure he can't see for six weeks." James and Mrs. Martin looked at her.

"Yeah I think my Mom is right, six weeks." Victoria nodded. James looked down at his wife and gave her a questionable look.

"What do you think he is a dog?"

"No I don't James," Elaine began taking her grandson from Victoria's arms. "Dogs can see when they are born."

Chapter 18

Five Years Later

James rested his hands on the kitchen table. Victoria sat across from him taking small sips of her coffee. The basic morning routine was being followed once again. James looked up and saw Michael dancing near the televison. At this time one of his favorite shows comes on.

The gloomy weather outside predicted rain, maybe a bad storm. There really was no telling. Sipping her drink loudly, Victoria distracted James. In the past five years she hadn't changed. Not one thing was different. Their lives boring and predictable. James didn't want to be predicable anyone!

While he worked his ass off, getting stories and listening to people shout his name twenty-four/ seven, Victoria often took to the mall buying new clothes for her already huge wardrobe. James shook those thoughts from his head. He had loved her before, when the baby had just been born and she hadn't been that big of a bitch.

James paused and questioned that. Did he really love her at all? Had he forced himself to love her?He stared over at Victoria. She wasn't the same girl that he met on his graduation, she wasn't the woman who he proposed to. He didn't love her anymore! There, he said it! In fact the only reason he married her was because of the baby. James glanced over at Michael.

The little boy was a sweetheart, but he had a lot of her in him. James looked back at Victoria. If he came home late she immediately thought that he was having an affair with someone. Sometime he wondered why she thought this, because if she assumed he was then she would be indicating that she possibly could have had one.

The doorbell rang suddenly. Victoria got up to answer it before James could even move. Minutes later she came into the room, a worried expression on her face.

"What's wrong?" A second later a tall blond figure emerged into the room. James jumped up and ran to the kitchen, his hand ready to grab the knife in the sink.

"Jamie, what is wrong? I thought you would be happy to see me." Erich sneered. He was supposed to be in jail, why the hell was he here?! He moved closer into the dining room looking around. "Nice house ya got here Jamie. I remember I used to live here. Remember that?"

"What the fuck are you doing here?" James demanded, his hand was grazing the knife. He saw that Victoria had taken a seat at the table.

"I came to see my son."

"What?" he asked confused. Victoria held her mouth quiet. Looking from Victoria to Erich the connection was made.

"My son. Michael. You know that little bundle of joy over there," Erich responded slowly and pointed to the child who was too into his show to even care what was going on. "Hadn't dear Victoria told you of our little rondeau while you were away in New York? Had she not told you that we met in a bar and I took her home?" an evil twisted grin that James had seen before appeared on his face.

James picked up the knife and threw it at Erich but he ducked out of the way. "You know Jamie, being in prison teaches you something. It's just not about making licence plates or getting into fights. It's about becoming a family, for which I did with them." Erich bent down and picked up the knife. "Now Jamie, I have a family. I have sweet Michael and beautiful Victoria. What do you have? Lavender is gone you gave her up remember?"

"Get the hell out before I call the cops," James gritted through his teeth. Erich held up his hands and moved to the door.

"I'll be going Jamie, but I just want you to know that Michael is mine. So is the beauty queen here." He stroked her long hair tenderly then waved goodbye and made his way out the front door. James stood stunned for a moment, letting his brain hear all that had told him.

He paced back and forth in the large kitchen. Victoria sat the kitchen table, trying to hold back tears. Anger, hate, and betrayal were the words that popped into his head as if a movie trailer had said them. He shook his head and looked at her. She looked up, her brown eyes begging for forgiveness.

"What have you done?"

"I'm sorry." she sobbed.

"It's a little too late for sorry Victoria!" James screamed at her. She sobbed louder. "You slept with him and got pregnant. Then you passed the baby off as mine!"

Victoria stood up and walked over to him and grabbed his right arm. "James I'm sorry! I'm sorry! I made a mistake. I didn't know who he was!"

"Me, me, me! Is that it Victoria? I made a mistake, I slept with a guy I didn't know while my fiancee was in New York, now I'm pregnant and I'll just say the kid is James'. Push-over James won't know the difference, he's just a sucker who'll believe anyone!"

"Shut up!"

"No! I'm tired of being pushed over and I thought you loved me, and you wouldn't do something like this to me! Tell me how many other men have gotten in your pants since we've been married?"

"James!" She pleaded.

"Why did you do this to me?"

"I was mad! I was mad at you because you wanted her to come and I just wanted to get revenge. I swear to you that I didn't know who he was!" James went back to pacing back and forth while she spoke. "I'm sorry, I'm sorry for everything!"

"You don't even know," James said slowly, he walked up to her and looked down upon her. "You don't even know what I went through. You don't know how for hours I was locked up and hit until I bled! You have not a clue of what he did. Did you even question why he was in jail? Of course not!" James screamed at her. He stepped away and startled making his way up the stairs for the bedroom.

Slamming the door behind him he ran to the closet and grabbed a suitcase from the back. Without thinking he just started throwing clothes into the bag not worrying if it all fit. He heard her footsteps while he was in the bathroom grabbing his toiletries.

"Where are you going?"

"Away," he said turning to her. "I'll be gone for maybe a week, in that time I expect that you will find a place to go. This is over, I'm going to be filing for a divorce."

"No please!" she begged, as she fell to her knees at his feet. "Please I'm so sorry!" James sneered at her and walked back to his suitcase. She stood up as he was lifting the suitcase off he bed.

"You're a bastard!"

"And you're a whore! Jesus Christ I can't believe you!" James yelled as he walked past her. He threw his bag in the car and drove away.

⁂

With the windows down in the new Lexus James had bought last winter, he cruised onto Fry Pond Road with the radio blaring. He pulled into the gravel driveway and slammed on the brakes. Looking over the house it was just as he remembered it last summer.

The old country home had been bought as an investment and was going to be rented out. So far no one had lived in it. James stepped out of the car and grabbed the duffle bag from the passenger's seat. Taking out the unmarked key from his pocket, he made his way up to the door and let himself in.

He really loved this house. Deep wood floors with a tremendous fireplace the living room was described as cozy and elegant. James looked out the window and into the woods. A pond and fire pit were the only clearing you could see among the trees. It needed cleaning, the furniture looked one hundred years old sitting there caked with dust. He would have to run to the store too, to get food for the time he was going to be there.

An hour later, James had returned from Stop and Shop with more than two months of food and three bags of cleaning supplies. When he was walking through the store throwing food into the cart he asked himself what the hell he was doing. In less than an hour of leaving Victoria, he felt a relief.

Did he really intend to stay at this house? Was he going to get a divorce from her? Nothing was holding him back! *Michael, well look how that turned out,* James thought putting away the shopping. He didn't know what to feel right now. Thinking about Michael he saw Erich.

The eye shape and facial expressions, even the way he said words sometimes. Was that even remotely possible?

"They belong together," James said aloud. They were both conniving, lying sneaks! By Wednesday morning everyone will hear the past of the story that wasn't true. Mostly likely sounding like, "James left Victoria and Michael. Victoria is so upset!" *Yeah well I'm upset too!* Though no one would ever know his story. How was he to say that the baby was Erich's and he had shown up the house.

"You're so stupid James!" he told himself. Why on the face of Earth had he thrown a knife at him? He should have beat the shit out of him the way he had gotten it. Those painful memories never fail to make an appearance.

Sucking in air he stopped and remembered. That night he had been scared. Terrified even. The cold chilling floor rubbing against his hurting back. James winced and tried to get it out of his head. Often at night he had been having dreams of that night. Was it a warning to him?

Maybe it was some kind of deja vu. James' cell phone that he hadn't realized was in his pocket had begun to ring.

"Hello?"

"James where are you? What's up you didn't show up for work today, I called the house and Victoria is sobbing. What is going on?" Sheen asked him desperately. Sheen had been there for him the past few years, always knowing when he should cut down on work or go out to unwind.

"Ah...Victoria and I are separated. I got a little surprise at breakfast this morning. Trust me its something you do not want to hear."

"Man I'm sorry. Anything I can do?"

"No I just want to be alone. I'm taking my vacation now. I have some things to do up at the other house. That's where I am now."

"How long you gonna be out there?"

"I have about two weeks vacation coming so I think I'll take it. Sheen, you know any good divorce lawyers?"

"Wow dude a divorce, I gotta know the story." Sighing James finished putting away the breads.

"Alright if you want to come up you're welcome but this time won't be like last time!" James warned him. The last time they had been up at the house Sheen had brought five cases of beer and drank ever single drop. He had been so drunk that James had to take him home and make sure he took aspirin.

"Promise. I'll be up later. See ya."

"Bye." James hung up and placed the phone on the counter. With a few hours he would be able to clean up and then hopefully look in the phone book for lawyers.

✦

"That is pretty heavy shit," Sheen said flatly. James sat facing him, his legs on each side of the chair. "So what are you going to do?"

James sat up straight then moved out of the chair. "It's over. I mean after everything that went on when I was a kid I see him again and he's the father of the boy I've been raising."

"James we've been friends for a few years, it always seemed like this big mystery with your brother. Why? Something happen between you guys?" James swallowed and let his head fall to his chin.

"Are you willing to listen?"

"Yeah."

"Are you sure?"

"Yes!"

"Fine. My brother had given me tickets to go see a band-"

"This is when you went out with that girl right?"

"Yes. Anyway, the tickets were fake. We ended up seeing the show and later on we found out he had told our parents where we were. The next day me and Lavender were downstairs in the basement and I went away for a minute and he was trying to rape her. I hit him and he threw me against the wall. I'll cut this part short...so later on I came home everyone was in bed sleeping, he dragged me down the cellar."

"Sheen you wouldn't believe it even if you seen it, huge room with torture shit. I was horrified. I spent the next two weeks in the hospital. I have one scar left and my tattoo is covering it."

Sheen sat speechless staring at James. "Wow!" James gave a little smile then went to get a drink out of the fridge. "So did he go to jail?"

"Yup, eighteen and a half years. I guess he got out early. I really don't care as long as he stays the hell away from me. He'll have a good time with that tramp, lets see if he can keep up with her spending."

"You're not scared that he'll come after you?"

"I don't know. But I can handle myself." He nodded and looked outside.

"So what's your love life going to look like now? You gonna get back with that girl?" James laughed.

"Lavender? She's long gone now Sheen. I'm kicking myself for being a dope...I guess it's one of those things you don't know what you have until its gone. Problem is I know what I had, I just wanted to have my cake and eat it too."

"What if she's single? What if she wants to see you?"

"And what if she's not? What if she had moved on like I had? Then what? Where do I go from there?"

"Well you wouldn't be losing anything if she is married or whatever."

"I can't show up at her doorstep."

"You want to though. Is it because you love her?" Sheen teased. James made a face at him.

"Grow up man."

"You love her. Come to think of it you've said you loved her when you talk about her. I was too drunk to realize what you were really saying."

"Yeah what's that?"

"That you adore her and want to be with her ever second of the day until you die!" Sheen dropped to the floor and played dead.

"You make me sound like a moron."

"You are a moron."

"Shut up!"

When James returned four weeks later to his house in Cranston, he found all of their things gone and divorce papers on the table. James rubbed his forehead and looked around. He had gotten the call yesterday that Grace needed to move out of the apartment that she was in to save up money for her car payment. Once again that will be taken care of, James thought.

When he had talked to his mother, she seemed strange, she sounded as if she was high. James had shrugged it off but he still wanted to find out. Going back to work he had a huge story sitting on his desk. He had to go and interview the head pediatrician at Hasbro Children's hospital.

"Just what I need to go sit with some know it all quack doctor."

Chapter 19

Setting off for the Hasbro Children's Hospital after his new habit of three cups of black coffee, James moved swiftly to the car. He guessed this is what they said about Mondays, that they were always bad. Saturday he had helped Grace move out of her dorm apartment and into his house.

When he arrived he parked and rode the elevator up to the sixth floor where the Head Pediatrician's office was. He secretly hoped that the interview would be quick, why he didn't know. He didn't have anything to do, most of his friends weren't talking to him because of the divorce- Nick especially.

If only Nick knew what a slut his sister was. Of how she tricked him and connived her way into his inner core. How could he have let her? How was he so stupid? James sighed and stepped off the elevator and into a cozy office waiting room. A older woman sat at the receptionist desk. Her short salt and pepper hair in curls.

James walked to her and placed his hands on the desk. "I'm here to see the Chief Resident, I didn't catch his or her name."

The woman looked up at him with a warm smile, "Your name?"

"James Martin, I'm with Providence Journal," said James as he showed her his press badge.

"Okay, well the doctor is with a patient right now, but she requested that you wait in her office. I'll take you there follow me." The elderly woman said standing up. James followed her down a long corridor, the walls were painted a light yellow and pictures of children hung on the walls.

They came to the end of the hall and the woman opened a stained glass door. He stepped inside and looked around. The maroon carpet, he could tell, was soft under his feet even with shoes on. More pictures of children hung on the wall, the back wall of the office was medical books in tall mahogany book cases.

"She'll only be a few minutes. Can I get you anything? Water, Coffee?"

"No thank you."

"If you need me I'll be up front, there is an intercom button on the desk, feel free to push it if you need something. My name is Rita."

"Thank you," he said watching her leave. James took a seat in one of the dark leather chairs in front of the desk. While taking out his notebook and pen his cell phone rang.

"James Martin."

"James, it's Grace, where are you?"

"I'm waiting to do an interview. Why?"

"Can you possibly explain why I'm just finding that you have the file from Dad's crime scene?!" Grace yelled over the phone.

James sighed, "How did you find out?"

"I was in the office ."

"So you were going through my things?" James asked angrily.

"He was my Father too James! I should know!"

"Grace can't I just have five Goddamn minutes to myself? I'm so tired of this! Just leave me alone for-" James cut himself short when he heard the door open. He turned around and his eyes widened. He stopped talking, all he could hear was Grace saying his name over and over again. James regained himself and shut the phone.

"Lav?"

" James," Lavender said walking over to her desk.

"What are you doing here?"

"I'm chief resident." He should have remembered that she was going to med school.

"You...look amazing."

"Thanks, you look good too." Everything came pouring back to him, he remembered the taste of her lips when he kissed her, the warmth of her body when he held her, the scent of her hair...

"Wow, I'm in shock from seeing you. I feel as though I'm looking a ghost."

"Um...thanks? So how have you been?" she said taking her seat across from him.

"Oh um...you could say okay. How about you?"

"Fine. How is everyone?"

"Grace is living with me to save up money and my Mom is fine.."

"That's great."

"Yeah."

"How is everyone on your side?"

Lavender smiled, she had missed Jeremy and Lizzie since she moved back here. "My Mom and Jeremy are good. Lizzie is all grown up now, she's in Harvard."

"That's amazing."

"I'm really proud of her." an awkward silence passed between them for a long time. "How is your married life, if you don't mind me asking?"

"We divorced, it's a long story. How about you did you ever marry?"

"No I was too busy for the dating scene. I'm sorry to hear about the divorce also. What about your child?" Lavender asked quietly.

"Yet another long story, the baby wasn't mine."

"What?!" Lavender exclaimed, her heart jumped with joy with his response. "It wasn't your baby?"

"No, he belonged to someone else." James gave a small laugh and looked at her. "I miss this. I miss how I could tell you everything that was going on in my life, and how you would always make it better. Do you remember the time that we went over to Rocky Point and you-"

"James please," Lavender begged. James stood up and walked around the desk and knelt at her knees.

"Listen to me. I spent too much time away from you; I want things back the way they were. Can we start over? I don't think that I could stand losing you again." James watched her desperately trying to not look at him. "Have dinner with me tonight, please."

"I...can't.... I have responsibilities."

"To what?... Have dinner with me. Please."

Lavender sucked in air and looked into his eyes, the eyes she loved, the eyes she saw every day... "Okay, Tonight."

"Good, I'll pick you up at seven thirty." James smiled and stood up from the floor. He watched her stand up and face him. He was taller by five inches.

"I have to go. Kids need taking care of and things....."

"Yeah, um...me too."

"So I'll see you tonight?"

"Yeah."

"Bye."

"See ya." Lavender smiled and walked out of the office. He stood there for a long moment, half shocked that she said yes, half unsure if he was doing the right thing. It would all come down tonight.

At four James called Lavender to get directions to the house, then went back to the house to do some work then get ready. Grace was locked up in her room ever since she heard James put the key in the lock. He was debating whether or not to bring her back food tonight.

He called Hemenway's on the way home for reservations, he got an outdoor table for them. The weather should be nice tonight, not too cold, or too hot. James started to get ready at six thirty and was done by seven ten. He had twenty minutes to get there, in which he only needed ten.

Before leaving he went over to Grace's room and knocked on the door. "Grace?"

"Go away dirtbag!"

"Grace open the door."

"No!"

"Please open the door." James said firmly.

"Make me!"

"Grace I can take this door right off the hinges if you would like me too."

"Then I'll move into the other room!"

James was getting angrier by the second. "Grace you're pissing me off now! Come out of the bedroom!" James waited a few moments and then stepped away from the door. "I'm going out. So you can come out when I leave if you want to act like the big baby that you are showing me that you can be right now. Goodnight!" Not a sound came from the room as James went down the dimly lit stairs. When he was downstairs he heard the doorknob turn on the bedroom door and a pair of size seven and a half feet running down the stairs.

He stood in the kitchen waiting for her to get there. She appeared, tears streaked her face, her shirt was wrinkled and hair tangled. Grace ran over to him and wrapped her arms around his long torso. He held her close and after a few minutes pulled her off him.

"I know Grace. I know how you feel. I swore I would get to the bottom of it and I'm going to...Look I gotta go, we'll talk tonight when I get home." He told her leaning down and kissing the top of her head. She shook her head and let her hands fall to her thighs.

He turned and left, not making a sound all the way to her house. Pulling up in front of 659 Mia Court he studied the house. It was a two story modern house with green grass lining from the front to the backyard. It was painted white with a soft blue trim. He stopped the car and got out. Before he even made it up the walk the door opened and Lavender emerged. She looked stunning, her hair was pinned up into a french twist and she was dressed in a short black skirt and a three quarter mint green colored top.

"You look beautiful." She blushed remembering the day he told her she was beautiful at the hospital.

"Thank you," Lavender said walking up to him. He looked down at her hand and grasped it. She squeezed his hand and started to walk down the rest of the walk. "So where to?"

"Hemenway's. Is that okay?"

"It's perfect."

"Good," James said. He walked around to the passenger side, opened the door and let her get in. After he shut the door he ran to the drivers side and hopped in.

"This is a great car."

"Thank you, the payments aren't that great though." Lavender laughed. "So are you ready?"

"Yeah, you?"

"Yes." James said slowly. He turned to look at her and their eyes met. He leaned in to kiss her lips, he kissed her full on without her objecting. After a moment they pulled apart and laughed. "I feel like I'm ten again."

"That's funny."

"Why?"

"Cause you didn't get your first kiss until you were fourteen."

☙❧

"Thank you," James said to the waiter as he brought the drinks they had ordered. The glass room of Hemenway's was packed, as was the outdoor area. Two menus were placed in front of them by the waiter.

"Order when you are ready." James nodded and opened his menu. After a little while, the waiter came back.

"Do you know what you would like to have tonight?" James looked over at Lav and saw that she already had her menu down.

"I'm going with the lobster," James told him.

"I think I'll have the snow crab," The waiter wrote this down and then took the menus.

"Good choice." James told her. "I should have gotten it, it sounds great. So....How did you end up taking a job at Hasbro?"

"Well I had been working in Manhattan for a year and a job opened at Hasbro and they looked at my record and with my grades and such they offered me the job. How about you, how did you make your way to the top?"

"I hit a big story and they promoted me. You know how big stories are in this state," said James.

"So how is everyone else? I haven't seen the old gang."

"Well Steven Gabriel is married to a girl he met up in Boston and Will is in the marines. Ray is out in Vegas with his family and Nick is still doing the same thing, getting with as many girls as he can. I haven't spoken to him recently."

"Why?"

"He says I abandoned Victoria and Michael, her son. He doesn't know what really went on though."

"What really did go on?" she asked curiously.

"I'll tell you later." The food arrived minutes later, each meal was extraordinary. James paid the bill and soon they found themselves driving back to her house. It was almost ten o'clock when they arrived back. James stopped the car in front of the house and stared into the dark street.

"Do you want to come in for coffee?"

"Sure," he answered her. They walked quietly to the front door. Lavender took out her key and inserted it into the lock. James walked in after her and looked around. It was tastefully designed with modern paintings, some he recognized from the New York apartment. He followed her into the living room where he saw a woman sitting up on the couch.

The woman turned around and James flipped. "Mrs. Ryan?" James asked uncertain of what he was seeing. She hadn't told him her mom was here! The older woman stood up and walked over to him, and placed her hands on his shoulders.

"My James, how handsome you are. how are you dear?" she talked to him as if she had seen him yesterday and as if she hadn't told him to stay away from her daughter. Her red hair was slowly turning a greyish-white and some wrinkles appeared near her light eyes.

"I'm fine Mrs. Ryan." James looked for Lavender who was turning off the televison that her mother had on.

"That's excellent James," she began. James and Lavender watched her walk to the coat rack and grab her coat. "Well Dears I must be going. It was nice seeing you again James. Lavender I'll call you tomorrow. Goodnight." He watched her leave and then turned to Lav.

"You didn't tell me your Mother was here." Lavender walked over to the couch and sat down.

"She's here for the summer until I get settled." James walked over to the couch and sat down next to her. An awkward silence passed them before anyone spoke. "So what happened with Victoria?"

James sighed and looked at her. "I married her, then Michael was born in March. Things were okay for the first three years, then she became secretive, staying away from me so on occasion I would sleep in my office not wanting to go home to see her. I was trying to avoid my unhappiness.

Then one morning, I was downstairs and Victoria sat at the kitchen, the next thing I knew Erich was in the house."

"I went berserk, I wanted to know what he was doing here, he said he came to see his son." At that Lavender gasped, for she had already figured it out. "He left and I questioned her, she had a fling with the guy not knowing who he was. She didn't know anything!"

"Please James don't yell," Lavender pleaded.

"Sorry. She passed him off as mine and everyone thinks that he really is mine and I abandoned him...... I blame myself for my father's death. I didn't even cry when he died. There must be something wrong with me! Everyone's life is being put on my shoulders and I don't want to carry it any longer, I shouldn't have to!" Lavender scooted over to him.

"There is nothing wrong with you James. There is nothing wrong," she whispered putting her arms around him. "There was never anything wrong with you."

James looked up at her and kissed her lightly. Lavender's hands held him close to her body. She kissed him hard. She wanted him, it was all she ever wanted, to be with him. James' kisses moved to her neck, his lips hungrily on her skin. Lavender caught her breath feeling his hands move up her shirt, massaging her breasts. "James-" He moved her shirt up more exposing smooth skin. Lavender lifted her arms over her head and let him take off her top. Left in her white bra, James placed his mouth on the swell of her breasts tasting her. Lavender's breath became heavy.

"Take me upstairs," she demanded. He stood up and followed her up the long stair case, they paused at the second landing kissing and touching more before they moved into the narrow hallway leading to her bedroom. When they neared her bedroom, she pulled away.

"I can't do this. You have to know. You have to know the reason I came to that church." She looked down and started to cry. Lavender grabbed his hand and pulled him down the hall and made him stand in front of the white door. Slowly she opened the door... James looked inside and saw a tiny body sleeping under a light blanket. James peered at the body and realized that it was a beautiful little girl. He turned back to Lavender. Tears took over her eyes.

"You married?"

"No James! No! God! I was pregnant. I was pregnant with your child!" James felt as though he was having a heart attack, thoughts came pouring back to him over the night in New York. James stared at the sleeping girl and looked back at Lavender, still in her white bra.

"But we-"

"It broke James."

"Why didn't you tell me?!"

"What the hell was I suppose to do James? Walk into your house and say that I'm pregnant and you can't marry her?"

"You were going to do that at the church though weren't you?"

"That was different!" Lavender protested.

"How was it?"

"Okay fine, it wasn't! Look, I'm doing just fine without you so if you want to just leave then I'll continue to raise and love her the same way I was doing before I saw you again."

James grabbed Lavenders arms and looked into her sad eyes. "I won't let you do that! If there is one thing I have learned from these experiences its that every single day of my life I have never stopped loving you! I won't abandon her either."

"You said it."

"What?"

"You said I love you."

"I do. I do love you." He pushed Lavender to him and kissed her deeply. He broke the kiss and looked at her again. "I want you to tell me everything, I want to see every picture of her."

"I would be happy to show you." Lavender smiled and then closed the door of her bedroom.

◈

"Her favorite sandwich is peanut butter and fluff, nice and healthy right? She loves Rugrats and Little Bear ."

James watched with awe as they sat downstairs watching a fire they had made grow dim in the early morning. Photo albums were scattered everywhere and different baby clothes , toys and such lay around them.

"Tell me the night she was born," James asked. Lavender laughed remembering it.

"That's an interesting story. A long, painful, interesting story if you get my drift. What's interesting about it is that Faye called me after Molly was born to tell me that a little boy shared the same birthday as my daughter. Michael Martin of Cranston Rhode Island."

"Mommy?"

Chapter 20

James quickly turned around and looked at the small girl standing there dressed in a long night gown. It was him. He was looking at the same blue eyes, same hair color, mouth, everything! Lavender walked over to her and lifted her up. She brought her over to the couch and sat back down.

His heart was beating out of his chest. It hadn't hit him until this second that Lavender had given birth to her and raised her while he took care of Victoria's child. Thoughts and feelings of uneasiness began to settle in his stomach. James stared at the girl and wondered what she knew. Had she ever asked about her dad?

Lavender stroked Molly's long, silky brown hair. Placing a kiss on top of her head she turned Molly to face her. "Do you recognize this man sweetheart?" Molly nodded in agreement and turned back to face James.

"He's the man from the pictures. My daddy." Resisting the urge to grab the unfamiliar child and take her in his arms James sat motionless on the couch. "I'm right aren't I Mommy?"

"Yes you are, this is your daddy." Molly hopped off the couch and walked a few steps over to James. Standing before him she smiled. Her tiny arms sprang to his neck and she was hanging to him hugging him.

"Mommy said you were gone but I just knew you would come to be with us! I just knew it!" His arms flew to hold her tight in his grip. All the nonsense that had been going on seemed gone and forgotten. James closed his eyes and listened to her breath. Opening them again he saw Lavender had tears in her eyes.

Molly pulled away from him and stared at her mother. "Why are you sad Mommy?" Lavender quickly wiped her tears and lifted her daughter back into her arms.

"I'm not sad honey. Sometimes when people are happy they cry."

"Are you happy that Daddy is here?"
"Yes. I am happy that Daddy is here."

On top of the world James seemed to float into the house. Locking the front door he heard the televison click off and the sound of sneakers running down the hard wood floor. Grace appeared, completely dressed and full of energy.

"So...how was the date? It must have gone well seeing you were out all night." a silly grin was wide across her face.

"I have news for you."

"Really? What is it?"

"You're an Aunt again."Grace's smile went to a frown.

"What? Who were you with last night?!" James laughed and hugged Grace. He had told her about Victoria and Michael when he had reported it to his Mom a few weeks after the separation.

"I went out to dinner last night with the love of my life." Grace seemed confused then after a few minutes of silence she caught on.

"Lavender?" James told her about Molly quickly before going up to shower. He had promised that he would be back later to see Lavender and Molly. Thinking about the past few hours, James couldn't really believe it. What was to happen now? Were they going to marry? If they didn't, what about Molly?

He had made it pretty clear last night that Lavender was the love of his life and there wasn't anyone else for him.

She hung on to his neck while he kissed her lips, after parting she let her mouth go to his ear. "By the way...I didn't get to tell you that the tattoo on you hip looks really hot..." James smiled and pushed her away.

"Want to see it again?" She kissed his lips quickly then looked away.

"Later, we have a guest." Molly came running down the stair case and crashed into James' body. James squatted down and took her into his arms.

"Hey Molly, how does going out to get something to eat sound. Then I'll take you over to zoo. Mommy hasn't taken you there yet has she?" Molly shook her head then looked at Lavender. "Mommy are you going to come?" Lavender smiled and looked at the boy who, when he was twelve got her out of bed to come see the fireflies in the woods. Her Mom had never found out she had been out past midnight..

"I think that Mommy is going to get some work done. Why don't you and Daddy just go, we'll do something later. Now go get changed." Molly ran upstairs and into her bedroom.

James walked further in the door and grabbed Lavender's hand. "Why don't you want to go?"

"You need to spend time with Molly. She wants to be alone with you anyway." James nodded and walked to the stair case.

"Is it okay if I go up and get her?"

"Be my guest." James walked up the staircase and made his way to Molly's room. The white door was open revealing a bright pink and purple wall paper. A play kitchen, dolls, books and videos were neatly around the room. Molly sat on the floor struggling to put on her shoes. The denim skort she was wearing went perfectly with the pretty blue top with flowers on it.

James walked in the room and sat down next to her. "Do you need some help?" She nodded and handed him her shoe.

"I can't tie like Mommy."

"When you're bigger you'll be able to."

"Will you teach me?."

"Of course." James finished with her shoes then picked her up and bounced her downstairs. Lavender was in the kitchen looking over a file of some sort. Looking up she smiled at them.

"Are you already to go?" James responded to her with a yes. Letting Molly down he watched her run to Lavender. "Have a good time sweetie." she told her hugging her gently. They all walked to the door and stood there for a moment.

"Do you want her back at a certain time?"

"Take as long as you'd like."

"Okay." James leaned down and kissed her lips slowly before going out the door.

"Look at the lion Daddy!" Molly squealed pointing to the huge lion sitting in the grass. The Roger William's Zoo was dead quiet today, the only sounds were from the animals and Molly.

"I know he's very pretty." Molly turned to him, on her face he could see Lavender's expression.

"Its *handsome* Daddy, not pretty." James laughed and took her hand leading her away from the lions. "What's your favorite animal?"

He thought about it for a minute. That brought back memories. Him sitting around with his friends playing with toy cars and animals. "I think that my favorite animal is a dog because they give lots of kisses!" He picked her up and gave repeated kisses on her rosy, cheeks. She laughed all the way out of the zoo and halfway to Newport....

James should have called before going all the way down to Newport. His mother wasn't home when they got there at three o'clock. So he thought he would take her to meet someone else who was very special.

"Where are we going?" Molly asked when they got into Cranston. Turning right onto his street he watched the car of Tony Rosenti, his neighbor, go by him.

"I'm taking you to meet someone who is very special."

"Who Daddy?" He loved when she called him daddy, at first it had seemed strange but as she said it more and more it became natural to him. Sure Michael had called him Daddy but this was *his* little girl saying it.

"Your Auntie Grace. I told her all about you."

"Is she nice?"

"Yes she's very nice." James pulled into the driveway, got Molly out of the car and into the house.

"Grace?!" James called from the doorway. He helped Molly take off the light jacket she was wearing and hang it on the coat rack. Molly tugged on James' jeans and began to speak.

"I have another Auntie too. Auntie Liz. She lives in New York with Grandpa and Grandma." Grace came some-what sprinting down the stairs. She paused and looked at Molly for a moment then came down slowly.

"My God... She's a clone of you. Just a girl though."

" She has Lavender's nose." James bent down wrapping his hands gently around his daughters arms. "Molly, this is your Auntie Gracie." Grace bent down reached to touch Molly's silky hair.

"She's like a porcelain doll...too precious to touch."

" I was taking her up to see Mom but she was not home do you know where she is?" Grace hesitated then looked behind her.

"Mom is in the kitchen. And uh.....she doesn't know about her. I didn't say a word." James stood up and let out a sigh. What was going to be her reaction? He had just found out that the son he had been raising wasn't his and now he had a child of his own. James took Molly's hand and lead her into the kitchen. His mother stood at the kitchen counter talking on the phone.

It was just like when she use to live here. His mother looked over at him and gave a little wave, then she saw the small hand in his hand. Quickly she hung up the phone and walked over to him.

"James who is this?" She asked trying to hide he astonishment. As if she were weightless, James picked Molly up again.

"Mom...this is Molly. Molly this is your Grandma." His mother's face went completely white. It wasn't possible that this child was Victoria's, had James been having an affair?

"James? I don't understand. This girl isn't your daughter!"

"Yes she is!"

"This is my Daddy," Molly said softly. She had kept quiet all this time. "My Mommy told me so." His mother walked over to James closer and up to the little girl in his arms.

"What's your name sweetie?"

"Molly Christine Springer." Sure that his mother would faint anytime James took his hand to her shoulder steading her. Looking from the girl to James the words she wanted to say were caught in her throat. Her son had a child with his childhood sweetheart. It was something she always saw coming but she never thought she would be in shock.

"Your Mommy is Lavender."

"Yes! Do you know my Mommy?" Molly exclaimed, her eyes lit bright with excitement. A flash back from the day of the wedding came to her. Lavender had looked like she gained weigh, of course she had only seen her from a far but something you can just tell. When in all the things that were happening then could she have gotten pregnant?

"I know your Mommy very well. You know she used to live right across the street." Christine Martin pushed a colored brown strand from her face. "Your Mommy is very lucky to have such a pretty and smart little girl like you." She saw her son smile and put his daughter back down on the ground.

"Molly sweetheart why don't you go see Auntie Grace upstairs. I know that she is dying to see you more."

"Okay Daddy." Molly ran out of the kitchen a moment later. James stood face to face with his mother. He didn't know if she was going to hit him upside the head or embrace him for being a good boy.

"James, what is going on?"

"Why is it that no one says hello anymore?"

"If that girl looked nothing like you I would think that you were lying to me but she is a replica of you when you were her age. I should know. What is going on? How is it that her mother is Lavender?!"

Sighing James walked into his kitchen and got himself a bottle of water from the fridge. "Before the wedding I went to New York and me and Lavender slept together. She was at the wedding to tell me about Molly. If what had gone on hadn't happened I would have been with Lavender and Molly 300 percent. Friday morning I went to do an interview and I saw Lav. We went out to dinner and I learned about the baby."

"James what's going to happen now? Are you getting married are you going to get to see her on weekends if you don't get together? The way that girl looks and talks to you, you can clearly see that she adores you."

"Mom, Lavender and I are going to work it out. Trust me I'm not going to screw this up. I've only been with this kid a day and I adore her just as much as she does me." His mother nodded and tearfully went up to her son, squeezing him tightly.

※

The night six months later would mean something special for James. Not only was it the day that the divorce was final but it was also a night for Him and Lavender to be alone. They had went out to dinner earlier and then they decided to go down to Narragansette Pier. Walking along, a light breeze blew while the waves crashed against the side of the rocks and tall pillars.

"I got the divorce final today." James told her breaking the silence between. She looked at her excitedly. She was happy for him, all the shitty things that the witch had done could go behind him. Something made her think that it could be a new start for them.

"So do you have to pay child support for Michael?"

"No."

"Are you still going to see him?"

"I don't know. I haven't seen him all this time. Why should I see him now?"

"You raised him for five years. You don't have a bond?"

Thinking about it for a second he came back with no. "She always had him. I rarely saw him. Lav can we talk about us for a minute." At the end of the pier they stood watching the waves for a moment.

"There is something I need to say-"

"Shoot."

"Want to know a secret?" Slowly she nodded. "When we were seventeen and you had just told me that you were leaving, I took all my money and went to a small, run down, jewelry store and bought a diamond engagement ring. I had it in my pocket at the airport," James kneeled down and pulled out a box from his pocket and opened it.

In it the ring was perfectly protected, though old, it sparkled and shined like it was just bought. Taking her left hand, he placed the diamond ring on it. Looking up at her James saw she was crying. "The decision was made in a heartbeat from the moment I met you. Lavender Springer, will you marry me?"

"YES! YES I WILL!" James laughed and stood up. She jumped into his arms, laughing, crying and so sure that nothing could ever tear them apart again.

Chapter 21

June 21, 1999

Lavender sighed as she pushed the tall file folders away from her. The dark wood desk was crowded with papers from different files of patients ranging from three months old to five years old. Looking down at her left hand she caught the sparkle of her engagement ring. Only one month away.

The planning was almost done. Ceremony, caterers, guest lists... everything except for her dress. Something she wanted to put off but she couldn't wait until the last minute! With everything going on for the wedding, taking care of Molly and on top of everything else work, she didn't think she could handle much more.

She smiled again, James had been so great with Molly. Picking her up from dance class, or taking her to school. One night she had asked him if he ever was in trouble for dropping out of work at crazy hours. "I'm the boss. I can leave when I need or want to." The image of James just walking out of the newsroom while everyone else was running like chickens without heads, made her laugh.

The private ceremony was being held at the Coachman, a pretty little place where it would be just enough for the people they were inviting. She had only invited the first hundred, James had invited the second, making it 200 people crammed into a room. It was mostly family and friends on her side. A few colleges here and there, some friends from college that she had been close with.

James had practically invited the whole newspaper! His family was small, and his plan was to make it up with people who worked for him. Lav knew that the one person that James needed to be there was his best friend. He had told Sheen Cortes that he was the best man but that might just end in tragedy.

Sheen wasn't the guy who had sleep overs in James' back yard or at his house when they were kids. Does Sheen know him like I do? Or like...... Nick does? Nick was who he needed. The second person in James' life that he could trust- well for a little while.

Lavender really didn't like Sheen. He seemed sneaky. But he was James' friend and she had to accept it. Nick needed to be there standing next to James. Not Sheen. She had urged him to call and explain what happened to him and then become friends again. *He had such a hard head, and he is so damn stubborn!* Lav shook her head and sat up straight. This chair was killing her back.

The other pictures on the desk were of her and James, Molly, also of her parents and sister. They were all coming in for the wedding. Even Liz who was getting out of a summer school course. It would be great to see them again. The last time had been when she moved here last year. Her mother had visited but not Jeremy and Liz.

Her mother had given her a heads up that Lizzie was deeply involved with a Harvard law student. Then quietly she had asked if Lizzie could bring him along. *What could I say no?* Lavender thought. Besides it would be good for her. When she had been sixteen a nasty break-up had broken her heart into two huge pieces.

A knock at the door signaled someone she hadn't been expecting. Her future sister-in-law Grace.

"Grace, what are you doing here?" Grace walked in and took a seat across from Lavender. Lavender saw that Grace and her James shared the same shape eyes and nose. Her long brown hair was pulled back into a pony-tail and the fashionable velour sweat suit she was wearing, had been her birthday present from Lavender..

"Lav do you have a minute?"

"I always have time for family." Grace nodded and placed the small purse she was carrying on the floor.

"Can I talk to you without saying anything to my brother? Or anyone else for that matter?"

"Is there something wrong? Are you okay? Are you sick?" Lavender asked concerned. She didn't look sick, just a little worn out. Foundation that could be seen around her eyes, didn't hide the deep bags.

"No I'm not sick I just needed to talk to someone. I can't talk to my Mom or James. So will you listen and not tell anyone?"

"I promise."

"Okay..." Grace said settling into the comfortable leather chair, a smile spread across Grace's face. "I met a guy, and he is fabulous! His name is Dan and he goes to school in Boston. I met him through a chat room and for the past six months we've been seeing each other every weekend. He told me he loved me." Lavender smiled at Grace.

"Grace, why don't you want James to know? This is wonderful news!"

"Um....he's only three years younger than James."

"Oh." Lavender looked down at her desk. An older guy was okay but Grace was still this tiny little girl who didn't know how bad guys could be.

"I was wondering if you can refer me to a gynecologist because I want to go on the pill. We've been having sex, but I just think that we could use more protection than just a condom."

Lavender sat there with her mouth hanging wide open.

"Lav?"

"Yeah?"

"Lav please don't tell anyone especially not James." Lavender looked around her desk, her eyes at Molly. She never regretted having her but if they had been more careful- She didn't want Grace to end up like the teenage mothers her age. Taking a pen from the side of her and a notepad, she wrote down names of a few doctors.

"Oh, thank you so much Lav!" Grace jumped out of the chair and ran to hug Lavender.

"Call me after you go."

"Will do, thank you!" Grace called going out of the office.

It had been almost a week since her encounter with Grace and the effects of her visit hadn't worn off. On Tuesday one of her days off, Lavender, Molly and her almost Mother-in-law set out to do the impossible- find her a wedding dress.

"It's hopeless," Lavender declared after three hours of searching every single bridal shop in Providence. "Maybe I'm not destined to find a dress I like, Maybe this wedding isn't supposed to happen at all." With Molly tightly holding her hand on her right and Mrs. Martin walking on her left they walked a narrow cobblestone street in Newport.

The dark cloudy skies indicated that it was going to rain soon and she surely was not going to get caught in the rain.

"I told you that you *will* find a dress here. This shop is going to have a dress for you I know it." Lavender felt like asking how she knew. What would make this store any different from the last? All the dresses she tried on were either too plain, or too extravagant.

When she was younger, she always dreamed of the big wedding with millions of people. Her idea of the dress would be the most expensive, outrageous, puffy sleeved thing in the world. She wanted something pretty but it was more about the man she loved. On Friday they were going to try cakes at the specialty bakery. "That should be nice," she had told James sarcastically, "Pack some more onto my hips."

"Are you saying that you're fat?" He asked her later on that night.

"I'm not any model."

"I have no idea what you see but it is a different image from mine," he had said it with her face in his hands. *That was James for you,* Lavender thought. Before she knew it they were outside the small boutique. The wooden sign above read TWILIGHT: WHERE DREAMS ARE PUT INTO ACTION.

"Have you ever been here before?" Lavender asked Mrs. Martin. She looked down at her daughter who was standing there pulling her coat around her tightly. Bending down to pick her up, she buttoned the jacket on her tiny frame and then headed in the store. It was getting cold and Molly would soon be falling asleep, seeing she hadn't taken a nap in the car.

The deceivingly large room, held what seemed like millions of wedding dresses, from plain to extravagant, and the kind she was looking for which was between both. Behind the counter was a short woman with light blond hair.

Molly rested her head on her mother's shoulder and buried deep into her neck. She did the same thing since she was a baby. Sometimes it reminded Lavender of when James would move from her lips to the base of her neck, trailing kisses along.

"Hello, and welcome to TWILIGHT, I'm Yvonne. Can I help you with anything?"

"No. We're just browsing," Lavender told her politely as she went looking at the dresses. Mrs. Martin followed behind her quietly. She saw her granddaughter's eyes slowly close as her mother picked up a pretty white dress.

"I think this is the one." Lavender told her picking up the dress and holding it up. It was a v-neck dress, that in the back came down to the lower part of the back. "I'm going to go try it on."

"Do you want me to take her?" Christine asked holding out her arms for Molly. Lavender looked at her daughter and smiled at her beautiful, sleeping face.

"I'll take her in with me. She'll be fine." Lavender made her way to where it said dressing rooms and disappeared behind it. The dressing room was brightly lit up with lights that reminded her of a tanning bed picture.

Setting Molly down gently on the dressing room bench, she took off her clothes and slipped the dress over her body. It seemed to drape in all the right places. Had she really found a dress this quick in one store?

⁂

An hour later, Lavender walked in the door of her house. Molly was still asleep in her arms when she walked up the stairs and into her bedroom. Lavender placed her on the kind sized bed, under the covers, then went into the bathroom to change up.

The rain had started to fall when they left the store and some how it didn't seem right. She changed out of her jeans and blouse and into a sweatshirt and pants in a few minutes then went to check the machine.

One from her Mother, then from a Faye, another from....Grace. Lavender held her head in her palms. What was she going to do? She promised she wouldn't tell James, but having his seventeen year old sister go on birth control was something he should know about, he was the one who was basically taking care of her. The little voice in her head told her to keep her mouth shut, if Grace wanted to tell him it was her business. Lavender walked over to the bed and laid down next to a still sleeping Molly. Why did it have to be her that she came to? A phone rang quick and hurried, she grabbed it.

"Hello?"

"I wouldn't think that you would be home." A smile formed on her worried face. He always did this to her.

"Why it that?"

"I knew you were going dress shopping today. I also knew it would take forever knowing you." James laughed.

"Where are you right now?"

"I'm working late. I wish I was home right now. What are you doing?"

"Something you want to do. I'm on the bed with Molly laying down. She's been asleep for a little while now. Passed out on my shoulder in the dress store."

"Did you find something?"

"Yes. Of course you don't get to see it."

"Why not?" Lavender smiled to herself. She may have left the virginal part of her behind but she wasn't going to do a single thing wrong concerning this wedding.

"You're not supposed to." The other end became quiet all of a sudden. She couldn't even hear him breathing. "James? Are you there?"

"Yeah um...I just ah...kind of spaced out. I'll see you later okay?"

"Yeah okay." Lavender slowly hung up the phone then looked back at Molly. Blue eyes stared up at her and long brown strands of hair fell into Molly's face. "Hey sweetheart? Did I wake you up?"

"No." Lavender snuggled close to Molly and pushed the hair from her face.

"Mommy found a dress to wear. You fell asleep before you could see it."

"Can I see it now?"

"No I left it at the shop. Are you hungry?"

"Yeah."

"What do you want?" Molly thought about it for a minute then jumped up from her quiet state.

"Peanut butter and fluff!" Lavender laughed and sat up. Molly was starting to jump on the bed.

"Moll, stop now. I have an idea, why don't we go get some pizza and bring it to Daddy. He's working late tonight."

"Yeah!" She exclaimed jumping off the bed and running to the room down the hall. Slowly, Lavender got up and went to her closet to change. Jeans and a sweater would be okay, it was kind of cold.

The rain still was pouring hard on the cars and houses and far off you could see lighting. *Good thing I parked in the garage,* Lav thought pulling on her boots. Molly came running back into the room her favorite stuffed animal, Wally the Walrus- tucked under her arm.

"Is Wally going to come and have pizza too?"

"He's hungry. I can bring him right Mommy?"

"Sure sweetie. Come on let's go." Lavender grabbed her purse, then made her way down the stairs with her daughter. The downstairs was completely dark, making it hard to see the dolls scattered across the living room. Lav tripped on one before turning around, squinting to see Molly.

"Didn't I tell you to clean this up before we left this morning?" When no one answered her back she went to the light. Molly always said something to her when she was asked. "Molly?"

Lavender clicked on the light and looked around. Molly wasn't in sight. Where was she? Had she not been there a moment before when she was coming down the stairs?

"Molly?....Molly?!" Lavender looked around the room. Something caught her eye in the kitchen, something on the window. Slowly she walked over to the kitchen window and looked closer. A note! What was going on? Grabbing it quickly Lavender felt as if someone had dropped a pinball machine on her head.

May your wedding be filled with joy and happiness. Heed the advice- don't let that pretty little girl go into the basement.

"Molly?! Molly where are you?!!"

"I'm right here Mommy. I was upstairs getting my shoes." Lavender turned around and ran to her little girl. She took her in her arms and ran out to the garage and into the car. Driving down the highway way passed the speed limit, Lavender decided not to say anything to James.

He didn't need anymore stress or strain.

Chapter 22

July 15, 1999

She didn't know why she was so nervous. In her mind this day had been replayed so much. The white sash around the waist of her dress was being wrapped tight around her fingers. Lavender looked out the dark window of the limousine. The sun beating bright on the streets outside and the clear blue clouds made the morning even more enjoyable.

Faye sat next to her in the limo, sipping on the champagne in the car. The pastel mint, maid of honor dress she was wearing was went beautiful with her thick red hair. Lavender looked over at Molly who was sitting at the end of the limo. She had brought Wally the Walrus, in which she had taken one of James' ties and wrapped it tightly around the animal's neck.

Lavender caught Faye's clear blue eyes staring at her. "What's wrong with you?" Lavender sucked in breath and faced her best friend.

"I'm so nervous that my legs are shaking." Faye started laughing and put the half full glass of champagne down into the cup holder.

"Lav you have no reason to be nervous. This is just what you have always wanted. Now it's finally coming true. Besides look at Molly." Lavender looked over at her daughter who was looking out the window. There was no doubt that she was madly in love with James and there was no way that she was going to get cold feet and back out.

"You're right. I shouldn't be nervous." but she still was. Lavender looked back at Faye and started to talk to her again.

"Mommy?"

"Yes Honey?"

"Where are we going?"

" We're going to the place where Mommy and Daddy are getting married."

"No, this isn't the way." Molly said looking out the dark window.

"Moll what are you talking about? They're taking us to the place were we went with the purple walls. Remember we went with Daddy?"

"I know Mommy. This isn't the way to get there. I remember." Lavender looked at her daughter questionably.

"Molly this is the way." Faye grabbed her arm and smiled.

"Lav? There is something you need to know." Lavender watched Faye grab the clutch bag from her side and take out a fancy piece of paper. She handed it to her friend and watched her read it.

The paper was from The Providence Biltmore Hotel. Lavender seemed confused as she read the first few lines.

Screw the other place. This is your wedding day and I thought I would make it even more memorable. Meet me at the Providence Biltmore at 12:30. I'll be waiting at the end of the isle.

Lavender smiled after finishing the note. That sneaky jerk. He changed the plans. The Providence Biltmore? How could he ever afford that? She knew he had got a major paycheck, but this!

Before she knew it she was in front of the Biltmore. The Bellhop opened the limo door and helped her step out. Molly got out before Faye and took her Mother's hand. Lavender bend down and looked her daughter in the eyes.

"Can you do something for me?" Lavender asked her. Molly nodded her head and looked back her mother. She had left Wally in the limo and taken the pretty white basket filled with yellow roses. "We're going to see Grandma, ask her to take you to Daddy. Then when you see him I want you to run over to him and give him a big kiss. Tell him that Mommy said that she was very excited."

Molly smiled at her Mom and linked her arms around her neck. Lavender's long brown hair, like Molly's was pulled back into a up do with curls hanging down-except that Lavender wore a long veil.

"I love you Molly."

"I love you too Mommy and you look very beautiful today." Lavender tried to stop the tears that were forming in her eyes.

"Thank you darling." Lavender stood up and walked into the Biltmore. In the lobby the bright chandeliers held her image as she looked up. The beautiful painted ceilings were stunning above her. Molly's small hand was still in hers. Lavender was unaware that her soon to be Mother-in-law was running to her.

"Oh my God! You look marvelous dear! And Molly you're so beautiful!" Mrs. Martin gushed to them. Lavender quickly explained about Molly and let her go with her Grandmother. Lavender and Faye were lead up the stairs into a room where every chocolate covered strawberry in the state was present.

"I have a great idea." Faye said to Lavender after stuffing three strawberries in her mouth.

"What's that?"

"Seeing you're nervous, I'll marry James. I would die to get this everyday!" Lavender laughed and looked out onto the view of the city. Only a few more minutes and then it would be final. She would finally be Mrs. James Martin. Finally.

⁂

James sat quietly on the couch. Sheen had gone to get some more wine for himself down at the kitchen. Sitting there in his tuxedo he thought about the last time had been doing this. How he had felt so helpless sitting there after she left him to think that he had gotten her pregnant.

In a way thinking back maybe she had know of his decision to call it quits at the last moment. Then he had changed his mind back and forth. Maybe she was able to see that his expression after she had told him said : I don't want this. James sighed and let his eyes close. Even with the sound of the door he didn't open his eyes.

"James?" A somewhat familiar male voice asked him. James opened his eyes and saw a five foot eleven inch man dressed in a black tuxedo, his short blond hair spiked up.

"I didn't think that you would show up." James said to Nick standing up from his place. Both stood awkwardly in the same stiff position. After listening to Lavender say to him over and over again, "Call Nick, Call Nick." He had finally called him and left a message to call him back.

They had talked once on the phone and Nick learned the story. The only thing James had left out was who the father was. That was something Nick had to find out on his own. He had invited him to the wedding only last night.

"Well I wasn't planning on coming here. At one o'clock in the morning after watching reruns on channel three, I decided that through everything we were best friends before my sister."

"I knew if I ever got married best friend would be there," Nick concluded. James smiled and walked over to him, then shook his hand. The door opened again and he watched his five year old daughter run into the room.

"Molly you look beautiful!" James bent down to pick her up while Nick eyed him. He had left that out on the phone too. She pushed her small, but full lips to her father's cheek.

"Mommy said she is very excited." James laughed and pushed a stray lock from Molly's face.

"Are you going to see Mommy now?"

"No, Gramma said she and Auntie Faye were getting ready. Grandma told me to stay with you because she had to go get something." James walked back over to the couch and sat down, placing Molly on his lap.

"Is there something that you didn't mention on the phone?" Nick asked him.

"Uh....yeah....this is my daughter. Molly this is Nick." James told her introducing her to him. Molly jumped off James' lap and went over to Nick.

"I heard about you. Auntie Faye talks about you when she and Mommy are talking about how Daddy sleeps." James' eyes went wide at what was coming out of his daughter's mouth. *Great, not only is Lav talking about our sex life she is letting Molly hear it.* Something she said though made him question.

"Moll why don't you go outside and see if the waiter there has something for you." She nodded and went out the door where the bellhop was waiting to take their order at anytime.

"Are you with Faye?"

"No." Nick answered quickly.

"Don't lie. You can't lie to save your life."

"I was with her once....or a few times."

⁂

After Molly and Faye walked down the isle it was Lavender's turn. The large room was filled with everyone they had invited. Lavender wondered how James had managed to get everyone to come here instead of the other place.

Jeremy stood at her left, her arm linked into his. Quickly scanning the crowd she saw her father sunken in the back of the last row. She hadn't wanted him to show up, there was no reason to she hadn't talked to him in all these years. With her Mother nagging her to invite him she had reluctantly made the call.

Lav smiled when Faye moved out of the way and she saw James. So handsome, polished in his black tux. Sheen stood next to him dressed the same. He didn't look nearly as good as James. A familiar face was looking back at her next to Sheen. Nick stood out between the two men as he was dressed differently.

Molly hung onto Faye's hand as her Mother walked down the isle. Lavender smiled at her for a moment then locked her gaze with the man of her dreams. This was it.

The memories of their first meeting to their first kiss flashed in her head. At that time all she wanted to do was to pass algebra, now all she wanted to do was marry the man before her and share every moment of her life with him.

Fly to the moon and back, write I LOVE YOU! in the sky! This feeling, uncontrollable, amazing, never going away feeling was mutual between them. It seemed to slip by, the Justice of The Peace saying words.

"Do you James Andrew Martin take thy Lavender Diane Springer as your lawfully wedded wife, to have and to hold from this day forward, from now until the hour of your death?"

"I do."

" And do you Lavender Diane Springer take thy James Andrew Martin as your lawfully wedded husband to have and to hold from this day forward until the hour of your death?"

"I do."

"Then by the powers vested in me I now pronounce you husband and wife. You may kiss your bride." James took his thumb and wiped the tear from her eye before leaning in, kissing her passionately.

James went for her hand and squeezed it as he continued to kiss her. She squeezed back then both pulled away. The guest were clapping but it seemed so far away, as if it were in another place. The only thing that James could hear was the beating of his heart, Lavender laughed and kissed him again. They walked out of the room, down the petal covered isle, leaving everyone behind.

"It took so long to get here." Lavender laughed.

"But it was worth the wait."

Chapter 23

"I'd like to introduce to you Mr. and Mrs. James Martin." James and Lavender walked into the Grand Ballroom of The Providence Biltmore as <u>I Can't Help Falling in Love</u> played. Her hand was buried deep into his hand, his arm around her waist. This song meant something long ago to them.

They had been sitting in the car at Rocky Point, flipping between radio stations when this song came on. On that night he had given her a bracelet at the mall. It was still in her jewelry box and right now on her wrist.

Leaning close to her ear James' cool breath brought goose bumps to her neck. "I hope you know that you owe me for this." She laughed and moved closer to his body. Out of the corner of her eye she caught Molly standing with Faye, swinging back and forth on her heels.

"Oh I know. And I plan to....tonight. After we arrive in Cabo." The thoughts had played over in his mind. Alone on the secluded beach cabana, sitting on the beach everyday...alone. His mother was going to watch Molly for the two weeks that they were gone so at least they knew she would be alright.

A few moments later the song ended and everyone went to the tables. The tall ballroom windows were half covered with the maroon fabric, keeping just the right light out. On the other side of the room, a ice sculpture of a angel was sitting on the long white table where the receiving line was.

Along the tables, clear crystal vases held bunches of yellow roses, with small white carnations. The long table held medium sized angel sculptures that were pure white with small flecks of gold on the eyes. Faye sat on her left while Sheen at James' right. Nick sat next to Sheen, somewhat feeling out of place. Molly ran over to her Mom and took a seat on her lap.

Sheen stood up and raised his flute glass in the air. "I'd like to make a toast," all the glasses were being held in the air at this point after Sheen requested it. "To James and Lavender. James has been a truly loyal best friend to me over the past years and I know how deep his love for this woman is. I may not know her as much as I'd like to but I sure plan to know her as well as I know James. I wish you the best of luck, and happiness. Salute!"

"Salute!" the guests responded taking a drink from their glasses. Suddenly someone unexpected stood up with his glass.

"I'd like to make another toast," Nick declared moving from the table and onto the middle of the floor. "I know I wasn't appointed best man but I think that I should say something," Nick started, few laughed when he said that, then he resumed, "since I was ten years old I've watched James and Lavender hang out. I know that Lav really didn't like me when I met her and I'm not quite sure if she even likes me now but I'm going to say this, Lavender and James are going to have the most perfect life."

"I have found that of all of the people I know I can say that James is the only one who I can really call my friend. He's been there for me all the way, even if we have had ups and downs. Anyway, I know that James know that Lavender is "The One" and I know that He won't ever let him go. James I want to say....there is no one who I can trust more. One more thing, I want you two to have a *really* awesome time in Cabo." Some of the guests laughed as they clinked their glasses together and took another drink.

◈

"I don't want you to go!" Molly sobbed into Lavender's chest. The airport was somewhat crowded at four fifteen in the afternoon. They had to hurry to get on the five o'clock flight they were to be on. His mother stood still trying to get Molly to let go of Lavender and with her.

"Sweetheart, Mommy and Daddy will be back before you know it. We're going to bring you back some really nice things."

"I want to go with you! I don't want you to leave me!" Lavender closed her eyes and tightened her grip around Molly's body. It was hard for her, never once had she left Molly alone for that long of a time. James bent down and moved Molly away from his wife.

"Moll, look at me. I promise you that the days will fly by. I told you that we would call you every single day and you can call us anytime you want."

"I don't want you to go though! I want to go with you!"

"Daddy and Mommy need to spend some time alone for a little while. You'll have fun with Grandma and you'll get to do lots of fun things."

Molly still was crying and she ran back over to Lavender. She quickly looked at her watch. They needed to get on that plane.

"Molly listen to me, stop crying and let us get on that plane. If you don't stop crying then we're not going to get you anything at all. Now please go with Grandma and we will call you when we get there." She stopped crying for a minute then from Lavender's shoulder she was staring her father straight in the eyes.

James touched Lavender's shoulder then took Molly from her arms into his. He kissed her goodbye and handed her to his mother. "Come on Baby Doll, let's go do something fun. Mommy and Daddy will call later."

He lead his wife to the check in counter then silently they walked onto the plane. Taking their seats she didn't look very well.

"Are you okay?"

"I don't know."

"If you want to stay here we can jump off this plane and spend our honeymoon here." Lavender shook her head and reached for his hand.

"No we're going. James...you wouldn't have even believe how hard that was for me." James took her hand to his lips and kissed it.

"I know. I know. This is out honeymoon though, the beginning of our life together and we really need this time together."

※

"It's even more beautiful than the pictures!" Lavender gushed as she and James set down the overnight bag in the beach cabana. One wall was painted a bright yellow, another a coral pink and blue.

"You need sun glasses in here," James joked setting his night bag on the floor. The bedroom was off to the right, while the large kitchen and family room were right in front of them. One of the bellhops was to bring the rest of the bags in from downstairs.

"I'm glad that we came. Besides I'm pretty sure we're going to want to go on more trips by ourselves often." Lavender walked over to him, wrapping her arms around his neck. He sure wished that the bellhop would hurry up. He kissed her quickly then took her into his arms. The doorbell rang at that moment.

When James opened the door he was surprised to see three bellhops carrying their luggage. They set it down in front of Lavender then stood at the doorway. "This isn't ours," Lav said looking at the tags on the suitcases.

"We had two big, grey bags, not three black ones." James told them. He didn't think they understood, seeing they just stood there with goofy grins on their faces. Lavender looked to James then went over to the beige phone in the kitchen. She quickly looked at the laminated paper for the front desk.

The three men took the bags back out the door leaving them alone. "They said there was a mix up, we should have our bags tomorrow morning. He said that he would knock off tonight's stay." James locked the door and put his back against it.

" Now we are alone at last."

"Such a classic line." Lav smiled as she walked to the bedroom. She took off her ice blue blazer and elegantly threw it on the bed. The matching skirt hit the back of her knee, reminding her that her garter was still on. "James I didn't take off the last part of my dress will you help me get it off?"

He appeared in the doorway of the bedroom, being dressed so causally he looked as if he had just walked out of a magazine photo shoot. His perfectly messed hair, that he had gotten when they slept on the plane still remained on his head. The casting of light from the moon outside the open balcony hit his face, illuminating his beautiful eyes.

Taking a seat on the bed, Lavender moved her left leg over her right and moved up her skirt to show him the pure white garter. "I forgot to take it off." He soundlessly walked over to her and kneeled. Gently he slid it down her smooth, silky leg.

Lavender ever so slowly laid down on the bed and felt him move his hands up her thigh. He took both his hands away and moved up her torso rounding off to her back. His touch felt soft against her tanned skin. Pushing up the white t-shirt she was wearing, James placed lavish kisses on her midriff.

Moving his lips up to her mouth they kiss passionately, a loud moan escaping Lavender's mouth. His hand found the zipper of her skirt, sliding out of it Lavender was half naked under him. Lavender watched him pull off his tie, while her fingers traced a button of his shirt before she unhooked them and ran her hands over his tight muscular chest.

"God you're so beautiful," he whispered, his grip pulling off her bra. When his kiss reached her collarbone, while his fingers traced the rest of her body, Lavender closed her eyes and pulled him closer to her.

"James, I can't wait any longer." James laughed and gently tugged at her lacy panties. Lavender looked at him and smiled coyly. "Seeing that I'm naked now, darling I think that you should do the same."

Sitting up she pushed him on the bed and started unbuttoning his shirt, then his belt holding up the dress pants. Lavender pulled down his briefs leaving his toned, naked, body under her.

James kissed her and grabbed her hips. He quickly turning her over so that she was under him. "You want to go the old fashion way?" Lavender smiled. "I brought "Cosmopolitan" with me. We can see what positions we can try."

"I want to make up my own positions." his hand moved between her thighs, making Lavender arch back. His tongue explored her, making her cry in pleasure. "I want to hear you moan Lav... moan for me," James whispered. Lavender moaned loud as he moved his fingers in her. James' mouth traced her body starting from her breasts ending at her thighs.

"Lav, I want you so bad-"

"So then take me," Lavender whispered in his ear. Her leg moved up the curve of his back holding onto him as he slipped into her. James' sweaty body moved harder against hers. She screamed louder, called his name as he rocked her world with intense passion. They were both out of breath as they came to a climax. Lavender held James's weight on her as she stared into his blue eyes. She moved a sweaty strand of hair from his forehead. Lavender's chest moved up and down as she took in deep breaths.

"I love you,"James kissed her lips, then her neck.

"I know." She laughed, pushing him off her and standing up. He rolled over on his back, letting Lavender crawl on top of him. "Can we do it again? Please??!!" She laughed.

"Whatever you want, Mrs. Martin."

"I want to be in control-" Lavender whispered grabbing James's tie from the floor.

◆

James was going to be pissed at her when he saw the state of the car. Grace hadn't meant to take the mustang out of the garage but her car was in the shop getting work done and she had to go meet Dan. She hadn't seen him since the night of James and Lavender's wedding and she planned to surprise him at the hotel he was staying at.

Grace parked and within minutes had gotten the room number from the front desk. Riding the elevator up she was giddy and scared at the same time. She wondered if she looked alright and checked herself out in the mirror. Her tight jeans hugged her body and everything was great except for the fact that she should have fixed her hair a bit more. Grace was smiling as she stepped off the elevator.

Dan was so great, he was loving, gentle, kind, smart, amazing! She had fallen head over heels. It only took a few steps to get to his room where she knocked on the door. After a few minutes of not answering she knocked louder. Dan appeared at the door. His blond hair was smoothed down on his forehead and around the nape of his neck and the dark brown eyes were open wide.

"Gracie?" She smiled and leaned in to kiss him. Her lips touched his but he didn't return the kiss. Grace pulled away and made her way inside the hotel room.

"What's the matter? Are you alright?"

"I'm fine." Grace looked around the hotel room. It smelled musty and lingered of hotel cleaning products. Dan had shut the door and walked over to Grace. She smiled and pushed him down on the sloppily made bed. Grace tore at his body until he was naked under her. While slipping off her shirt she heard a loud crash from the bathroom.

"What was that?"

"I don't know." Grace stood up and walked over to the closed door. "Grace-"

Grace opened the door and then fell dizzy. A short-haired blond woman with bright blue eyes looked back at her with a half smile on her face. She was only dressed in a blue bra and matching underwear. Grace turned back to look at Dan who was forcing his pants on and then she looked back at Lizzie.

"Grace, I can explain." Dan said calmly walking over to Grace. She felt like she was going to cry and she didn't know if she was more angry than sad.

"Trust me Grace its not what it looks like!"

"How- Why? How could you?!" Grace turned to Dan. "When?!"

"Gracie, let me explain we met at your brother's wedding-"

"You said you loved me! You said we were going to get married!,"Grace cried.

"Look If I can just get my things and leave-" Lizzie said quietly.

"Yes, you do that!" Grace yelled. " You tramp!"

"Dan?"

"Gracie, please let me say something-"

"Stop saying that and just fucking tell me and start explaining! I think I have a right to know why my boyfriend is with my sister-in-law's sister!"

"We met at your brother's wedding,"

"Were you with her when you didn't show up for a half hour?!"

"Listen to me, we were at the same bar last night and things went a little too far-"

"Have there been other women you have been with since we've been together?"

"Um...."

"There have! Oh my God! I can't believe you!"

"Grace please, don't leave me! " Dan protested. "I love you!" Grace closed her eyes and tried to hold back tears.

"I've got to go,"

"Grace please! I love you." Grace ran out of the hotel room and into the parking lot. How could this have happened? He said he loved her! Grace started up the car and drove out of the parking lot. At the third red-light the woman in the Lincoln Town Car rear ended the 1973 Mustang Convertible sending the air bags into Grace's face.

Chapter 24

"You smashed my Mustang." James repeated for the tenth time. It was sitting in the garage of the country house where they had just moved into. Grace winced every time he said those words. Lavender was standing next to him just as shocked. When the insurance company and the police had called him, they rushed home thinking that something more serious was wrong.

"James I'm sorry, it wasn't my fault."

"My car....." Grace had never seen her brother like this before, He looked like he was about to cry!

"It was just a car what's the big thing? You have the money to get another one," Grace replied thinking aloud. James took his view away from the smashed in rear and looked at his sister as if he was going to murder her, which he just might do.

"The big thing? The big thing is I've had this car since I was sixteen years old. Thirteen years I've had this car! I've moved about three times with it and had some of the best memories of my life in this car! No Grace it's no big deal! I can just go and buy another 1973 red Ford Mustang Convertible in almost mint condition!" James' face was blood red and his eyes were popping out of his head. "Your stupidity has done more than smash a car, its taken my and my wife away from our honeymoon where we spent four fucking days! It's not even the car, Grace you could have died! You could have been paralyzed for the rest of your life! Didn't you think of your safety? I told you before I left that I didn't want to near that car!"

Lavender pulled at his arm trying to move him out of the garage. James pulled away from her and stared at his sister. "I don't want to see you right now. Leave." Grace stood up straight and nodded. She walked through the open garage door, head hung and tears in her eyes.

James hit the close button then made his way through the basement /office. The cold, grey, concrete floors matched the grey metal desk in which he took a seat. He rubbed his head, hoping that the on coming migraine would magically disappear. Lavender was silent as she took the seat across from him.

Afraid to say anything to him, she sat there waiting for him to make the first move. After a long time and getting all the small wrinkles off her skirt with her hands, she spoke up, "are you alright?"

"No." She stood up and started to walk to the staircase leading up to the kitchen and family room.

"Do you want something a drink or something to eat?"

"No." Trying not to show that she was pissed at him, Lavender walked up the stairs and into the living room. The glass french doors looked out onto the wooden patio and into the deep woods. Before the wedding when they were moving their stuff in, she had met the people who lived behind them.

Lavender couldn't see the house from the windows. God forbid if anything ever happened here no one would be able to help them. The next house was about five minutes down the road and it was only occupied by a very old woman. Lavender adored the house but she wished it was in a different area.

She walked down the two stairs and found herself in the living room. A old brick fireplace at her left, a long maple sofa at her right. Lavender looked up at the stained glass window in back of the TV. It was a rose with a long green stem. Often she found herself staring at it.

Moving away from that room she looked out onto the other french doors that went out to the long porch. It showed a different view, the small pond and fire pit. Drawing herself out of the room she went upstairs into their bedroom and looked at the still packed suitcase on the bed.

Lavender wished that they were still in Cabo, drenched in suntan oil and soft sand. She wished none of this happened, now she didn't know what to think or what to say to him. He loved that car. The day he got it was a day she would never forget....

James had his licence a whole hour when he arrived home from the DMV. His Mother had taken him and when Lavender looked out the window she could see that he was driving alone in a shiny red Mustang Convertible.

Earlier he had not been sure if he was going to pass, but the look on his face and the car he was sitting in told her he had. Rushing down the stairs nearly knocking Jeremy's coffee over she swung open the door and raced to the parked car.

The sunglasses he bought at the beach earlier that summer covered his eyes. A few months ago his Mom went with him to one of the car lots. Instantly he had fallen for the 1973 Mustang in candy apple red.

"I don't believe I know you," she teased him, "you must be new around town."

"I would say I am babe. Want to jump in for a spin?"

"Well you know....I have a boyfriend. He lives in that house right there. I don't know if I should go. Besides my Mommy told me not to get into strange cars with strangers." Lavender smiled at his beautiful white smile.

"How about me and your boyfriend have a little chat later. As for your Mom, tell her I'm not a stranger. Just an acquaintance." James had then reached over and opened the passenger door....

Some memories. Lavender was half way done unpacking his clothes when she felt a presence behind her. Turning around she saw him standing at the door the same way he did when he had been at her apartment, six years ago.

Lavender gave a half smile and then went back to unpacking. He walked over to her, placing his hands around her hips and his lips on her neck. Tucking her neck to the other side she felt secure in his grip. Still words were not exchanged between them. "So?" she asked him putting his shirts to the side of the bed.

"So....I've been thinking."

"About?"

"About the car....the honeymoon and a few other things."

"And what is going on?"

"It's time for me to let go. I knew I wasn't going to have the car forever. Maybe this was just the way to get rid of it." Lavender turned around and saw the sadness on his face. He could have it fixed and he knew that.

"The honeymoon?"

"My Mom doesn't know we came back this early. We can drive somewhere. It won't be Cabo but at least we'll be alone." Lavender shut her eyes and thought about it.

"Why don't we just stay here? We can't do that to your poor mother and besides it will give me a chance to get used to this place."

"Whatever you want to do is perfectly fine." James placed a kiss on her lips before letting her go. He walked up to huge window in their bedroom. Looking out he saw a squirrel sitting on the deck below. Good thing she didn't see it because she would have a fit.

James could tell that she wasn't too keen on living up here. Never had he thought she would be afraid of a tiny spider. Although she had found it in the bathroom...he would have to get the exterminator out here.

"How about a nice quiet evening in? I'll go and get Molly tomorrow." Lavender told him moving the suitcase off the bed. She grabbed the remote and turned on the new big screen TV. Both flopping down on the bed they switched through channels. Upon hearing the doorbell ringing frantically, Lavender went downstairs and opened the door.

Faye stumbled in the house sobbing. Her shirt was torn at the shoulder and a trace of still fresh blood hung onto her sleeve. The once sleek red hair was pulled this way and that. When Lavender saw her face she cried out in shock.

At that point she could hear James' feet coming down the stairs. Faye's black and blue eyes were puffy and swollen as it was but crying made it worse.

"What happened?" James asked seeing Faye.

"I don't know." Lavender put her arms around Faye bringing her into a hug. As she was trying to silence the tears so she could talk to her, the doorbell rang again. James went to get it and came back with Nick.

"Faye what happened? Who did this to you?" James had gotten Lavender the ice packs from the freezer as soon as he came back. Faye had a seat on the bar stools at the counter.

"Kyle." Lavender shook her head. Kyle Miller, the younger man Faye had been dating moved in with her a few months ago. He was a prison guard who knew how to fight when he had to.

"What went on?"

"We were fighting and then he pushed me down the stairs. He came after me and hit me. I got away and came here." Faye sobbed. Lavender looked to James then to Nick. Wait where was he?

When had he left?

"Faye we should get you to the hospital," James said quickly taking her hand. "Lav go get something from the closet so Faye can wear it. Grab my shoes too please I'll meet you in the car." James grabbed the keys watching Lavender disappear into the hall and up the stair case.

In the car Faye sat in the back quiet. James looked through the rear view mirror and caught her glance.

"I know what it feels like."

"How the hell would you know?!"

James gave a hidden laugh and looked back at her. "I was fourteen when I almost killed. I can remember bleeding and tasting every ounce of it."

"Why are you telling me this?"

Lavender got in the car before he could answer and in another minute they were off.

⁂

Holding Lavender's hand in the waiting room outside of Faye's hospital room, James sat stiff. A call on his cell phone a minute ago told him that Nick Brenden was being searched for. Seems as though he went and beat the shit out of Kyle Miller. Lavender was antsy sitting there.

"Do you have ants in your pants or something?" he asked her. Lavender glared at her husband and went back to moving around.

"What's taking so long?"

"I don't know."

"I hate hospitals. I hate them! Why did I ever become a doctor? You know what they did to me when Molly was born?"

"What did they do?"

"They wanted to deliver in the ER! I told them I wanted the maternity ward, finally they listened to me. I still remember this bitchy nurse. She had these huge beaver teeth. I fought with her for the first ten minutes because as she said 'you have to hold the baby a certain way.' I bet the broad doesn't even have kids of her own I told her to give me my baby or I'll knock her into next week, her and those beaver teeth. Are you listening to me James?"

James looked over at her and nodded his head. A tall woman dressed in a doctors coat and black slacks came up to them a moment later.

"I'm Doctor Petermen," she told them. Long curly black hair hung down from a pony tail in the back of her head. "Faye's doctor...Wait are you Lavender Springer from Hasbro ?"

"Yes I am. It's Martin now."

"Its such a pleasure to meet you. Um...anyway Faye seems to be fine. We got her all cleaned up and the baby is fine."

"Baby?" James and Lavender asked at the same time.

"Uh...yes. You can go in and see her if you'd like."

"Thank you Doctor."

"James I think I should go in first."

"Okay...fine." Lavender quickly made her way into the room. Faye was laying down in the hospital bed, hand sprawled across her chest. Lavender couldn't tell if she was sleeping or awake.

"Faye?"

"Hey..." Faye looked up at her best friend and gave a smile.

"How do you feel?"

"I'm alright."

"Listen you can stay with us tonight-"

"That's really nice of you Lav but I don't think I should."

"Why? Where are you going to go?"

"I just don't want to intrude on you two."

"You're not....."

Faye moved around in the bed. Her foot itched but she didn't have strength to move down and scratch it.

"I didn't know Kyle was like that. I thought he was kind, gentle. You know, Lav you have it made."

"I know."

"James is such a great guy. He's there and he adores you and Molly. I wish I could find a guy like that."

"Faye...tell me what happened. Why did he push you?"

She swallowed hard then looked up into Lavender's eyes. "Your eyes are so pretty."

"Tell me Faye! Tell me why the son of a bitch pushed you! Stop beating around the bush."

"Okay....I found out I was pregnant the other day. I told Kyle and he said I should get rid of it or he'll get rid of it for me. I told him to get out. That's when he pushed me and hit me."

Lavender looked at Faye who was now beginning. The man was a monster! Who would do that to get rid of a baby?

"I know about the pregnancy. The doctor told us everything is fine."

"I left something out Lav."

"What is it?" Lavender looked over Faye. Now seeing some kind of glow. When her grandmother had found out about Molly she had taken her aside and looked at her. *"I knew I saw a change in you Lavender."*....

"Kyle isn't the baby's father."

"Who is?"

"Nick."

Chapter 25

Brad Lursen had always been the runt of the litter. He was born to a poor family in the winter of 1967. His mother died during his birth. Bradley had seven older siblings. The oldest starting at seventeen and the youngest at five. With dark brown hair and bright hazel eyes Brad was always labeled as the best looking of them.

His Father was a heavy drinker with a beer belly to prove it. The family was scattered, always moving from one home to another or as soon as the landlord wanted the money his Father never made. Brad had always been good, never stealing like his brothers and sisters or committing crimes.

Some say it was because since they could remember, Brad had been drawn to the church. He considered going into priesthood, but then turned it down once he had made some friends. In school he had okay grades, teachers didn't care enough to help him raise the grade in science that always brought him down.

As Brad became older he found a friend from a rich Cranston community. He had labeled Erich Martin a friend. He hung around sometimes with him and was always the quiet one. After Erich's arrest at seventeen Brad never saw him again.

He got a low paying job at a small bar and lived above it in a small rental room. All his family had either died or gone to jail, leaving him alone. Working as a bartender was fun sometimes, hearing peoples' stories, risks they took, or things they had seen. Brad always wondered what his life would be like if he could have traveled and seen the world.

On a cold night sometime in December of 1993, Brad received a call. The bar had been empty all night. The only sounds were coming from a couple who had rented a room upstairs in the rooms. He was standing there towel drying the beer glass in his hand when the phone began to ring.

He didn't feel like answering it. Why should he? The boss wasn't there to watch his every move and no one in the bar to notice. Still something told him to pick up the phone. It didn't stop ringing even after a few minutes. Reluctantly, he picked up the receiver.

"Hello?"

"Is Brad Lusren there?" a raspy male voice asked.

"Speaking."

"I have a message for you."

"Excuse me?"

"I have a message for you. You must go to the prison and ask to see an inmate named Erich Martin." The words seemed to be delivered slowly to him. Erich Martin? Why of all people would someone want to see him?

"I'm sorry but you must have the wrong number or something."

"Be there at two-thirty tomorrow afternoon." The caller hung up after that, leaving Brad with the dial tone. Brushing a bead of sweat from his forehead, he rested his back against the wall. What if he didn't want to show up? Then what would happen. Going back to the beer glass, Brad stayed quiet all night.

The office in the downstairs basement was somewhere to go when he needed or wanted to be alone. It must have been close to three in the morning when James hit the light switch for the basement. With Lavender and Molly sound asleep upstairs, James found this may be yet another perfect time for him to do this.

Passing the two refrigerators that held frozen meats and stuff they might need sometime in the future, James walked through the open doorway and into the office. Nearing the file cabinet, it almost seemed routine to him. All the nights he would walk over and pull out the big manilla folder, spread it on the desk and get no where by the time the sun rose.

Doing the same this time, he took a seat at the desk and opened it once more. **Robert J. Martin** was at the heading along with death date. Pushing his way though the paper work he looked at the photos taken from the crime scene.

Shutting his eyes for a moment, James remembered the first time he had seen these. After pleading and pulling a few stings, he had gotten the police reports and files. On the first night, locked in the office at the other house he had stared at the photos of his father's car turned over and wrapped around a tree.

At first it had hurt to look at them, now it was nothing. He knew it was wrong. He knew he should still feel sad, but over all he felt was angry.

Angry at the brakes, his father for not sitting with the seat belt that hadn't been fasten. Most of all he was pissed at himself. Just because he had to hold his ground they hadn't talked for all those years.

He could remember his father saying that he will be sorry when he is gone and in his head James silently answer him back with, no you will. Going back to the file he read over the paperwork..

The last time he had been down here it had been early at night and Lavender saw him pouring over the file. She hadn't said anything to him, she had just stared and tried to see what his expression said. After a moment she had left him to be and brought Molly upstairs for bed.

The question still remained of how, who and why someone tampered with the brakes. Turning the pages the autopsy pictures came next. This always made him feel as if he was going to die soon and that his body would look like that. Swollen and different colors. Now he had more things going for him and he refused to leave.

His daughter and wife made him snap back and remember that it wasn't going to happen. Not for a very long time. Sure a lot of people said that but then they ended up in the casket the next week. Live life to the fullest! His mother's words ran through his head. Quickly James shut the file and put it back into the cabinet. Glancing over at the calender he saw that it was getting really close to Christmas. Only another ten days.

Thanksgiving had gone well for them. His mom and sister, who he was now talking to, came over along with Faye. It felt weird being in Faye's presence. She was pregnant and it was Nick's kid. Nick still didn't know.

Day by day Lavender tries to convince her to tell him but she isn't ready yet. James sometimes wondered what Nick might do when he find out. If they marry it would mean Nick would have to give up his take them and leave them ways.

Nick had always liked Faye ever since they were kids. When they were in ninth grade he had asked her out and she rejected him. That was the only time he had ever been rejected in his life.

Lavender had done most of the Christmas shopping already, taking him along without Molly so that they could get her toys and clothes. Still they hadn't taken her to see Santa Claus and she was going to keep at them until they did. Too many things were going on right now, with both of them working and shopping things seemed to never get easier.

"The sick season," as Lavender said. It meant having she had to spend more time in the city at work. That left James with Molly at dance class, to cook dinner, to get her off to bed, then finally settle himself to read over a book that always put him to sleep.

As James went upstairs he could see that the snow was still falling from last night. The white powder was untouched as it piled on the ground covering the grass and flowers. The snowman Molly and Lavender had made last weekend still stood at the edge of the woods with the thin twigs sticking out for arms.

Even with the heater on the house was too cold. Sometimes a fire would take the chill out but on most mornings it didn't even give off heat. Since snow had began to show in late November, they had been walking around in sweaters and two pairs of pants. Sometimes he really hated the winter months then other times he wished it would stay like that year round.

Before James went down to the basement he had flicked the switch on the black coffee pot so that when he came up he could bring something back for himself and Lavender. Tip-toeing up the stairs and passing Molly's closed bedroom door he walked into the master bedroom. The thick covers were piled so high they covered Lavender from head to toe.

Placing the coffee on her night stand along with his, James moved the covers back to see her. The long sheer nightgown she had been wearing the night before was still off her and thrown to the floor. *She must be freezing*, he thought as he went over to the deep walk in closet.

Pulling out her red terrycloth robe he looked at it. She really needed a new one but he knew she would never give this one up.

Gently touching her bare skin, James let his strong hands move over her arms, and chest. Her eyes shot open and she seemed disoriented for a moment. "Good morning angel." The smile that he loved crept across her face. "How did you sleep?"

"Good," Lavender brushed a strand of hair that was falling on his forehead. "Last night was fun. Is that the word I should use to describe it?"

James smiled back at her. "Something like that....I wish that everything was over. You didn't have to go to work, I didn't have to go to work. I wish that we could just stay in this house. No one bothers us up here."

"It will calm down soon, don't worry." taking the robe from him she put it on and tied it at her waist before getting up. "What time is it?"

James looked over at the wall clock near the door. "Almost four-thirty."

"What are you doing up?"

"I wasn't doing anything." Lav looked over at him questionably.

"Fine." James stood up and walked into the bathroom. His twenty-nine year old face looked older and he figured after he shaved he would go back to looking like his regular self again. She appeared behind him, placing her arms around his shoulders and lacing her fingers together to hold on to him..

"Are you okay?"

"Yeah, why wouldn't I be?"

"James I know that I've been spending too much time at work and I'm sorry."

"It's not work," James told her quickly. Lav unlaced her fingers and walked out of the bathroom mumbling something that sounded like asshole.

"What did you say?" he asked walking out of the bathroom.

"Nothing."

"What is your problem lately!?"

"Nothing." James shook his head and walked back into the bathroom and looked in the mirror. Her moods lately had changed. She became angry or just frustrated. He couldn't understand it and it was too early in the morning to try.

⁓❦⁓

The town of West Greenwich had one gas station where James went every time he needed gas. It was run by one of the Greenwich natives, Old Chuck Little. Chuck had a white moustache on his upper lip and a thin layer of white hair that he combed to the left side of his nearly bald head.

Chuck was never seen without a newspaper in his hand. Today with the snow almost up to his knees James walked into Chuck's tiny old convenient store.

"Morning Chuck." He looked up and nodded. "I need twenty on three." James placed a twenty dollar bill on the scratched counter. He watched the old man take the money and put it in the register.

"Thanks Chuck." James once more opened the door and stepped out into the snow. Another car was sitting next to his at the next pump. It was a beat up old sedan the color of red wine. The driver was nowhere in sight.

Maybe it was the journalistic side of him, then again it could be just ordinary curiosity but something about the car didn't seem right.

Shaking the thought from his head James went to the pump and started to put the gas into the car. A flicker of red caught his eye, making him turn to see a medium tall man dressed in a plaid red shirt. His pants were torn and his hair unruly. *What the hell was he doing out here dressed so lightly?*

"Excuse me sir....are you alright?" James called out to him. The man turned to face him. Something about him vaguely familiar. "Sir?"

"I'm fine!" his horse voice barked. He walked over to the sedan and opened the door. James focused on the man. He seemed like someone he once knew. The eyes and nose, even under all that wild hair seemed familiar. James walked over to him. His arm resting against the open door.

"Are you sure you are alright? You really shouldn't be out here dressed so lightly."

"Look I told you I'm fine. Now screw!" James took a step back and turned his back to the man. That voice....... Turning around again James looked at him.

"Are you Brad Lursen?" Boy did he change! The last time he had seen him was when Erich had some friends over right before the incident. The man before James was not the clean cut boy that had been over at his house visiting the asshole.

"Can you just leave me alone?"

"I'm sorry....do you remember me? James Martin, I used to live in Cranston." Brad looked up and gave a grin.

"Sure I remember you. You're one of the reasons I'm like I am."

"Excuse me?"

Brad swung his legs out from the floor of the car and out into the snow. James' pants were slowly getting soaked up to the knees and the heavy coat he was wearing didn't keep out the cold that was going right through him.

"I got fucked over real bad. All the things I owned gone...I was forced to live on the street as a beggar. But here you are living the good life with your beautiful wife and darling little daughter. I'd watch that precious little girl if I were you." With that James grabbed the neck of his shirt.

"Look you stay away from them!"

"I'm trying to warn you!" James shoved him back, Brad's back hit the loose snow and went flat the asphalt. He whimpered in pain.

"Go anywhere near my Goddamn house or my wife and kid and I will beat the shit out of you. Got that!?" James walked back to his car and sped off. At the stop sign he saw Lavender come to a stop. He knew she saw him but tried her best to ignore him.

If she wanted to be the biggest bitch in the universe that was just fine with him.

An hour later he found himself at his desk. Phones were ringing off the hook and the reports were running wild around him. His secretary Nancy ran up to him first.

"Mr. Martin this note came for you." James took the folded white paper from the young woman's hands and silently read it.

Merry Christmas Jamie

Chapter 26

Christmas Eve Day

It was likely that today, being the last shopping day of the holiday season would be the day that James goes to the Providence Mall to get Lavender's gift. Even though over the past week and a half she had been the most unbearable human being on the face of the planet he still wanted to get her something special.

When he went downstairs Molly was sitting at the kitchen table eating a bowl of cereal. The navy blue long sleeve dress was the same dress that she had worn when Lavender had taken her to get her Christmas picture taken. The crisp white lace matched with the white mary-jane shoes she was wearing. Lavender was dressed in her red robe, hair tied up into a bun on the top of her head, as she stood in the kitchen looking over the paper.

"Morning."

"Morning Daddy." James saw Lavender glance up then went back to the paper. James sighed and walked into the kitchen. "Molly Mouse you ready to go?"

"Where are we going Daddy?"

"I have to go run some errands."

"Oh. Okay."

"Why don't you go and get your coat from upstairs." Molly left the table and quickly ran up the stairs. James turned and faced his wife, who was now staring at him.

"Where were you at two o'clock this morning?"

"I was here."

"You weren't in bed. You were down in the basement again. Am I right?"

"Drop it."

"No James I won't drop it! At all hours of the night you're down there looking over that file!"

"I can look over the file as long as I damn well please!"

"Well I am tired of you looking over that thing like it's the map to all the gold in the world!"

"I'm tired of you being such a bitch lately!"

"I knew it was too damn good to be true. You're just like all the other men and here I thought you were different!"

"What the hell does that mean!?"

"You know very well what it means! You never were like this, suddenly you just make this big turn around over night! I don't understand it!"

"There is nothing for you to understand!"

"James you're just a big asshole!" He turned around and left the kitchen. Taking fast steps he went down to the basement. A moment later he heard her running after him. "Get back here!"

"Why? I'm just an asshole. Why the fuck did you marry me then?"

Lavender stood a few feet away from him. "Right now I don't even know why James. In fact I wish I didn't." He had his back turned to her at this point. James shook his head and walked past her back up the stairs. Molly was back from upstairs with her jacket zipped up around her.

"Come on let's go."

"I didn't get to say goodbye to Mommy first."

"Molly get in the car **now**." She ran to the door and out to the car. The snow almost took her under once she climbed down the stairs. James picked her up around her middle and walked to the car.

Pulling out of the driveway he looked at all the Christmas decorations they had put up three weeks ago. The lights had taken him two days to put up. Three sets were around the top of the house, five sets went around the huge pine trees around the house, and two sets were around the tall Christmas tree inside.

He had video taped Lavender and Molly putting on the strings of popcorn and glass ornaments. Everything was fine then. Why now was everything screwed up? Did she regret marrying him? And in the first place why did he ask? In the front yard was a light up nativity scene. Above that Lavender had hung the glitter star Molly had made in school.

"See Molly," she had told her, "It just like the story of the night God was born. Remember I told you the story?"

Before he knew it he was on the highway. There was hardly any traffic there which surprised him.

"Is Mommy mad at me?" Molly's high voice asked. James took a second to look over at her then went back to the road.

"No, she's mad at Daddy."

"Why was she yelling at you?"

James drew in a breath and then let it out. "She didn't like something I did."

"What did you do?"

"Molly it's a grownup thing."

"Oh....Mommy's been mad for a long time hasn't she?"

Stealing another glance at his daughter James listen to her. "Mommy said she's been feeling sick. That's why she is mad."

"I don't think that she is sick Molly."

"She told me so."

"Molly how much did you hear when we were talking."

"You were yelling-"

"I know we were yelling, but can you tell me how much you heard?" Molly suddenly got quiet and looked down to the car floor.

"She said she didn't like marrying you." Molly suddenly began to cry.

"Why are you crying?"

"Because....I.....don't want... you...to be aggravated." She said through sobs. James began to laugh. Grace had used the word a few times when she was over and Molly must have caught on.

"Molly stop it. Everything is fine. Now I want to see that beautiful smile on your face. I'm sure that Santa Claus won't want to see you crying." She suddenly stopped crying and nearly jumped out of the seat belt.

"We're going to see Santa!?"

"Yup, now sit back down the right way or I'll have to call Santa on the phone and tell him not to bring Molly Martin any toys this year."

"No Daddy! Don't call Santa!" James had to laugh at what he just did. He waited a long time to do that. Every time near Christmas his Mother would do it to him.

"I won't call," he said with a grin.

Stepping out of the hot, foggy bathroom, Lavender took a breath of fresh air. The steaming shower she had taken turned the mirrors so foggy that you couldn't even see anything. With the white terry cloth towel wrapped around her she made her way over to the walk in closet.

Lavender thought that if she kept herself busy then she wouldn't think about what had happened between them. She had cooled off a bit since he left but still not fully. She only said the truth, did he really think something was going to pop out at him from that file.?

Never had she looked at it. As far as she knew it was just a file. What was in it was a mystery all its own. It had to be something big for him to keep at it. She stood in the closet looking for something to wear and decided on the silk dress pants and the green cashmere sweater. Later she would change into the dress she had bought on a sale rack in Macy's.

It would be a family Christmas, Jeremy and her Mom had came in from New York, and her Mother-in-law and Sister-in-law were expected to show up. In the past week Faye had told her that she decided to tell Nick about the baby as a "Christmas Present". Lavender expected that Nick might want to get some protection gifts this year.

She never saw him as a father. In fact she never saw him even remotely ready to settle down. Lavender just didn't want Faye to get hurt. After dressing she went downstairs. Not a soul around to speak a word.

Eyeing the basement she slowly walked down there. Lavender knew where the file was. She knew the combination to the lock on the file draw too. She needed answers to why he had done this big turn around.

Her mouth hung open as she looked through the file. He was looking for answers himself! Reading every page things became more clear.... Suddenly the doorbell rang upstairs. Shutting the file quickly she ran up and answered the door.

Sheen stood there, hands stuffed deep in his pockets. "Sheen what are you doing here?" Lavender moved aside so that he could come in out of the cold. Desperately she was trying to shove the theory that she had of the death of her father-in-law aside.

"I came to see James." Lavender turned her back to him and started to walk into the kitchen.

"James took Molly out. I don't know whe-" Suddenly she felt his cold hands around her body as he pushed her down to the ground. A moment later she felt the blade of the cold knife against her neck. He rolled her over and sat on her legs and placed his arms over her flat arms.

"Seems as though your worst thoughts have come true. Being all alone where no one could hear you scream. You know, James knew you didn't want to be here. He didn't say anything for his own selfishness." A twisted smile came over his dark complexion.

"You bastard! I knew there was something wrong with you!" Lavender tried to get out of his grip but moving and trying to kick.

"Heard your conversation with him this morning. He was really pissed off when he left. I think you really got to him when you said that you wished you never married him."

"Let me go!" Sheen let a hand go to the knife on the floor. He then held it closer to her throat.

"You better shut the fuck up. With one quick phone call I can have little Molly face down in the snow."

⁂

James looked around the mall. The bright lights and decorations were magical. On the speakers "Feliz Navidad" played. People moved in and out of every store, bags banging against each other as they walked.

Molly hung onto his hands as they made their way through the crowds. Outside of Lord and Taylor a bunch of people sang "We Wish You a Merry Christmas." That clashed with "Feliz Navidad " and it did not sound very good.

"Daddy are we going to see Santa now?" Molly asked.

"We have to get Mommy something for Christmas sweetie then we'll go see Santa."

"But Daddy I want to see him now," she whined.

"Molly we will go see Santa after we get Mommy her present. Don't you want to help me pick it out?" She crossed her free arm over her chest. James pulled her into Tiffany's a moment later. From where they were upstairs they could see the long line for Santa Claus.

They could also see the big guy himself, sitting posing for pictures and asking all the children what they wanted for Christmas. The people in the store looked like the rest that were at this mall, holding bags and purses, some even small children.

James stopped in front of one of glass cases to look at a gold necklace that had four diamonds that hanging down. When James and Lavender had been in there the last time they went to the mall, Lavender had seen it and instantly loved it. James released Molly's hand and looked down at the necklace.

"Can I help you sir?" James stood up and faced a boney faced woman. Her name tag read Emma.

"Yes I'd like to purchase that necklace."

"Very well sir," the next thing they heard was a glass shattering. "Excuse me I'll be right back." James nodded and bent back down to look at the necklace. It would be beautiful on her.

"Only the best for your mother Molly." James turned around to see his daughter. But she wasn't there. "Molly?....Molly?" He stood up and looked over the crowd.

"Molly?" he called. Where was she? James ran out of the store and looked around. "Molly!" Some people started to look at him. He ran back in the store and looked around one more time. Panicking James looked around, where could she have gone? Sprinting he ran to the escalator and took it down to the first floor.

When he got to where Santa was stationed he really began to lose it. He thought for sure that she would be here this is what she wanted to do! Spotting a security guard near the entrance to the line for Santa Claus he raced over.

"Please help me, my daughter's wondered off and I can't find her anywhere!"

"Okay, what does your daughter look like?"

"Brown hair, blue eyes. She was wearing a navy blue velvet dress with white lace on the front. Her hair is straight." The officer made a call on his radio. Soon all the security officers were looking for Molly.

James ran around to all the stores she liked to go in. None of them had seen her. What was he going to do? What if he didn't find her? *"No James, don't talk like that!"* He told himself. He kept looking running around in the stores looking for her calling her name.

He tried the bookstore, the food court, the major department stores. This wasn't like her to wander off, no matter how bad she wanted something. Why didn't he take her to see Santa first? Then maybe this wouldn't have happened.

Trying to remain calm became harder as the search grew cold. "The Dance of the Sugar Plum Fairies " began to play when his cell phone rang.

"Hello?" he asked angrily. When no one answered him he asked again. All he could hear was breathing on the other line.

"Who the hell is this?!"

"You can tell them to stop looking for Molly. She's alright for now."

"Who the fuck is this!? Answer me!"

"If I were you I would get home right away."

"Is this Brad? I told you to stay the fuck away from my family!"

"Molly's crying right now James you want to hear her?" In the background he heard Molly sobbing.

"I want my Daddy! Where is my Daddy?!"

"Molly!" James yelled through the phone.

"How sad that she can't see her Daddy....You better hurry home time is ticking. You know Lavender's waiting there too..."

"You shit head bastard! I swear to God that you're gonna pay!" The dial tone was heard a second later.

Chapter 27

Security had locked all the doors. And James needed to get out of one of them. Crowds of people blocked the exits trying to find out what was going on. He had to fight his way through the crowd.

"Excuse me! Excuse me!" He called fighting past them. James made it to the front of the doors where two officers were standing. "I'm the one who lost my daughter. I know where she is and I have to get out of here."

"We're going to have to get the boss to open the doors." James moved closer to them.

"If I don't get through those doors and find my daughter then I'm going to sue this whole damn mall!" One looked to another then took a key from a small ring. They unlocked the door and James shoved his way out of the mall.

In the parking garage he quickly turned the key in the ignition and sped out of the closed in area. The highway was backed up. Somehow he needed to find a way to get home quicker...

He jumped off the highway at the nearest exist and followed the streets to the less busier part of the highway. A grand total of five red lights were ran before he got to the highway entrance.

Turning on to Fry Pond Rd. the car nearly went off the road into a snow bank. Just making it, he drove a little more to his driveway then turned in. There was no car there, and not a foot print. Sprinting up the wood porch stairs he scrambled to get his keys.

Opening the door, all was quiet. Visible from the kitchen was Lavender tied to a chair, tears falling down her face. Her hair was messed and her pant leg was soaked with blood. She didn't see him open the door. Running down the long hallway he called out to her. As soon as he rounded the corner his head was hit with a heavy brass sculpture...

<hr />

He could feel the blood slowly drying on his head and neck. His arms were limp and his legs were bound. Slowly James opened his eyes and looked around. Lavender was still in the same spot as when he came in here. Blinking his eyes and tilting his head back he moaned. The pain was horrendous!

"Well, well, well...look who decided to join us..." James looked over to his right and saw Erich sitting at the kitchen table. Quickly James looked down and saw his feet where bound tight with rope and duct tape and his hands were the same around the back of the chair.

James looked over at Lavender and saw her face still with tears. She was bound the same as him.

"Where is she? Tell me where she is! Where is my baby girl?!" Lavender screamed.

"Where's Molly? What have you done to her?"

"You really have a charming little girl there Jamie boy. Very smart, yet very stupid like you. Like father like daughter, you both easily walk into traps." James let out a moan again, if Erich didn't kill him then the pain coming from his skull would.

"Where is she?!" he demanded with the little strength he had left.

"She's upstairs in her bedroom. We'll bring her down shortly right Sheen?" Out of the hall Sheen appeared, a few bloodstains covered his shirt.

"Sheen?!"

Erich walked over to James and looked him in the face. "This is something that I haven't seen in a while. That night you were so helpless and here you are the same. Although this time you're grown up but still the little faggot that you were then!" Erich slapped James hard across the face.

"What the fuck do you want from me!" James screamed.

"What do I want? I want to see you dead like I wanted to see you dead before! Now it's just harder!"

"Why did you want me dead asshole?! Please enlighten me!" Erich walked to the other side of the room.

"You want to know. Okay I guess I better start from the beginning.... Bet your Mommy and Daddy never told you that I'm adopted. Yup I am. Born September 19th 1965 as Joel Degario. I was a twin. My whore mother, Carol Degario, put me up for adoption and kept my sister. My sister later on died with our real father in a car accident. What a coincidence that my mother, Carol is also Jeremy Ryan's first wife and she was the mother of my step-sister Elizabeth. Oh and Jamie did you know that she dated your Daddy?"

"Did you also know that your Father named me from something my Mother told him when they were kids? See my Grandfather's name was Edward and my Uncle's name was Richard or Richie as he liked to be called. He remembered that when they named me. Sick isn't it? So I messed around with it and Erich is how I became to be known."

"Anyway...I ended up with Christine and Robert Martin, who couldn't have children of their own. I was just fine until three years later she gets pregnant and has a boy. After you came into the picture it was all down hill from there. I hated you. You took everything away from me. The attention, the love, everything! Yet here was the catch....the first born son received all the money once the money maker perished. So when you were fourteen I tried to kill you. They didn't even know about my little house of horror in the basement. That's how stupid they were."

"You had money away, they wouldn't leave you with nothing!" James choked out.

"You put me away for a long time Jamie. You and your slut wife here. She just couldn't keep her mouth shut. Typical woman.- I gotta thank you for something though Jamie. See without you I would have never met the people I did-" Suddenly a noise came from upstairs. Erich nodded to Sheen and without words spoken, Sheen made his way upstairs.

Sheen ran down a moment later. Molly's small arms were over her head. Sheen held her up by her hands and let her body hang. She kicked backwards at him but missed every time. Erich came up to her and let his hands run over her mouth.

"Such a pretty little girl you are....and so young to lose her parents. You know I think that we should keep her here to watch her Mommy and Daddy die their slow painful death. What do you think Sheen?" Molly opened her mouth and bit down on the skin that was covering her mouth.

He stumbled back and held his hand. "Son of a bitch! She bite me! Throw her down in the basement. We'll deal with her the same way I dealt with her bastard father!" Sheen opened the basement door and laterally threw Molly down the stairs. Erich looked at his hand then walked over to Lavender.

"Look at what your daughter did to me. She tore the skin! Do you believe that?" Erich walked back over to the middle of the floor. "While I was in prison I got this great idea. I said to myself, 'Erich let's fuck around with James' life even more!' So I got this really cool idea. Well In 93, I was getting out of prison early. I was a very good boy in prison you know- and one day who comes to see me? Why it's your Dad. And do you know what he said? He offered me a half a million dollars to screw and never come near you again."

"So I said yeah and with that money I hired a friend of mine. See Sheen had been in prison for killing his younger brother at the lake. Sheen was getting out before me so I came up with this plan. Pay him off to screw around with Daddy's brakes so that he dies too. Well I bet you didn't know that on the morning he died he was coming to see me and make them keep me behind bars."

"He never got there so I didn't stay behind bars Jamie. So for a while I kept a low profile. Until I heard that you were getting married. I figured this is part two of my plan. With my key sources I found her at that club that night. I took her home to your house and messed around in your bed. Never expected to get her pregnant but that worked out just fine too. Let's call this next part another coincidence."

"Sheen came to be friends with you. From what I understand he took you out drinking, got you a tattoo and you let him in on everything in your life. How big of a mistake was that?" Erich went over to Lavender. He put duct tape on her mouth, then quickly he ripped the tape off her mouth. She cried out in pain.

"Did that hurt? I've sorry." He smiled his twisted smile then pushed his blond hair from his face. Sheen laughed too.

"You bastard you betrayed me! You killed my father and I thought you were my friend!" James yelled at Sheen.

"All is fair in war and money." Sheen relaxed back on the basement door.

"Oh yeah about that Sheen," Erich said. Whipping out a gun he shot him in his head five times, "I don't share money." He laughed again. Lavender's eyes were wide with shock. On television you see this kind of thing happening but you would never expect it to happen in your own home!

Erich looked around. Then saw the open bathroom door. "I'll be right back, don't anyone move," he laughed. After he had disappeared Lavender looked at James.

"James I'm so sorry. I didn't mean to say those things. Please forgive me!"

"Lav it's okay. Everything is going to be alright. You'll see. I'm gonna get us all out of here."

"Don't let him hear you." James gulped and felt a shooting pain into his head.

"Dammit! God it hurts!" He tilted his head back again and tried to stop the pain. What ever he did to try to make it go away didn't help.

"What about Molly? Do you think she is okay?"

"I don't know Lav. We can only hope she is."

"James I don't want this to be the end. It can't end like this. It just can't." she sobbed. He closed his eyes tight trying to think of a way for them to escape. Erich has a gun how were they ever going to get away? A few minutes later Erich came back.

"So where did I leave off? Oh yeah we were up to now. Today I just happened to have someone follow you to the mall and kidnap your daughter. The way it happened was while you were looking at all those expensive jewelry pieces in Tiffany's your daughter was making her way down to see Santa Claus. I had Victoria go get her. Oh Vicky darling, why don't you come in here?"

Victoria came walking in from the front door. She wasn't the same woman he had once knew. Now she was fatter, her hair was stringy and blah. Clearly she had let herself go. She looked James straight in the eye, then looked to Lavender.

"You bitch! You put another one of your hands on my daughter again and I'll..."

"You'll what Lavender? Come after her while you're strapped to the chair? You know speaking of kids our are the same age. Well Victoria why don't you tell them what happened to little Michael?"

Victoria was on the verge of tears. When she had seen James' beautiful daughter today she felt like dying. Her baby was gone killed by the asshole who had fathered him. That day when she found Michael in the bathtub dead she had knew that he had killed him. Erich had blamed it on the child but Michael always hated the water and taking baths.

"He died. A few months ago. Drowned."

"Such a sad story Victoria," Erich told her. He then pushed her in back of him and knocked her to the ground. "Wasn't that a sad story you two? We should get out the violin shouldn't we. In a little while you can say goodbye to your kid too. I've come to the decision that you're going to watch me kill her."

"No!!!!!! Please don't touch Molly!!!!!!"

"I'm sorry but I have to. See, she's James' heir. She would get all the money. So my plan is that with her out of the picture then I can get your husband out of the picture. You, I have to keep alive so that you can send all the money over to me. Then I'll kill you in front of everyone at the bank."

"Please. You can have all the damn money, please just let us go!"

"Now would that be any fun? Of course not. I want to see you rot."

James lifted his head. He was getting dizzy, his head was bleeding more now. "You're going to rot in the lower depths of hell you ugly mother-fucking bastard!" James took a sharp breath and tried to keep consciousness.

⁂

She had never been down in the basement without the light on. Molly felt around the bottom of the stairs for the light switch. She knew it was on the wall next to the fridge but never has she studied it to know the exact place.

Finally she found it! Something needed to be done. Her Mom and Dad were in trouble! Molly didn't understand what that man could possible want with her Dad. When she had seen him he looked like he was going to be sick. Making her way into the other hall she found herself in the office.

Why was this happening? It was Christmas! This had never happened any other Christmas! What was going to happen to Mommy and Daddy? What about Gramma and Grandpa? And Grandma and Auntie Grace? All Molly knew was that she had to help her parents.

She remembered something that she learned in pre-school. If there is an emergency call 911. Molly ran over to the phone and picked it up. 9-1-1, she dialed. An operator answered on the other line.

"911 please state your emergency."

"My name is Molly Martin. A man is in my house with my parents tied up. I think he is going to hurt them!"

"What's your address?"

"29 Fry Pond Road West Greenwich, Rhode Island."

"We'll have someone there quickly." Molly hung up the phone unaware if she was supposed to or not. All she wanted was for her parents to be okay. Before she had her long list of things she wanted for Christmas now all she asked of Santa was to help her rescue her Mommy and Daddy.

Before she had heard someone fall on the door. Probably her father's friend who had locked her in her bedroom. He had been around here before and she always stayed upstairs. *Mommy didn't like the man either* Molly though. Lavender once told her that she thought he was sneaky. Suddenly Molly began to cry what if she never saw her Mommy again?

What if she never saw Daddy again? Who would play with her and take her to the movies? Who would come in and kiss her after Mommy put her to bed? What about who was going to let her sleep in their bed when the lighting and thunder is happening outside? She hoped the police would come soon.

✦

James didn't think he would make it much longer. Through his blurred vision he could see Erich's hand holding the gun at him. This was it. This was the end of his life. Everything he never did would never get done. Breathing heavily he tried to block out the mutters of Erich saying that he was going to get all the money he had.

His eyes began to flutter close when he looked up at Erich.

"Say goodbye Jamie!" The repeated gun shot came just as the police lights were seen through the stained glass rose in the window. James looked up from Erich's body that was now bleeding all over the floor to the woman with the gun standing in back of him. Victoria's hand shook with the gun.

"That's for Michael."

Chapter 28

Victoria still stood shaking as the police opened up the doors of the house. Someone was behind him untying his hands. He looked over at Lavender who was now pushing past some police officers yelling that Molly was downstairs. When they wouldn't move Sheen's body out of the way she ran outside in the cold night and went through the garage.

The lock was on there old and rusty, making it easy for her to push her weight on the door so it would open. Bright lights were coming from the ceiling and the air condition was on in the room making it colder.

"Molly!? Molly where are you?!" Lavender yelled. She ran deeper into the basement looking for her daughter. "Molly! Molly where are you!?" A second later a tiny body crawled out from under James' desk. Molly ran over to her mother crying. Lavender held her tight against her chest.

She pulled Molly away from her and looked over her body. "Molly does it hurt anywhere? Can you move your feet and legs? What about your arms?"

"I'm okay Mommy." The bright lights of an ambulance were seen from the open basement door. Lavender picked her up and ran outside. She didn't want to take Molly back in the house but she had to see what was going on.

"Molly I want you to put your head on my shoulder and don't open your eyes until I tell you okay?"

"Okay." Just to be sure Lavender held a hand on top of her head. Running in the house she looked at the scene around her. It was like she hadn't been here. James was no where in sight but the body of Erich and Sheen still laid were they had died. Before she had ran down to get Molly Victoria had been dragged out of the house by police.

Lavender walked Molly upstairs and put her in her bedroom. Going over to the closet she grabbed warmer clothes for her.

"Can I open my eyes now Mommy?"

"Yes." Molly blinked and looked around. Her mother knelt in front of her and started to put a pair of leggings on Molly.

"Where is Daddy?"

"I don't know sweetheart. I have to go see."

"The police came quick."

Lavender looked up questionably at her daughter. "How do you know?"

"I called."

"You called?"

"Uh huh. I told them the address and everything." Shocked Lavender continued to stare at her daughter. Out of the corner of her eye she saw a short man standing at Molly's bedroom door.

"Excuse me for interrupting Dr. Martin, I'm Detective Jenkins." Lavender stood up and. Molly still sat on the bed feet dangling in the air.

"Molly I'll be right back." Lavender walked out of the room, closing the door behind her. Lavender rubbed her arms trying to get warm.

"Dr. Martin I know this is a very upsetting ordeal for you but I'm going to have to ask you a few questions."

"Where is my husband?"

"He's been taken to Kent County Hospital. He's suffered some head trauma. I really don't know what his condition is." It felt as though her heart had stopped. Lavender ran back in the room and brought Molly out, keeping her head on her shoulder once more. Rushing past the man she heard him call out something to her. In the car she put Molly in her car seat and sped away down Fry Pond Rd.

⁕

Molly had fallen asleep in her Mother's arms when Doctor Lillian Bradford came out to see Lavender. It was hours that she had been waiting to know what was going on with James and now just might be the time. Beside her James' mother sat, tapping her foot against the hard cold floor.

"Dr. Martin?"

"Yes?"

"I'm Dr. Bradford, your husband's doctor."

"How is he?"

"He has a mild concussion surprisingly and a broken rib. Mostly likely he'll be out of work a month at the most. I want to keep him here overnight. He should be able to go home in the morning."

"Thank you Doctor."

"Can we see him?" his mother asked her.

"Certainly. One at a time though. We gave him some medication to ease the pain so don't be surprised if he doesn't act himself." Lavender nodded and watched Dr. Bradford walk away.

"You go in first. Give me Molly and then I'll go in after you," his mother said. Lavender handed Molly to her quickly then slowly walked to James' room. The door felt a thousand pounds when she opened it and stepped inside. He was sleeping so perfectly. The back of his head wasn't visible but she could see the white bandage resting on the pillow.

Walking over to him she just stood there looking. Gently she ran her fingers over his forehead, pushing away the stray hair. Lavender pulled the chair from the other side of the room next to the bed.

"I'm not sure if you can hear me, but if you can then great. Today when all this happened you were one of the first things that I thought of." Tears started to swell in her eyes. "If I had died before you got there, then my last words to you would have been that I regretted marrying you. I hope you know that it was a lie. Marrying you was the best thing I've ever done. I don't think I really know how great I have it. When I was young I watched my Father beat my Mother then come after me and I knew you were different I knew you would never hit me or hurt me. I have always known you were special."

"I look at Faye and wonder what I would do if I were her. If I didn't have you in my life I'm sure that I would be lost somewhere... Every chance I get I thank God that I've found you. Look at me I'm rabbling and not making sense." She wiped the tears that were running on her face, then looked back at James.

"Perhaps this never would have happened if we never met-"

"If we hadn't you might have not ended up with the beautiful daughter you have and the idiot husband laying in the hospital bed." James smiled opening his eyes. She gave a small laugh and shook her head at him.

"How long had you been listening?"

"The whole time."

"You jerk." James moved his hand over to her hand that was resting on the bed. "You have a guardian angel over you. This is one of the many times she's helped you."

"I know who she is."

"Do you?"

"Uh huh. She's sitting in the room with me. Every time something bad happens to me I think of you." She started to blush uncontrollably. "What about you? Are you okay?"

"I'm fine."

"What about Molly?"

"She's asleep outside the room. You know she's the one who called the cops."

"What?"

"Yeah she told me when I saw her."

"She gets her brains from you."

"I'd like to think it's a little bit of both of us." James tried to sit up but winced at the pain from his side. "Lay down, otherwise you'll just get hurt more."

"Thanks Doctor."

"Anytime."

"What's going on back at the house?"

"I don't know, I didn't stay long enough to find out."

"He's for sure dead?"

"Yeah. Gone for good."

"That had to be the best Christmas gift...wait Christmas, what about Molly?"

"We'll figure something out."

"She never got to see Santa Claus."

"There is always next year."

"But we're in this year. I promised her that she would get to see him."

"James I think that she'll be happy that you are alive."

"My cell phone is in my jacket can you get it for me?"

"You can't use your cell phone in here."

"Watch me."

"Who are you calling anyway?"

"Santa Claus."

Sitting at home on Christmas Eve, Roman Jones was peacefully quiet. As a janitor for the Providence Journal he enjoyed the quiet instead of the hustle and bustle of news reporters. The phone started ringing loudly as just as he was finishing the jigsaw puzzle.

"Hello?"

"Roman? This is James Martin." Now this was something he didn't expect. The young editor had always been kind to him, always said hello or goodbye when he saw him. Sometimes he would even have lengthy conversations with him.

"Mr. Martin, Merry Christmas!"

"Merry Christmas to you Roman. Listen I hope I'm not bothering you-"

"No, No, not at all."

"Okay, well at the Christmas party you dressed up as Santa Claus, I was wondering if you still had that outfit?"

"I have it. Why?"

"I need a big favor."

"Anything."

"My daughter didn't get to see Santa Claus and I would really appreciate it if you could come and just say hi or something to her."

"Don't even say anymore. I would love to do it!"

"Really? Oh thank you! You're great!"

Molly woke up when the tap on her shoulder continued. She rubbed her eyes and sat up. Looking around she saw she was in a room. Her Mom and Dad were sitting there watching her.

"Daddy?"

"Yes sweetheart?"

"Are you okay?"

"I'm fine."

"Mommy did you tap me?"

"No I didn't but look behind you at who did." Molly turned around and smiled. "Santa!" Roman Jones's long white beard and red suit made him look like Santa was supposed to look.

"Ho, Ho, Ho! Hello Molly! I was on my way to your house when Rudolph told me that you were here! I had to turn around and find you! I was waiting for you at the mall today, but I didn't see you. Now I seen that you walked away from your Daddy and went with a stranger. Now that is something you're not supposed to do."

"I know." Molly said quietly.

"You won't do that again will you?"

"No I won't Santa."

"Well then other than that on my list of good little children you're at the top! Now why don't you tell me what you want for Christmas?" Roman sat down on the chair and let Molly sit on his lap. James and Lavender smiled as Molly named off everything they bought her.

"Well Molly that was some list! I'm sorry to say that I have to go deliver more toys to other children. Before I go though, I want to say that you are a very smart girl for doing what you did for your Mom and Dad."

"Thank you Santa."

"Ho, Ho, Ho, You're welcome Molly! Merry Christmas Everyone!" Roman waved to them as he walked out the door. She ran over to Lavender and jumped in her arms,

"Mommy it was Santa it was really him!"

"I know! Wasn't that great?" Molly let go of Lavender and went near James.

"Daddy how did he know I was here?"

"I don't know, he just knows."

"Where were the reindeer?"

"I guess they are on the roof."

"Oh."

"Molly, your Mother and I would like to say that without you we don't know what might have happened to us. You're a very smart girl and we're glad that you did what you did."

"We're very proud of you Moll. You showed a lot of courage today." Lavender told her stroking her hair. Molly smiled and looked at her parents lovingly. Her mother picked her up and kissed her on the cheek. "Well Moll, Daddy has to get his rest. You can come back tomorrow and see him."

"Am I going with Grandma?"

"Yeah. I'm going to stay here with Daddy. I'll see you in the morning."

"I want to say goodbye to Daddy," Molly said pushing away from Lavender. She went over to James and kissed him on the cheek.

"I love you Daddy."

"I love you too Molly Mouse." James hugged her the best he could, then let Lavender take her. She returned a moment later without Molly. Taking a seat on the chair next to the bed, she smiled.

"It seems like only yesterday she was born. The first time I held her I knew she was different. She took a long time to talk but when she did it was sentences and speeches." Lavender laughed. "You know that she'll never forget what you did tonight with Santa."

"I know. I plan to do the same for you."

"You're going to call him and make me sit on his lap?"

"No."

"Then what?"

"Go downstairs and you'll see." Lavender uneasily looked at him, but curiosity took her down the elevator and outside. A white horse with a carriage attached to the back, stood there. The driver was no other than Nick Brenden.

"Is this part of your big radio job?"

"Something like that. The station had it and a friend called in the favor," Nick smiled. "Get in you have this carriage for an hour or until they realize that I took it and then they're going to fire my ass."

" You're not suppose to swear on Christmas," Lavender laughed. "I'll be right back" She then ran to the elevator then to his room. His smile was unforgettable when she walked in. Running over to hm she kissed him passionately and whispered that she loved him in his ear.

Chapter 29

Walking down the narrow corridor of the Rhode Island prison, James felt like he was a prisoner here too. *Only a few more steps.* He repeated to himself. Just the ride here made him sweat. It was already two weeks into January and he was back on his feet. "This way." the prison guard's gruff voice told him. James followed him to the room where in a few minutes he would talk to Victoria. The room was dark and the one window it had didn't give much light. He took a seat on the hard wooden chairs and waited.

Victoria was escorted into the room by two burly security guards on each side of her. She too took a seat, only it was across from him. The prison clothes looked filthy on her body.

"Hi," she said quietly. James nodded and kept his gaze on her. It was hard to believe that he had once been married to the woman before him. Her eyes were pale and full of sadness. Her whole family had disowned her because of what she did.

"How are you?"

"Fine. I'm holding up...how are you?"

"I'm okay."

"How is your family?" She could never bring herself to say Lavender's name.

"They're good." Staring at her now, James felt nothing to her. He had heard of old love being renewed when one saw that person but he felt nothing to her. Maybe it was because he never loved her in the first place.

"Do you know how Nick is?"

"Nick's good."

"What about my parents-"

"Look, I didn't come here to talk about this," he said heated.

She looked down and then back up at him, "I kind of guessed that you didn't. When they told me that you were here I knew you wanted something from me."

"I just want some answers...Victoria I was wrong to marry you. It was my fault just as much as it was you. This may hurt but you and I both know that I really didn't love you."

"I know. You loved her from the moment you saw her. Or so Nick says. For a while I wondered what she had that I didn't."

"She never lied to me."

"Everybody lies James."

"Lavender never lied about a baby that wasn't mine."

"What was I supposed to do James? What would you have done?"

"Don't try to turn this around. Now I came here to get answers to what happened!"

"I'm not trying to turn it around!"

"Dammit you always do this!"

"What do I always do?"

Sighing James closed his eyes. "How did you get Molly to come with you?"

"I told her that she was going to get to see Santa Claus."

"How did you know that she wanted to?"

Victoria put her head down sighing, "He bugged the house. They were watching it twenty-four hours a day. They had hidden camera's in every room. Ever wonder why Sheen brought you so many wedding presents?" Victoria paused. "He filmed you when you showered, when you had sex, there wasn't anything that wasn't seen." James closed his eyes, they were watching them, learning their routine, learning their weakness. Molly.

"What did he do to her?"

Victoria shook her head."Nothing."

"I know he did something what was it?"

"He gave her sleeping stuff, I don't know. All I know is that when she was asleep he had me put her in her bedroom and lock her in there."

"I want to know how you could do that? She's only a baby."

"Did I say I wanted to do it?" James let out a breath and stood up.

"What happened to Michael?"

"I told you he died."

"How did he die?"

"He killed him okay!?" Victoria shouted out. "I came home and he had killed him in the bathtub!" James got quiet.

"I'm sorry."

"It's too damn late for sorry. If you hadn't walked out on me maybe this never would have happened!"

"I don't care Victoria! Get that through your head! It's over! Tell me one more thing-"

"I'm not telling you anything."

"Where is Brad Lursen?"

Victoria bit her lip. She had watched Erich strangle him. "I don't know."

"You cant lie to me. I can tell when you are. Now where is he!?" James demanded. His hands were plastered down on the table. Victoria looked on his left finger and saw his wedding ring. Once before it had been her ring to him. Now it was Lavender's ring.

"He's in the pond off the highway going to your house." James stepped back. Instead of being an ass he should have listened to Brad Lursen, only later had it hit him that it was too late. He told the guard that he was leaving, but she suddenly grabbed his arm.

"James..."

"What?" James demanded.

"I just wanted to say-"

"What? Say it so I can leave!"

"I just wanted to say that you have a beautiful daughter."

"Fuck you." James swiftly walked out of the room, finally closing the door to his past.

Grace stepped into her apartment, getting out of the cold January air. Her usually warm wool coat was still buttoned around her when she saw him standing in the doorway. Smiling she stared at him. His boyish brown ringlets framed his forehead and neck while bright hazel eyes kept her dreaming of him. He walked over to her and kissed her cold lips. Grace felt herself melt in her boyfriend, Brandon Armstrong's warm embrace.

Through their poetry class at Brown University, Grace and Brandon had met when school started up in the fall of last year. It had been two months since the incident with Dan, who she thought was the love of her life, it had left her scared and not willing to have another relationship. Until the day Brandon "accidently" spilled his coffee on her. Since then they had been inseparable.

"I didn't think that you would be home so soon. I didn't even finish setting the place up." Brandon said helping her out of her coat.

"What were you setting up for?" She asked flirtatiously. Brandon took her hand and lead her into the bedroom. Grace's mouth flew open at the sight of the place. Tons of candles were the only source of light in the room they shared while, the sweet scent of vanilla burned from incests. "What is all this?"

Brandon stood in front of her and smiled. Bending down on one knee he took a black box from his back pocket. "Grace Nicole Martin, will you give me the honor of becoming my wife?" He asked placing a beautiful three stone diamond on her left hand. Grace stood speechless for moments.

"I asked both your mother and James before asking you, I thought I should do it the old fashion way but if-" he began standing up.

Grace jumped into his arms. "Yes! Yes! I love you!" She screamed as loud as she could. Brandon kissed her and held her in his arms for the rest of the night.

⁂

Parking in the driveway, James walked to the front door of the new house they had bought. Located back in the city, they bought a house close to the neighborhood where they had grown up. The house was a bright yellow with white trim and large windows. Lavender loved it as soon as they looked at it with the realtor.

Opening the door he heard the newly familiar bark of Molly's puppy, Lady. The half German- Shepard, half Labrador was only a puppy but she was already growing quickly. The dog had been a Christmas present from Grace. Lady came to a sliding halt at James' feet.

He bent down and pet Lady on the head then stood back up. Molly came running down the entry hall. When she saw him she ran to him and hugged him.

"Hey Molly Mouse, what are you doing?"

"I'm painting."

"What are you painting?"

"I'll show you Daddy." Molly took his hand and led him into the playroom they had made for her. All her toys were neatly put away, thanks to Lavender. Molly held up a paper. On it was a big black smudge with a red line near the top.

"Is that Lady?"

"Yeah see her tongue?"

"It's very pretty."

"I made it for you so that you can take it to work." James smiled and took the painting from Molly.

"Thank you very much. As soon as I go there tomorrow I'll put it on my desk." He bent down and kissed her. It was hard to believe that she was already going to be six years old. "Molly where is Mom?"

"She's outside with Auntie Faye."

James walked out the room and went into the kitchen, where from outside of the french doors he could see his wife and her best friend sitting on the wooden porch looking out on the endless spread of forest in the back of their property. Opening the door they both turned around.

"Hey what's going on?" James asked them. He walked over and placed a kiss on Lavender's lips before settling down on the iron chair. The sun was beating down on them even with the umbrella up.

"I'm engaged!" Faye squealed. She threw her left hand in James' face. The ring was silver with a diamond.

"No way, Nick ready to commit?" James laughed. Lavender looked at him and smiled.

"I was just telling Faye what married life is like."

"It's gruesome and horrible!" he joked. Lavender hit his arm playfully. "So when is the wedding?"

"We're getting married in four weeks. We've already met with the wedding planner and we want as soon as possible before the baby is born. Naturally you two would be the best man and maid of honor."

James looked over at Lavender and shrugged. "Good deal, so any names picked out yet?"

"Dylan if it's a boy and Alexandra if it's a girl." Faye smiled. "They gave me the choice but I opted not to know."

"I did the same thing with Molly. Though I knew it was a girl." Lavender smiled.

"So you didn't finish, what was his reaction when you told him about the baby?" Lavender asked Faye.

"He was happy. I guess that is the best way to put it. He made a big change. He started picking out names, though I told him I already had some picked out." James smiled then stood up and went inside.

On March 17, Nick Brenden married Faye Waters in a loud ceremony at the Quidnessett Country Club. It was also the day Faye delivered her children. Lavender held Faye's hand on the way to the hospital.

"I can't Lav- I can't! I'm not ready to have the baby yet!" Faye's white wedding dress had been changed to a top and pants right before her water had broken.

"Yes you can," Lavender looked at Nick who was driving. His hands shook on the wheel as he wove in and out of traffic. "You're so ready Faye! You are going to be fine, were almost there." Lavender looked out the back window. James was in their car along with Molly, trying to keep up with Nick. She smiled to herself and received a perfect image in her mind.

"Are you sure we're almost there?"

"I promise."

"You can't promise! You a doctor! Doctors lie!" Faye yelled. It wasn't long after that Faye and Nick disappeared into the delivery room. Two hours later, Nick walked into the waiting room, where Molly, James and Lavender, still in their wedding attire, sat. His face was pale but a huge smile was on his face.

"Well?" Lavender asked holding on to James' hand.

"Twins."

"What?!" James and Lavender asked at the same time.

"Yeah, surprised me too," Nick laughed. " Faye knew all along...I'm the father of twin boys, I can't believe it!"

"Can we see them?" James asked.

"Yeah come on," Nick said wiping his sweaty hands on the blue hospital garments. James took hold of Molly as he and Lavender followed Nick to the nursery window. In the front were two twin boys, each with blond hair and blue eyes. Lavender bit her lip holding back the waves of emotion from inside her.

"They're beautiful Nick- what are their names?" Lavender asked quietly.

"Dylan and Alex." James held Lavender's hand tighter as they looked at Nick's sons.

"Is Faye alright?" James turned to Nick.

"Perfect- she's happy to be drugged." Nick laughed and continued to look at his best friends. "Faye and I talked it over a while ago and we want you guys to be the God-parents." Lavender turned and looked at Nick with a smile.

"Of course, we would be honored," Lavender looked over at Molly who was in James' arms. She was rubbing her eyes and yawning. "Nick I think we're going to get Molly home. Call me when Faye is okay." Nick nodded and watched them walk out of the hospital.

Lavender was quiet on the way home, only the low hum of the car radio was heard. She turned and looked in the backseat. Molly was passed out in her seat. Smiling she turned back around and fidgeted in the seat.

"You okay?" James asked looking over at her.

"Yeah I'm fine."

"You didn't look fine back at the hospital."

"I was just concerned about Faye." He turned into the driveway and then turned off the car.

"What a day huh?" Lavender nodded and proceeded to get Molly out of the backseat. As quietly as she could she walked up the darkened stairs and into Molly's bedroom. When taking off her dress, Molly's eyes opened wide.

"Mommy?"

"Yes?"

"Are we home now?"

"Yes sweetie, go back to sleep." Lavender placed a t-shirt over her daughter's body and tucked her into the bed. "Night Molly."

"Mommy?"

"Yeah?"

"I can't wait," Molly yawned and fell back to sleep. Lavender smiled and let the tears fall.

"Neither can I."

St. Petersburg, Florida
One week Later

Molly, Grace, and Brandon walked in front of them on the beach the warm waves touched over their feet. Hooked hand in hand they silently walked. Molly's spring break couldn't come at a better time for them. Grace and Brandon accompanied then for their spring break as well. " I never thought that her wedding would be this soon." James told her. Lavender laughed.

"Remember when she caught us making out in your garage?"Lavender laughed.

"Yeah. I still can't believe that Molly's already six."

"You? What about me? I'm the one who was with her the longest." laughing James entwined his arms around Lavender's waist. "I love you James." He turned to look at her. After everything they had been through together it was finally perfect.

"I love you too Lav."

Lavender put her arms around his neck and went to his ear. "Oh yeah.... we're having a baby."

About the Author

Danielle Deneault was born March 22, 1991 in Providence, Rhode Island . She now resides in Las Vegas, Nevada.

Printed in the United States
46826LVS00002B/127-144